TAINTED BLOOD

STILL SHOCKED BY the death of their comrade Abel, Reiner and his cutthroat companions, the Blackhearts, are horrified to learn that there may be a spy amongst them.

Imprisoned and forced into dangerous missions under threat of death, they are press ganged into working as bodyguards for their 'employer' Count Manfred as he journeys to Talabheim, where the forces of magic are running wild. With enemies all around and a traitor within, can the Blackhearts solve the mystery and save the city from destruction?

A WARHAMMER NOVEL

TAINTED BLOOD

NATHAN LONG

To the memory of Fritz Leiber

A BLACK LIBRARY PUBLICATION

First published in Great Britain in 2006 by
BL Publishing,
Games Workshop Ltd.,
Willow Road, Nottingham,
NG7 2WS, UK

10 9 8 7 6 5 4 3 2 1

Cover illustration by Christer Sveen.
Map by Nuala Kinrade.

A CIP record for this book is available from the British Library

ISBN13: 978 1 84416 371 7
ISBN 10: 1 84416 371 7

Distributed in the US by Simon & Schuster
1230 Avenue of the Americas, New York, NY 10020, US.

Printed and bound in Great Britain by
Bookmarque, Surrey, UK.

See the Black Library on the Internet at
www.blacklibrary.com

Find out more about Games Workshop
and the world of Warhammer at
www.games-workshop.com

THIS IS A DARK age, a bloody age, an age of daemons and of sorcery. It is an age of battle and death, and of the world's ending. Amidst all of the fire, flame and fury it is a time, too, of mighty heroes, of bold deeds and great courage.

AT THE HEART of the Old World sprawls the Empire, the largest and most powerful of the human realms. Known for its engineers, sorcerers, traders and soldiers, it is a land of great mountains, mighty rivers, dark forests and vast cities. And from his throne in Altdorf reigns the Emperor Karl-Franz, sacred descendant of the founder of these lands, Sigmar, and wielder of his magical warhammer.

BUT THESE ARE far from civilised times. Across the length and breadth of the Old World, from the knightly palaces of Bretonnia to ice-bound Kislev in the far north, come rumblings of war. In the towering World's Edge Mountains, the orc tribes are gathering for another assault. Bandits and renegades harry the wild southern lands of the Border Princes. There are rumours of rat-things, the skaven, emerging from the sewers and swamps across the land. And from the northern wildernesses there is the ever-present threat of Chaos, of daemons and beastmen corrupted by the foul powers of the Dark Gods. As the time of battle draws ever near, the Empire needs heroes like never before.

Gengrad

laurelorn forest.

Middenheim.

middle mountains.

Wolfenbu

Talabheim.

Altdorf.

The Empire

Nuln.

The Moot.

Grey Mountains.

Averheim.

Black fire

Karak Norn.

ONE
The Tide of Chaos

ABEL HALSTIEG'S BODY lay at Reiner Hetsau's feet, his face frozen in a rictus grin, eyes wide, bloated tongue sticking through bared teeth. Abel's limbs were twisted to the breaking point by the poison that filled his veins. Reiner's companions – Pavel and Hals, Franka, the girl who disguised herself as a bowman, Gert and Jurgen – stared at the corpse as well. Reiner looked at them, knowing one of them had poisoned Abel, and had the power to poison the others with a word. But which one? Who was the spy?

They raised their eyes to him. Hals and Pavel grinned, as if sharing a secret. Gert's eyes twinkled with malicious glee. Jurgen glared. Franka smirked. Dread dragged at Reiner's heart. Were they *all* spies? Was he alone? Was there no one he could...?

Reiner jerked awake, heart thudding. He blinked around the moon-rimmed darkness. He was in his bed in Count Manfred Valdenheim's Altdorf townhouse. Only a nightmare. Then he chuckled bitterly. What did one do when one's nightmares were nothing more than the truth?

Someone tapped at the door. Reiner rolled over and stared. That must have been what had wakened him. He wished he had a dagger, but Count Manfred allowed the Blackhearts no weapons in his house. 'Who is it?' he cried out.

The door opened. A slight figure eased in, candle in hand. It was Franka, still in her boyish kit, though the other Blackhearts now knew her secret. 'Only your valet, m'lord,' she whispered, closing the door and tip-toeing to the bed. 'Come to polish your... sword.'

'Eh?' said Reiner. His head was still clouded with the nightmare.

Franka smiled. 'Come, now. Surely a man as worldly wise as his lordship can't be so obtuse?'

Reiner stared at her blankly. She sighed and sat on the eiderdown, setting the candle on his bedside table. 'Very well, I will spell it out. Yarl has been dead a year. My mourning is over. Indeed, I waited a year and a week, so as not to appear in an unseemly hurry. But now...' She paused, suddenly shy. 'Now, I am my lord's to command.'

Reiner blinked. Since the Blackhearts' return from the fort in the Black Mountains he had been so trapped in his tortuous thoughts that the subject that had filled his waking moments – and his sleeping ones as well – had gone completely from his head. He remembered counting the days – the hours – until he could be with Franka, but now, though his lust for her was more enflamed than ever, now...

'Perhaps,' he said. 'Perhaps we should wait yet a little.'

'Perhaps...?' Franka burst out laughing. 'Reiner! What a joker you are! You almost...' She paused. Reiner wasn't smiling. 'You aren't joking?'

He shook his head.

'But why?' Franka asked, baffled.

Reiner couldn't look at her. If she was only one of the legion of doxies and camp followers he had dallied with over the years they would already be hard at it, but Franka wasn't the sort of girl you used and threw away. 'We… we aren't free. It would ruin it. I don't want to be with you when we have to hide what we do.'

Franka scowled. 'Is this the same man who wanted to have at me in a tent surrounded by our unwitting companions? Weren't your arguments exactly to the contrary, saying we would be stealing moments of freedom? What has got into you?'

'Poison!' said Reiner. It exploded from him before he could stop it. '*Poison* has got into me.'

Franka shrugged. 'But, it has been these many months. And you made no bones about it before.'

'That isn't the poison I mean,' said Reiner. 'I mean the poison of mistrust that has plagued us since–'

'Since we found Abel.'

Reiner nodded. 'One of us is a spy for Manfred. One of us cast the spell that poisoned Halstieg. You've seen how it has hurt us. I'll wager our companions spoke not ten words to each other on our return to Altdorf.'

'*You* certainly didn't,' said Franka. 'But I understand. Gert and Jurgen are good companions. I'm as reluctant as you to think that one of them might be Manfred's creature.'

'Who's to say it must be Gert or Jurgen?' snapped Reiner, then cursed and clamped his mouth shut. Too late…

Franka looked up at him, blankly. 'What do you mean?'

'Nothing. Forget I spoke.'

'Reiner. What do you mean?'

Reiner looked at the floor. 'I know I am a fool, but I haven't been able to get it out of my head since that day. Manfred might have turned one of us – one of the first lot – made some promise, offered freedom, gold, what-have-you, in exchange for spying on the rest.'

'But, Reiner,' said Franka. 'All that's left of us is Hals, Pavel, you, and myself. Surely you can't suspect–' She

froze as a thought came to her, then stood abruptly,
trembling. 'This is why you don't want to be with me.'

'No, I...'

Franka stalked to the door. Reiner threw off his blankets and charged after her. 'Franka, listen to me!'

She opened the door. 'What is there for you to say? Do
you truly think I am a spy for Manfred?'

'No! Of course not!' Reiner couldn't meet her gaze.
'But... I can't be sure.'

There was a pause. Reiner could feel Franka's eyes
burning into him. 'You're mad,' she said. 'You've gone
mad.' She stepped into the corridor and slammed the
door.

'Yes,' he said to the closed door. 'Yes, I believe I have.'

THE BLACKHEARTS WERE fed in the servants' hall to keep
them out of sight of Manfred's frequent visitors. These
days the companions, who had once bantered and
argued like Altdorf fishwives, ate like grim automatons,
as they had since returning from the Black Mountains.
Franka kept her eyes on her plate. Hals and Pavel muttered in each other's ears, heads together. The brawny
sword master Jurgen stared into space as he chewed.
Gert shot sad glances at the others. The barrel-chested
crossbowman was a born teller of tales, and it seemed to
physically hurt him not to have anyone to talk to.

It was a relief therefore, when, the next day at dinner,
just as Reiner was swabbing his plate with his bread, boot
heels sounded on the stairs and Manfred entered the
kitchen, ducking his silver, leonine head under the blackened beams. The cooks and footmen vanished at a wave
of his hand, and he sat down at their table with a sigh.
Reiner saw that he was tired and worried, though he kept
his face as placid as ever.

'I go to Talabheim tomorrow,' he said, 'accompanying
the elf mage Teclis on a diplomatic mission. You will
accompany me, as my servants.' He smiled as they reacted
to this. 'It would defeat your purpose if I called you my

spies, wouldn't it? And I am adding four to your number, who you will meet tomorrow.'

The others tensed at this news. Things were strained enough without adding strangers to the stew.

'You believe you will have need of spies in Talabheim?' asked Reiner. 'It is not a foreign land.'

Manfred looked down and toyed with a table knife. 'This is not to be spoken of, you understand, but something has happened in Talabheim – an eruption in the energies of Chaos so strong it woke the great Teclis from his sleep last night here in Altdorf. He fears that if it is not stopped, Talabheim will fall to Chaos, if it hasn't already.' He jabbed the table with the knife. 'And when the tide of Chaos rises, it is my job to suspect agents of the Ruinous Powers. This is where you come in.' Manfred looked up. 'I head a Reikland embassy which will offer aid to our Talabec brothers in their hour of need. But while we are there, making speeches of mutual support, you will be hunting for the cultists and criminals and conspirators that I feel certain will be found to be the cause of the trouble.'

He sighed and stood. 'We leave tomorrow before dawn. Sleep well.' With a heavy tread, he walked up the stairs again.

Reiner and the others sat silently.

'A tide of Chaos rising in Talabheim?' said Pavel, at last, scratching under the patch that hid his empty eye-socket. 'And we're riding straight for it? That's fine, that is.'

'At least it ain't the cursed mountains again,' growled Hals.

'Maybe we'll all die this time and get it over with,' said Franka, staring at her plate.

Her sadness stabbed Reiner in the heart.

TWO
An Honorable Profession

REINER SAT IN Manfred's opulent coach, waiting for the count's train to get underway. It was still as dark as pitch, and the coach yard flickered with yellow torchlight. Reiner was dressed in a plain grey clerk's doublet, which still smelled faintly of clerk. An inkwell hung from his belt, and a beautiful parchment case rested on his knees. Through the coach's windows he caught glimpses of Pavel, Hals and Gert filling their new positions – Pavel whistling on the buckboard of a provisioning wagon, Gert huffing as he loaded cured hams and sacks of flour onto it, Hals securing chests and baggage on a second wagon, his bald head shining with sweat.

Other men also assisted in the preparations. Reiner eyed them closely. They were not servants of Manfred's household. Were they the new Blackhearts? There was a swaggering, barrel-chested fellow with a bristling red beard seeing to the horses. A meek youth of about the same size, but with a slow, moping gait, followed redbeard around, helping him and laughing obsequiously at

12

his constant jokes. Standing by a mule loaded with leather satchels was a thin young man in the grey robes of the College of Surgeons who blinked around him in a daze. Beside him was a tall, wiry villain with darting eyes who looked utterly unconvincing in the smock and leggings of a surgeon's assistant.

Manfred climbed into the coach, accompanied by Jurgen, in the uniform of the count's guard, and Franka, in page's livery emblazoned with Manfred's gold lion. Jurgen sat next to Reiner, trying vainly to keep his broad shoulders from crowding him. Franka sat beside Manfred. She wouldn't meet Reiner's eye.

Manfred smiled as he saw Reiner's costume. 'I believe you have found your calling at last, Hetsau. You look every inch a clerk. Perhaps one of those fellows who write letters for the unlearned at a pfennig a sheet.'

'Thank you, m'lord,' said Reiner. 'It is at least an honourable profession.'

Manfred scowled. 'There is no more honourable profession than defending one's homeland. It pains me that a noble son of the Empire must be forced to the task.'

'If I recall, m'lord,' said Reiner, 'we were not asked.'

'That is because I am an astute reader of men.' Manfred rapped on the ceiling. 'Kluger! Let's be off. We're late as it is!'

The coachman's whip cracked and the coach rolled forwards. Reiner saw Hans and Pavel out of the window wheeling their wagons around to follow Manfred out of the gate.

THE PROCESSION WOUND through Altdorf's cobbled streets in the pre-dawn grey. The grand palace of Emperor Karl Franz loomed in the mist like a gigantic griffin guarding its nest, the buildings of the Imperial government clustering around it like its brood. After passing through the merchant quarter, they came to the river and the Emperor's private docks, a gated enclosure hemmed in on three sides by barracks, stables and warehouses and on the fourth by the river.

As they entered, Reiner began to understand the importance of their mission. He had assumed Manfred would travel with, at the most, an escort of knights and swordsmen, but the yard was crammed to bursting with the men-at-arms of half a dozen different nobles, all trying simultaneously to load their horses, wagons and equipment on four large, flat riverboats.

Torchlight glinted off the helms of Count Manfred's ten knights and those of the twenty spearmen and twenty archers from his Altdorf retinue, but these were a mere fraction of the assembled force. Here were the greatswords of Lord Schott, a captain of Karl Franz's honour guard, arguing with the knights of Lord Raichskell, Master of the Order of the Winged Helm. Behind them, the handgunners of Lord Boellengen, undersecretary to Baroness Lotte Hochsvoll, Chancellor of the Imperial Fisc, were engaged in a heated shouting match with the Hammer Bearers of Father Olin Totkrieg, representative of the Grand Theogonist, Esmer the Third, while the hooded initiates who accompanied Magus Nichtladen of the Imperial Colleges of Magic watched impassively.

Each lord also had an entourage of secretaries, valets, cooks and grooms that rivalled Manfred's own, as well as wagons full of chests, strong boxes, and provisions. Reiner had seen whole armies set out with smaller trains.

In the centre of this mad jumble was a white island of stillness that made Reiner and Franka catch their breath. Elves. Though Reiner considered himself a well-travelled, well-educated man, he had never seen an elf before. The fair did not leave their homeland often, and when they did, they didn't mix in at the Three Feathers or the Griffin. They met with heads of state, were feted with official banquets, and sailed home laden with fine gifts. So, try as Reiner might to remain cool and aloof, he stared along with everyone else at the six statuesque warriors in silver breastplates and white surcoats who stood motionless before the gangplank of the lead boat.

The elves' faces were as set as carved ivory: sharp, proud and cruelly handsome. Long, thin swords hung at their sides, and curved bows rose from leather scabbards on their backs. It was hard at first for Reiner to tell one from the other. They seemed cast from a single mould. But as he looked, he began to notice subtle differences – a beaked nose on this one, fuller lips on that one. He hoped, however, that he wouldn't be required to remember which was which.

'Wait here,' said Manfred. He stepped from the carriage and crossed to a half-timbered building. Reiner and Franka's gaze remained fixed on the elves, who looked neither right nor left, nor spoke among themselves.

'I thought,' said Franka softly, 'that they would only be men with pointed ears, but... they aren't men.'

'No,' said Reiner. 'No more than we are apes.'

He and Franka exchanged a glance, then looked away.

To hide his discomfort, Reiner turned instead to Jurgen, who looked down as if daydreaming. 'You seem unimpressed by our fair cousins, Rohmner.'

'I am impressed,' said Jurgen. 'They have great control.'

'Control?' Reiner asked. It was rare for the taciturn swordsman to volunteer an observation.

'They are aware of everything, and distracted by nothing. It is a trait to emulate.'

Reiner chuckled. 'You're well on your way, laddie.'

The clamour of the courtyard abated. All heads turned. Reiner leaned over Jurgen to see out of the other window. From the half-timbered building came Manfred and a cluster of officials, in the centre of which was an elf in snow-white robes and a high, mitred cap. He walked with a slight limp and steadied himself with an intricately worked white staff, but there was nothing weak about him. His demeanour commanded attention – majestic and terrifying at the same time. Reiner couldn't take his eyes off him. Though the elf's face was as smooth and unlined as those of his guard, there was an impression of impossible age about him, a depth of wisdom and pain and terrible knowledge in his opal eyes that could be seen even across the dark quay. The men babbled at his heels, all trying to catch his eye.

'But, Lord Teclis,' cried Lord Boellengen. 'We must come. The exchequer must assess the damages!' He was scrawny and chinless, with a bowl of grey hair, and looked, in his parade armour, like a turtle in too big a shell.

'The Emperor has asked me to survey the situation personally,' barked Lord Schott, a squat soldier with a trim black beard. 'I cannot disobey him.'

'The Grand Theogonist must know the extent of this plague of Chaos!' bellowed Father Totkrieg, a white bearded warrior-priest in black robes over polished armour. 'We will not be left behind.'

'If there is Chaos to be fought,' said the towering Lord Raichskell fiercely, 'the Order of the Winged Helm will not be denied the fighting of it. It is not honourable to stay in Altdorf while daemons stalk Talabheim.' His blond beard hung down over his enamelled green plate in two thick braids.

'The investigation of arcane threats is the responsibility of the colleges of magic!' said Magus Nichtladen, a sunken cheeked grey-beard in a rich burgundy robe. 'We must be allowed to do our duty!'

Teclis was deaf to them all. Accompanied by his guard, he walked up the gangplank onto the rover boat, spoke briefly to Manfred, then disappeared below the deck.

Manfred stalked back to his coach and slammed in, furious. 'Self-important fools,' he said, dropping into his seat. The coach began to roll forward, manoeuvring to ascend a ramp onto the back of the first riverboat. 'It was to be Teclis's guard and mine. A legation, not an army. Now we are more than two hundred. But if any of them are left behind the Emperor will never hear the end of it.

Sometimes I don't blame the fair ones for sneering at the pettiness of men.'

THEY SAILED NORTH and east up the wide grey Talabec, winding slowly through farmland toward Talabheim, the City of Gardens, an independent city-state buried deep within the dark forests of Talabecland. Reiner looked forward to seeing it, for it was one of the Empire's marvels, a city built entirely inside an enormous crater, the walls of which were said to be impenetrable.

The riverboats passed green pastures and brown fields in which gaunt peasants ploughed under the stalks of this year's crop to make mulch for next spring's planting. The earth was fresh in many a country graveyard as well, for it had been a hard year in the Empire. Many farmers' sons had come home from Archaon's invasion in coffins if they came home at all. And there had been famine even while the wheat ripened on the stalk, for much of last year's grain had been sent north to feed the armies, and the farmers of the north whose farms had been burned by the invaders had come south and turned to banditry, stealing the rest.

Reiner, Franka and Jurgen were kept busy all day, acting as Manfred's servants, while the count held council with Teclis and the other members of the legation in his stateroom. Late in the afternoon, at the point the river entered the Great Forest, Manfred ordered the boats to land and the servants to make camp. No one thought less of him for this caution. Greater armies had disappeared without a trace under the thick canopy of the old forest, and even the river was not safe as it wound between the looming trees. As it was they would be within it for five days and nights before they reached Talabheim. There was no need to press their luck by passing a sixth night in its shadows.

Manfred had a great tent erected in a fallow field, and dined with the other leaders. Reiner and Jurgen were dismissed and joined their comrades around a campfire, where Reiner was at last able to meet the new recruits. Only Franka, who was kept busy serving Manfred pheasant and wine, was not in attendance.

Pavel and Hals had already become friends – or at least amiable sparring partners – with the big redheaded groom, exchanging cheery insults with him as they spooned stew out of the pot as Gert chuckled appreciatively beside them.

'One Talabecman is worth ten Ostlandmen,' the redbeard was saying.

'In a pissing contest mayhap,' said Hals. 'The only thing the Talabecland pike ever successfully defended was a brewery, and they surrendered after the beer ran out.'

'Ha!' countered redbeard. 'The only thing Ostland pikemen defend is their sheep, and only if they're faithful.'

Reiner laughed. 'Hals, who is this fiery fellow you war with?'

Hals looked around, and it hurt Reiner to see the mistrust that crossed the pikeman's face when he saw who addressed him. 'Er, aye, captain,' he said. 'This is Augustus Kolbein, of Talabheim. He's one of us. Kolbein, this is Captain Hetsau, our leader.'

Augustus nodded and touched his forelock with a hand like a ham. 'A pleasure I'm sure, captain,' he said. 'Though I can't say I'm happy with the terms of service.'

'Nor are any of us, pike,' said Reiner. 'And while I'm pleased to have so strong a soldier with us, I am sorry you had the misfortune to be pressed into our cursed company. But, come, tell us how you fell foul of the Empire.'

Augustus grinned, making his beard bristle even more. 'Ah well, it's entirely my own fault, captain. Y'see I have a temper fiery as my hair, and there was a Reiklander captain of sword at a tavern in Altdorf, some nose-in-the-air jagger – er, beggin' yer pardon, m'lord,' he said, colouring suddenly.

'Never mind,' said Reiner. 'Don't care for the type myself. Go on.'

'Aye, sir. Well, he were badmouthing Talabecland some-thing terrible, saying we was all drunks and yokels and that we, er, performed unnatural acts with trees and the like, and I was taking it well enough. We Talabeclanders have thick skins about that nonsense. But then he had to go and say things about the countess, calling her a Taalist whore who rutted with filthy woodsmen and I don't know what else. Well, I saw red and the next thing I know I'm in the brig and the latchkey is telling me I broke the delicate little thing's neck and spooned out one of his eyes with me thumb.' Augustus shrugged. 'I've no doubt I did, but spit me if I recall it.'

Reiner nodded. 'Maiming a superior officer. Aye, there's no doubt you belong with us. Though again, I am sorry you've come to such a pass.'

The pikeman shrugged. 'Better this than the noose.'

Reiner grunted. 'You may come to change your mind about that.'

The others looked away.

Reiner turned to the big, moonfaced youth who sat next to Augustus. 'And you, lad,' Reiner said. 'What's your tale? Are you a killer of men, an eater of children? We've had all kinds with us over time, so fear not that you will shock us.'

'Thank you, captain sir,' said the boy in a high, nasal voice, 'Thank you. My name is Rumpolt Hafner, and it's an honour to serve under you, m'lord.' He ducked his head. 'Er I, I'm sorry to say I'm not much of a villain, though I will try my best not to disappoint you. And, er, I would certainly do murder if I met again the rotten blackguards who brought me to this.'

'You cannot disappoint me if you do your best and put your trust in me as I put my trust in you,' said Reiner. It sounded false as he said it, and Hals and Pavel shot him sharp looks over the fire as it sank in. He was glad Franka wasn't there. 'But tell your tale and we shall judge how much a villain you are.'

Rumpolt's lower lip stuck out. 'I still don't know why mine was a hanging offence. All I've done is steal a banner.

It was a dare. I'd just joined Lord Loefler's handgunners in Stockhausen. There was another there who were Loefler's rivals, Lord Gruenstad's Men, and my sergeant and his comrades said if I truly wished to be one of their company, I must perform a brave deed against them.'

Hals and Pavel smirked.

Rumpolt clenched his fists. 'They told me I must steal Lord Gruenstad's banner and stand it in the camp privy! How was I to know taking a banner is considered stealing the Emperor's property?'

'It ain't just that, lad,' said Gert, his hands crossed over his heavy belly. '"Tis a company's honour. They defend it with their lives on the battlefield. You think they'd take kindly to some wet-behind-the-ears booby sticking it in a midden?'

'But I didn't know!' moaned Rumpolt. 'And when I was caught, and told the captain that the sergeant and his fellows had put me up to it, the villains denied knowing anything about it.' His looked around at them pleadingly. 'Surely you can see I've been wronged?'

Pavel, Hals and Augustus looked away, disgusted. Reiner heard Augustus mumble, 'How could he not know?' and Pavel reply, 'It ain't a question of knowing.' Jurgen as usual said nothing, and the other two new Blackhearts, the shy 'surgeon' and his hawk-faced assistant didn't seem to care.

'Well lad,' said Reiner, soothingly, 'never mind. There's more than one of us who claims he's innocent, so you're in good company. Welcome to you.'

'Thank you, captain,' said Rumpolt. 'I'll do my best. I swear it.'

Reiner turned next to the wispy-haired young man in the surgeon's robes. 'And you, physician, what is your name?'

The fellow jumped at being spoken to. 'Er, my name is Darius Balthus-Rossen. Of Nuln, originally.'

'You haven't the look of a soldier,' said Reiner. 'Surely Manfred didn't recruit you from the brig.'

'No, m'lord. He found me in the Altdorf city jail.' He shivered. 'An hour before my hanging.'

'And why were you to be hanged?' asked Reiner.

The young man hesitated, glancing around uncertainly.

Reiner sighed. 'We are a company of convicts and lost men, lad. You cannot be more evil than some we have called comrade.'

The scholar shrugged, splaying his hands. 'I am nothing, a student of plants and the mysteries of life's natural processes. I haven't killed or maimed anyone, or stolen anything, or betrayed the Empire. I'm not a villain at all, really.'

'You must have done something,' said Reiner, dryly. 'They were going to hang you, after all.'

Darius hesitated for so long Reiner thought he wasn't going to speak at all. 'I... I was found in possession of a forbidden book.'

'What sort of book?' asked Reiner, though he already had an idea.

'Er, ah, it was nothing. Nothing. A treatise on the medical uses of certain, er, unusual plants.'

'Then why was it forbidden?'

'Because,' said the scholar, suddenly angry, 'my learned professors are blind, hidebound, incurious demagogues who have no interest in learning anything they don't already know. How can the world's knowledge expand if one is forbidden to try new things?' He clutched his thin hands into fists. 'An experiment isn't an experiment if it's been done before. We know so little of how the world works, why plants and animals grow, how the winds of magic twist that growth, how they twist us. The "wise men" are too afraid of the unknown. How–'

'Magic,' said Reiner, interrupting him. 'So, you are a witch then?'

Darius looked up and saw the others staring at him uneasily. 'No,' he said. 'No, I am a scholar.'

'A scholar of magic,' Reiner pressed.

The young man sighed. 'You see? Fear of the unknown. Had I been a baby eater, you would have shrugged and welcomed me, but because I have studied the arcane, no matter how academically, I am a pariah.'

'But are ye a witch?' asked Hals, menacingly.

Darius's shoulders slumped. 'No. No, I am not. Though of course you won't believe me now. I am a man of theory. I have less practical knowledge of the art than a village wise woman. I certainly can't hex you, if that is what concerns you.'

Hals and Pavel made the sign of the hammer, Gert spat over his shoulder.

Reiner coughed. 'Then why are you here? Manfred certainly didn't take you out of the Altdorf jail for your knowledge of plants.'

Darius shrugged again. 'The count told me that I was to see to your wounds. I have some small knowledge of physicking. My father was a surgeon. I can set a bone and patch a wound.' He looked down at his surgeon's robes with a weak smile. 'I seem the only man here whose garments are not a disguise.'

There was silence around the fire. It was clear the others didn't believe him.

Reiner didn't either. If Manfred had wanted a surgeon, he could easily have found one in a military brig who had battlefield experience. Darius had clearly been chosen for another reason. 'Well,' he said at last, 'it seems you have shocked us after all. But give me your word that you will keep your witching to yourself and I will welcome you. And I ask the rest of you,' he said, glancing around, 'to let the lad prove himself by his actions, like you have with all our other comrades.'

Darius sighed. 'I am not a witch. But nevertheless I give my word.'

'Can you magic the poison from our blood?' asked Rumpolt.

Reiner's heart lurched. Out of the mouths of babes! He hadn't thought of that. By Sigmar, if it was true!

Darius laughed. 'If I could, would I be here, enduring this interrogation?'

Reiner sighed. How foolish a thing hope was. Manfred would never choose a witch with so much skill. He turned to Darius's hawk-faced assistant, who was throwing twigs into the fire.

'And you, friend,' Reiner said with as much cheer as he could muster. 'Have you any dark secrets to share? Or at least a name?'

The man looked up with weary contempt. 'I ain't your friend, jagger. Nor friend to any of ye,' he said, his eyes darting to the others. 'Dieter Neff's my name. I'm here because 'twas a less certain death than the noose. And I'll be gone soon as I sort beating this poison, so there's no reason for how-de-dos and telling tales.'

'Dieter Neff!' said Reiner, with a laugh. 'I know of you. You're the "Shadow of Elgrinstrasse," the "Prince of Murder," with a hundred notches on your belt. I saw you once in Stossi's Place when I used to skin the marks there.'

'A hundred and seventeen notches,' said Dieter.

'So they caught you at last,' said Reiner.

'Never,' Dieter sneered. 'I was sold out by an employer who didn't care to pay when I done the job.' He threw another twig on the fire. 'He'll get his…'

Reiner waited for Neff to elaborate, but the man just stared into the fire. Reiner sighed. 'Well, if Master Neff won't speak, I can certainly tell you what I know. He is the best thief and assassin in Altdorf, known for getting into and out of places other men cannot. He once stabbed a man to death in the middle of Lord von Toelinger's annual banquet in full view of ten score armed knights and got out unscathed.'

Dieter barked a laugh, though he didn't look up. 'Y'don't know the half of it, jagger. The burgher I killed was the man who hired me. And I didn't kill him.'

'Eh?' said Rumpolt. 'What do you mean?'

Dieter paused, and Reiner could see he was weighing his contempt for his audience against his desire to brag.

'Berk was a wool merchant named Echert,' he said at last. 'Owed a lot of dangerous people money, so he decides the best thing to do is die. So he hires me to fake killing him and make it look good.' He shrugged. 'Not my usual line, but I like a challenge, so I worked it out. Told him to go to that banquet, then jumped him during the fish course. Cut him up something horrid, but no stab wounds. Screamed very life-like too, 'cause I hadn't said I was going to bleed him. Then I tells him to lie still, and his servants run in and drag him out before anyone gets a close eye on him. Worked like a charm. He was off to Marienburg in a closed coach before they'd given up searching for me.'

Darius snorted. 'This Echert better hope we all die then, for you've betrayed his secret to us.'

Dieter's eyes blazed. 'I ain't never betrayed a client. Echert's dead. Died of the lover's pox two months after he ran, stupid berk. All that money he paid me, wasted.'

Pavel, Hals and Augustus laughed. Darius shrugged. Jurgen stared off into the darkness beyond the fire.

'Well,' said Reiner. 'While you may not intend to stay with us long, Master Neff, you may find the riddle of Manfred's poison harder to crack than you expect, so welcome. We are glad to have a man of your skills with us.'

'I take care of my own skin,' said Dieter. 'The rest of ye can fend for yourselves.'

Reiner sighed. 'Then you likely *will* be taking care of your own skin, for no one else will be eager to do it. Carry on, lads. I've done my bit.' He sat back and took a mouthful of stew, then swallowed hastily as he had a thought. 'Er, one last thing.'

The others looked up.

'I tell you now so there's no trouble later,' Reiner said. 'One of our number is a woman.'

'What?' said Rumpolt, looking around at the others.

Reiner laughed. 'Not these ruffians. Our archer, who plays page to Manfred at the moment. We have kept her secret, and so shall you.'

'An archer?' asked Augustus, dismayed. 'She's a soldier?'

'Aye. A better one than some men I've known,' said Reiner. 'But hear me. If you get any ideas, forget them. The man who hurts her answers to me.'

'And me,' said Hals and Pavel in unison.

'And me,' said Jurgen.

The new men looked at the others curiously, but nodded.

As Reiner returned to his stew he heard Augustus murmuring unhappily to Hals and Pavel.

'I know it ain't right,' said Hals. 'But she won't listen.'

'And she can shoot,' added Pavel.

Jurgen spoke in Reiner's ear. 'Someone watches us.'

Reiner looked around. 'Who? Where?'

'I know not,' said Jurgen. He nodded toward the river, in the blackness beyond Manfred's camp. 'But they are there.'

Reiner stared in the direction the swordsman had indicated. He could see nothing. He shivered.

THREE
The City of Gardens

AFTER FIVE DAYS' sailing up the river, while every eye swept the banks for furtive shadows, Manfred's boats, on the morning of the sixth day, rounded a bend and Reiner saw the towering crater that was Talabheim's impregnable natural defence. It was an awe-inspiring sight, rising hundreds of feet above the carpet of trees, and of so wide a circumference that the wall didn't appear to curve. It stretched like an endless cliff into the distance in both directions.

Augustus beamed from the rail. 'Taal's fortress.'

'Taal's drinking cup, more like,' said Hals, laughing.

Augustus chuckled good-naturedly.

An hour later, oar-boats guided them to slips among the docks of Taalagad, Talabheim's port, a weathered little town huddled in the shadow of the crater wall. It was a damp, dingy place that seemed to consist of nothing but warehouses and taverns. The taverns were crowded, but the warehouses were deserted, for trade appeared to have come to a standstill. Piles of crates and barrels and burlap sacks sat under tarpaulins on docks and around the tariff houses, unclaimed.

The lords and their retinues disembarked and made themselves presentable while word of the legation's arrival was sent into Talabheim. Reiner looked up at the crater, which filled nearly all his vision. A road zigzagged a third of the way up it to a huge fortified gate, the entrance to Talabheim's fabled Wizard's Way, so called for the rumour that it had been cut by sorcery, not human labour.

After a long wait, a company in the red and white of the Talabheim City Guard made their way down the road, pikes glinting, to the docks. They looked tired and haggard, like men too long at the front of some great war. With them was a long-bearded ancient in rich robes and a velvet cap. He bowed low to Manfred.

'Greetings, Count Valdenheim,' he said. 'I am Lord Dalvern Neubalten, the countess's herald. I welcome you to Talabheim on behalf of her Excellency and her court.'

'You are most gracious, Lord Neubalten,' said Manfred, bowing in turn. 'We thank her for her courtesy on behalf of her emperor, Karl Franz.'

'Thank you, count,' said Neubalten. 'The countess has been informed of the reason for your visit, and grants Lord Teclis and your legation leave to enter the city. She asks, however, that you instruct your companies to hold here in Taalagad until you have met with her. I will escort you to her when you are ready.'

'Certainly,' said Manfred, bowing again. He withdrew to speak with Lord Schott and the others.

'Leave our companies outside?' asked Lord Schott. 'In this flea pit? Does she mistrust us?'

'She insults us if so,' said Grand Master Raichskell. 'We are sent by Karl Franz himself.'

'Merely caution, I think,' said Manfred. 'It is a foolish leader who lets two hundred armed men into her city without parley.'

'But did not Lord Teclis say it was dangerous within?' said Lord Boellengen, looking nervously up toward the gate. 'Will we be safe?'

'Sigmar is with us,' snorted Father Totkrieg. 'There is nothing to fear.'

Half an hour later, the companies quartered by the river, the emissaries gathered in their carriages, their servants and luggage in a train behind them, ready to travel.

'You'll walk, Hetsau,' said Manfred, returning to his carriage with the herald. 'Lord Neubalten will ride with me.'

'Very good, m'lord,' said Reiner. He bowed Neubalten into the coach.

Manfred pulled Reiner a few paces away and lowered his voice. 'Your duties begin now,' he said. 'You will be at my shoulder, quill in hand, when we are presented to the countess, but your true purpose will be to observe her court, noting names and temperaments. Whatever occurs within Talabheim, you can be sure the members of her Excellency's parliament will be trying to gain advantage over their fellows by it. We will use these rivalries to foil the Talabheimers' attempts to save themselves from their predicament.'

Reiner frowned. 'You don't want to save Talabheim? Then why have we come?'

'You misunderstand me,' said Manfred, impatient. 'That is precisely what I want. I want Teclis and the forces of the Reikland to be the ones to save Talabheim. You are here to make sure that Talabheim finds it impossible to save itself.' He nodded at the city guards, lined up to escort them into the city. 'These woodsmen have become a deal too independent of late. They must learn that they are better off within the Empire than without it.'

'I shall do my best, m'lord,' said Reiner. He smiled as Manfred returned to his coach. Ever the manipulator, Manfred. He undoubtedly calculated the political effect of what he had for breakfast every morning.

Reiner joined the baggage train with the rest of the Blackhearts, sitting with Augustus and Gert on a provision wagon as the procession got under way, climbing the zigzag road to the immense fortified gate known as the High Watch. They passed under its cannon emplacements and the sharp points of its portcullis, then disappeared into the darkness of its wide mouth, as if marching down the gullet of some legendary behemoth.

TALABHEIM HAD GONE mad.

Even from the exit of the Wizard's Way, high on the interior wall of the crater, Reiner knew it. Columns of smoke rose all over the city, which stretched out below him, rising to a pall of murk that hid the crater's far edge, thirty miles away. Strange colours glowed within the cap of smoke like occluded lightning, but there was no accompanying thunder. Reiner had seen the like once before, over a Kislev battle field, when his pistol company had faced a horde of northmen. He shivered. Hals and Augustus spat and made the sign of the hammer. Darius cringed away from the clouds.

The city climbed the inside of the crater almost to the Wizard's Way, tumble-down hovels and primitive dwellings cut into the very rock lapped up the slope like filthy debris left by a retreating flood. Below these, growing larger and more prosperous away from the wall, were houses and buildings and manor houses, and everywhere, parks and gardens and open spaces. It was the greenest city Reiner had ever seen. At the edge of his smoke-hampered vision it dwindled away entirely into forest and wild land – the Taalgrunhaar, Taal's sacred forest, that featured so prominently in jokes about Talabecmen and their wild revels.

As the legation wound down a switch-back road that matched that on the outside of the crater, Reiner saw narrow paths leading off into the nearly vertical slum. Furtive figures haunted these alleys, ducking behind precariously perched shacks as the procession passed. The air reeked of death and rotting vegetation and stranger things, and Reiner's ears were assaulted by wailing cries and distant crashes. The wall of the crater loomed over his shoulder menacingly. He felt hemmed in, trapped inside a madhouse.

Things only got worse as they reached level ground. The tree-lined street their escort led them down had once been handsome and well kept. Now many of its buildings were nothing but charred skeletons. Others had all their windows smashed. Furtive faces peered from them, watching the passing legation with empty eyes. A pile of naked bodies burned in a square – men, women and children – all ablaze. One body had a fang-toothed face where his stomach should have been. Corpses hung from a gibbet erected before a livery stable.

Reiner heard a choking sob beside him. Augustus was staring around, tears running into his red beard. 'What has become of it?' he moaned. 'What has become of it?'

Reiner nodded. 'Aye, terrible.'

'What do you know of it?' the pikeman snarled. 'This is my home! And it's–' A sob cut off his words. 'It's murdered. Murdered!'

A man in rags broke from a house and bolted for an alley. His head was a sack of loose flesh that bobbed with each step. Peasants armed with clubs chased him down and beat him mercilessly as he screeched and wept. The Talabheim guards marched on impassively.

Augustus turned away. 'This cannot be. Talabheim is the fairest city in the Empire. The city of gardens. The–' He stopped suddenly. Across the street was a gutted tavern. Only the front door and the placard above it, blackened beyond reading, still stood. 'The Stag and Garland!' Augustus cried. 'And is old Hans the barman dead then?' His fists clenched. 'Someone must pay for this. Someone must die for this.'

Closer to the city centre the streets became more populated. Priests of Morr, their faces covered in burlap, threw bodies onto pyres. Brazen thieves carried paintings and silver out of houses. A man with tin charms in the shape of hammers cried that they were 'blessed by the

Grand Theogonist himself,' and guaranteed to protect against madness and mutation. He did a brisk business. Gaunt peasants crowded around a wild-eyed priest of Taal, who shook a wooden staff wrapped in holly leaves.

'Are not the waking of the trees and the destruction of the Sigmarite temple signs of Taal's displeasure?' he cried. 'Taal is angry with us for allowing the upstart Sigmar to be worshipped in his land. This is Taal's land, and we have betrayed him by kissing the feet of the foreign tyrant Karl Franz. Repent, ye faithless ones! Repent!'

Before his words faded out behind Manfred's train, the bellowing of a priest of Sigmar haranguing another mob reached Reiner's ears.

'Is not the waking of the trees proof that Taal is a daemon?' he roared. 'What but a daemon would set its servants upon its worshippers? What but a daemon would drive men mad and twist their bodies with foul mutations? What but a daemon would raze Sigmar's new temple? We must bring torches to the forests, brave Sigmarites, and destroy their hidden temples as they have destroyed ours!'

'Sigmarite scum!' growled Augustus under his breath.

'You speak against Sigmar?' asked Gert, moustache bristling. 'You seek a black eye?'

'That's enough,' said Reiner sharply.

'But captain, did y'not hear–?' said Gert.

Reiner cut him off. 'I heard a pair of ranting fools. And you are a pair of fools if you listen to them. Now have done.'

Both Gert and Augustus opened their mouths to protest, but a sudden movement to their right distracted them. Hollow cheeked men, women and children spilled from an abandoned building, hands outstretched.

'Food, sirs!' bleated one.

'A pfennig, for your pity,' called another.

'Help us,' wept a woman.

The guards shoved and kicked them back, knocking them to the cobbles. The beggars lay where they fell, clutching their bloody heads and wailing. They hadn't been beggars long. Their clothes were dirty, but still whole, but already hope was gone from their eyes.

'Can these truly be men of Talabheim?' asked Augustus, dismayed. 'Talabheimers don't beg. They don't back down from a fight. What ails them? They should be robbing us blind. Or trying to.'

'They've seen too much, I'll warrant, and it's broken them,' said Gert. 'I've seen it before. An entire company of Ostermark sword. They'd fought some... thing, in the defence of Hergig, and though they beat it, afterwards it was as if the thing had torn out their hearts and left the rest of them whole. Worse than death, to my mind.'

Augustus shivered, then nodded. The two men seemed to have forgotten their argument.

In the centre of a weedy park, a jeering crowd surrounded a naked girl tied to a stake. They threw cobbles and clods of dirt at her as she wailed and begged for mercy. There were bundles of tinder at her feet and a fellow in a pointed red hood danced around her with a torch. She was very beautiful, though her face and body were bruised, but her legs were furred and hoofed like a goat's, and she had a hairless purple tail. Her high thin voice penetrated through the howls of the mob.

'Please! I ain't done nothing,' she whined. "Tisn't my fault. It just happened.'

The hooded man touched his torch to the hay and it went up in a rush. The girl began to scream. Reiner turned his head, but the sound stayed with him.

All along their route were barricaded streets manned by weary guards, some wearing the red and white of the city watch, others in the livery of this lord or that, or in no uniform at all, protecting streets or neighbourhoods from invasion. At some streets it seemed the guards and barricades were there to keep the inhabitants in. Beyond these was wholesale destruction, and slinking shapes that might once have been men.

Further on, they passed between the great grey stone edifice of the Grand Courthouse of Edicts, where the Talabheim parliament convened, and the Hollows, in the bowels of which those convicted in the courts served out their sentences. The gibbets and punishment cages in the forecourt of the courthouse were so thickly hung with corpses that it looked like a butcher's window.

Rising over the low, dormered buildings of the Law district, Reiner could see the buildings of the temple quarter, known as the City of the Gods – golden Myrmidia brandishing a spear at the top of a granite column, Shallya's slender white steeple, Taal's upthrusting rowans, and high above them all, Sigmar's stern stone bell-towers. It looked a calm, serene place, until Reiner noticed the pillars of smoke rising among the spires.

Soon after, the procession came to a high stone wall with a large, well-defended gate. Knights on horseback sat at parade rest before it, and trebuchets were mounted on turrets to either side. Over the wall Reiner could see the gables of fine houses and the tops of tall trees. A procession of priests of Morr was exiting the gate. They carried a handsome coffin. Reiner smirked. The rich, it seemed, were not burned like tinder in city squares.

The captain of their escort exchanged words with the gate captain, and Manfred's train passed once again into another world. The horror and clamour of the merchant district fell away instantly, replaced by quiet calm and stately beauty. Large, elegant manor houses surrounded by extravagant gardens lined the empty street. Everywhere upon the houses were swirling designs of oak leaves, vines and acorns, and ornate beam ends shaped like the heads of stags, boars, and bears. There was no one abroad in the neighborhood, and Reiner began to realise that what he had mistaken for calm was actually paralysis. The nobles hid in their homes, waiting for the storm to pass.

The procession came to a stop before another high stone wall, even more well defended than the previous one, and after more challenges and conferring, they were admitted. Inside was a grand estate, with extensive grounds, gardens, groves and out-buildings and, in the centre, a sprawling, ivy-covered old manor house, as big as any five of the noble houses they had just passed stuck together. And indeed, that was exactly what it looked like. Reiner could count at least seven distinct architectural styles in the portions he could see, representing additions made in as many centuries.

'This is the countess's residence?' he asked, turning to Augustus, confused.

The pikeman nodded. 'Aye, the Grand Manor.'

'But, but she doesn't live in a castle?'

"Course she does,' said Augustus. 'Look around you.' He swept his hand around toward the walls of the crater, now miles away, but still visible through the trees in all directions. 'The greatest castle in the Empire.'

'Ah, of course,' said Reiner.

'Was a castle once,' said Augustus. 'Back in Talgris's time, when the crater wasn't fully tamed. You can still see the old keep there.' He pointed toward the centre of the manor, where a fat, rough-hewn barrel keep reared its ugly, crenellated head over the civilized gables and dormers of the later additions. 'Still use it for the dungeon and the treasure vaults, and kitchens and the like too, but nobody quarters there any more. Cold and drafty.'

Their escort led them up a tree-lined avenue past barracks buildings and fortified sentry posts, and came to a halt in a gravelled forecourt on the west side of the Grand Manor where a company of the countess's greatswords waited for them.

Manfred stepped out of his carriage with Lord Neubalten, and Reiner took up his place three paces behind them. The courtyard grew hushed as Teclis joined them. It seemed Talabecmen were no more immune to the awe elves inspired than their Reikland cousins.

The legation crossed to tall double doors, where the greatswords waited for them, all dressed in green and buff, with brightly polished steel breastplates. Their captain, a tall man, with a narrow head of close-cropped blond hair and the grim eyes of a veteran stepped forward and saluted.

'Lord Teclis, Count Valdenheim,' said Neubalten, 'May I present Heinrich von Pfaltzen, captain of Countess Elise's personal guard.'

The captain clicked his heels and bowed, doing his best to remain unmoved by Teclis's presence. 'M'lords,' he said. 'The countess awaits you.'

The legation, escorted by the greatswords, followed von Pfaltzen through a series of broad carpeted corridors. Rich tapestries of woodland scenes were hung at regular intervals, and archways opened into richly appointed sitting rooms, libraries and galleries. It was magnificent, as befitted the seat of a countess, yet it maintained a slightly rustic ambiance, like that of some royal hunting lodge.

At a pair of tall, intricately-carved wooden doors, von Pfaltzen was challenged by two halberdiers in elaborate green and buff livery. He announced that Lord Teclis of Ulthuan and Count Manfred of Emperor Karl Franz's court in Altdorf and their retinue begged the countess's permission to enter.

The halberdiers saluted, and said that the countess granted her guests leave to enter, then swung open the heavy doors.

Lord Neubalten bowed Teclis, Manfred and the party into a high, handsome throne room. A green and yellow stained-glass clerestory painted the long room with mellow golden light. Rows of wood-clad pillars carved to resemble tree trunks rose up to spreading branches that supported a patterned green ceiling so that the room looked like a sun-dappled forest glade.

The herald led the party down between the pillars to a raised dais under a green velvet canopy, while von Pfaltzen and his men took up positions to either side of it.

Upon the dais, sitting on an ornate oak throne, was Countess Elise Krieglitz-Untern, ruler of the free city of Talabheim. After all the beauty of the Grand Manor she was a bit of a disappointment. Squat and broad and dowdy, even in a green and gold dress of exquisite workmanship, with lumpy features in a round, red face, she looked more like a fish-wife than a countess.

No wonder the common folk were reputed to love her, thought Reiner. They could claim her for their own. The one evidence of her nobility was her bearing. She carried herself with enough regal hauteur for three countesses – her posture ramrod straight, her bulbous nose high and proud, her eyes hard and flashing.

Noble courtiers stood in clusters around the dais. Everyone was staring at Teclis, who seemed to glow with his own inner light in the shadowy green room. Even the countess stared.

Lord Neubalten stepped forward and began announcing the names of those who came before the countess, giving all their titles and honours. Bored, Reiner glanced around the room, doing as Manfred had ordered, trying to judge the character and importance of the lords and ladies of the countess's court by their dress and manner. That one with the neatly trimmed beard was undoubtedly a pompous ass. And that one, with the slouching shoulders, a born rogue if ever there was. And the woman standing behind the pillar with the young lord at her side was…

Reiner's heart stopped. The woman was Lady Magda Bandauer, the devious witch who, when he had last been in her presence, had tried to kill him with the power of the cursed banner, Valnir's Bane. Reiner's hand went to the hilt of his sword, but then he released it. The bitch certainly deserved to be hacked to pieces, but perhaps this was not the place. What was she doing here, he wondered? Did these poor fools know the evil they had welcomed into their court?

Magda turned, as if she felt Reiner's eye upon her. Her gaze swept past him at first, then jerked back, and the look of fear that sprang to her face was gratifying, even if her discovery of him was unfortunate. They eyed each other silently across the throne room before the voice of the countess brought Reiner back to the business at hand.

'Lord Teclis,' she was saying. 'Wisest of the fair, most benevolent counsellor of men, we welcome you to our humble court and to the free city of Talabheim, jewel of Talabecland.'

Teclis inclined his head. 'I thank you, countess.' His voice was soft, but carried with unnatural resonance.

'And welcome also to you, Count Valdenheim,' she said in a much colder tone. 'Though we admit bafflement at your presence here with so great a force and with no prior notice of your coming.'

Manfred bowed low. 'Thank you, countess, and I beg you to accept my apology for this unheralded visit. We come at the great Teclis's request, and with the most peaceful of intentions. The fair one warned Karl Franz that some great evil had befallen Talabheim, and in a spirit of brotherly concern, the Emperor has sent this humble embassy to give you what assistance we can.'

The countess's face remained impassive, but Reiner could see that she was taking Manfred's diplomatic hyperbole for what it was worth. 'We are moved by the Emperor's concern, but there was no need for him to trouble himself. While we would welcome the wisdom of Lord Teclis at any time, we have the situation well in hand. We expect to divine the cause of this disturbance shortly, and are fully capable of defending our city until that hour comes.'

'You do not have the situation in hand,' said Teclis, as softly as before. 'The currents of Chaos in Talabheim daily grow stronger, your subjects die in the streets, and you haven't the manpower to stop this, only to protect the less affected neighbourhoods and the homes of the wealthy. And if the cause is what I believe it to be, not even your greatest scholars can put it right.'

Reiner saw the countess's eyes flare at this bald statement of fact, but there was little she could say. Teclis was an elf.

He had no need to trade in courtesies, for his status was unaffected by political manoeuvring. He had seen many emperors come and go, and would likely see three more ascend the throne in Altdorf. 'We welcome any aid you can give us, great one,' she said through tight lips. 'But if, as you say, there is nothing human efforts can do, would it not have been just as well for you to come alone?'

Manfred spoke up before Teclis could reply. 'The Emperor would not allow so noble a guest to travel alone within his domain. Nor would he allow the niceties of courtesy to delay aid for our fair sister Talabheim if it were necessary. We came in force, but with the hope that we would not be needed. And while your soldiers may indeed have the situation well in hand, there is no reason to turn away reserves when they are here to help.'

'To interfere, you mean,' said the countess. 'To take credit for Talabheim's victory over this trouble.'

'Countess,' said Manfred. 'I assure you...'

'And I assure you that your help is not needed. You have delivered the great Teclis to us, and we thank you for that. You may now retire, certain that we will keep him safe and will bring no shame upon the Empire while he is our guest. Thank you.'

It was an unmistakable dismissal, but Manfred only bowed and drew a rolled parchment from his doublet. 'Countess, it grieves me that I must remind you that, while Talabheim is a free city, it still resides within Talabecland, and that Talabecland is a state of the Empire, subject to its laws and to the commands of its Emperor.' He held up the parchment. 'Though gently worded, this document is not an offer of aid, but a command from Karl Franz, signed by his own hand, ordering your government to allow his representatives to assist you until they have determined that the danger to Talabheim, and the Empire, has passed.'

Manfred passed the parchment to Neubalten, who took it to the countess. She passed it to a scribe that scurried forward from behind the dais. He read it quickly, then whispered in her ear while her knuckles grew white upon the arms of her throne.

'This is an outrage,' she said at last. 'The Emperor over-steps Imperial law. The duchies have the ruling of their own lands, and need brook no interference from the Emperor unless it is a matter that affects the whole of the Empire. This is clearly Talabheim's problem, and–'

'Forgive me, countess,' said Teclis. 'I take no sides in the affairs of men, but you are incorrect. Though this distur-bance happens in Talabheim, if unchecked it will affect not only Talabecland and the Empire, but also the stabil-ity of the whole world. I would not be here else.'

The countess paled. 'Is it truly so serious?'

Teclis nodded gravely. 'It is.'

'Then,' she said, flashing a sharp look at Manfred, 'on your authority, fair one, and your authority alone, do I submit to this unwished-for interference by these foreign lords.'

'Thank you, countess,' said Teclis. 'I would meet with those of your court most concerned with this affair at your earliest convenience, to learn what they have learned of it.'

'Certainly,' said the countess. 'I will call an emergency meeting of the parliament tonight. We will make enlight-ening you and the Emperor's embassy our business. Until then, if you will follow Lord Neubalten, he will make all arrangements for your lodging.'

Teclis and Manfred and the rest of the Reiklanders bowed and stepped back.

'Thank you, countess,' said Teclis.

'Most gracious, your eminence,' said Manfred.

As the party followed Neubalten out of the throne room, Reiner leaned into Manfred. 'M'lord, do you recall Lady Magda Bandauer?'

'How could I not?' said Manfred, frowning. 'The woman brought my brother to war against me. Why?'

'She is here,' said Reiner. 'With the young man in blue and burgundy to the left of the dais.'

Manfred looked discretely over his shoulder, then nodded, his face grim. 'I see.'

'M'lord,' said Reiner. 'It would give me great pleasure if you were to order me to remove her.'

'And it would give me great pleasure to so order you,' said Manfred. 'Unfortunately, the young man is Baron Rodick Untern and Lady Magda wears his colours. As much as I might wish to destroy my brother's corrupter, it would be impolitic at this moment to murder the wife of the countess's cousin.'

FOUR
A Great Opportunity

THAT EVENING, THE Parliament of Talabheim met in a large wood-panelled chamber within the Grand Courthouse of Edicts. Countess Elise sat at the northernmost seat of a large U-shaped table. The members of her parliament – representatives of Talabheim's noble families, the merchant guilds, the city's temples, the colleges of magic, the countess's exchequer, as well as the three generals of the Hunters' council, Christoph Stallmaier, commander of the Taalbaston, Detlef Kienholt, commander of the city guard, and Joerg Hafner, commander of the militia, her minister of trade, and her minister of public works, filled the other seats. Extra seats had been added to accommodate Teclis and Manfred, and more were set along the walls for the other Reiklanders. Reiner sat with them, trying to put names, faces and titles together.

Arch Lector Farador, the voice of Sigmar in Talabheim, was speaking. 'The brothers of the Order of the Cleansing Flame have wrung many confessions from captured mutants, but little have come of them. It appears some lied, even under torture, and though the confessions of others led us to new nests of mutants and heretics, we have yet to find the villain who has set this curse upon us.'

'The brothers of Taal have not been idle either,' chimed in Heinrich Geltwasser, the temple of Taal's representative. 'Though we scorn the uncivilised methods of the Sigmarites, we have prayed to Father Taal unceasingly, and performed ceremonies to quiet the trees. We have admittedly had little success.' He shot a dark look at Farador. 'Too many of our faithful are being drawn away to other religions, and our prayers haven't the strength they once did.'

'Prayer cannot take the place of action,' said Farador. 'If you had been hunting mutants instead of dancing naked in the forest, this crisis might already be over.'

'Do you mock the mysteries of Taal?' cried Geltwasser.

'If the exchequer weren't so tight-fisted,' said Lord Otto Scharnholt, a thick-jowled dandy with rings on every finger, who was Talabheim's minister of trade, 'we would have more troops in the streets and they would be better outfitted.'

M'lord has grown rich from the office, thought Reiner, eyeing his broad belly. Takes a cut from every cargo that comes through Taalagad no doubt.

'And where does the minister of trade expect these monies to come from?' asked Lord Klaus Danziger, the Countess's exchequer, a sober, long-faced fellow in a black doublet of the plainest cut. 'The treasury is empty, m'lord. Empty!'

'Fathers, lords, please.' Teclis's soft voice easily cut through their barking. 'Your attempts to quell the disturbance are to be commended, but the madness and mutations are not the result of a lack of faith, and cannot be defeated by soldiers. A great eruption of Chaos energy has occurred somewhere in the city. Only when the eruption is found and... capped, will the mutations cease and the madness fade.' He looked around the table with his penetrating stare. 'Here is what I must know. In what area of the city are the mutations most prevalent? Have any ancient ruins or strange artefacts been uncovered within the limits of the city? Have any weapons or artefacts of great power been stolen? Any of these may point to the source of the disturbance.'

All the parliament members began speaking at once.

'Pfaffenstrasse crawls with mutants,' said the master of the wool merchants' guild.

'Pfaffenstrasse has nothing on Girlaedenplatz,' said the master of the union of coopers and wainwrights. 'They are thickest there.'

'It's those filthy peasants in the Tallows,' said Scharn-holt. 'My tenants there have gone mad. They've burned down my property. The trees...'

'There are none in the Manor district,' said Danziger primly. 'They wouldn't dare.'

'It comes from the woods,' said a Sigmarite.

'It comes on the wind,' said a Taalist.

'It comes from the wells,' said the master of the bakers' guild.

'Gentlemen, please!' The countess rapped her mace of office on the table. 'You will all be given a chance to speak. Now–'

'Your pardon, countess,' said Teclis, holding up his hand.

The room quieted and turned to him. Teclis pointed a long finger at a haughty mage in green and gold robes. The man swallowed nervously.

'Your name, magus?' asked Teclis.

'I, lord? Er, I am Magister Lord Dieter Vogt, representative of Talabheim's College of Jade Magic.'

'You said something just now, magister lord,' said Teclis. 'Please repeat it.'

'Er, well, I, I said some members of our college found a large stone recently. But nothing came of it,' he added hurriedly. 'It had no power at all.'

Teclis placed his hands flat on the table. 'I see.' There was the faintest tremor in his voice. 'And where did you find this stone?'

Magister Lord Vogt coughed, acutely aware that Teclis was displeased. 'Er, well, when the Temple of Sigmar collapsed...'

'The temple did not collapse!' cried Arch Lector Farador. 'It was destroyed by cultists!'

'It wasn't,' said the minister of public works. 'You built it over a sink hole. It fell in, then smashed through into the caves.'

'A sign,' said Taalfather Geltwasser, 'as if any were needed, that the Sigmarites' faith is founded on unsound doctrine.'

'What caves are these?' Teclis asked the minister of public works.

'Er, well, yer lordship,' said the minister, ducking his head. 'We didn't know about 'em until the temple opened 'em up, but there are caves under the city. Haven't yet had a chance to look about much, what with all this madness.'

'The caves are where we found the stone, m'lord,' said Magister Lord Vogt. 'When men were sent into them to look for survivors, it was discovered that the stones of the temple had smashed open an ancient crypt set into the floor of the cave. Our college was asked to determine if the crypt was an arcane threat.'

'It was elven,' said Teclis.

Lord Vogt looked up in surprise. 'Er, yes. It was. How...'

'And it contained a rune-covered stone the height of a man.'

'Indeed, fair one,' said the mage. 'Much of the crypt was destroyed by the falling temple, and the runestone was dislodged from its pedestal, but miraculously it was intact.'

Teclis breathed a sigh of relief at that. 'So you have the stone then.'

Vogt nodded. 'Yes, lord. Our scholars thought it might have some magical properties, and so brought it back to our lodge to examine it, but it had no magic and seemed to serve no higher purpose.'

'No higher purpose than maintaining the stability of the world,' said Teclis. He sat back, pressing his chest with his hand as if he were in pain, then looked up. 'What your scholars uncovered is a waystone. It appears magically inert because its purpose is to draw away magic. It absorbs emanations of magical energy – Chaos energy – and shunts it into… another place. Its removal is the cause of Talabheim's trouble. Without it, the source of the Chaos energy under your city spreads unchecked.'

'But, Lord Teclis,' said Magister Lord Vogt. 'Talabheim is one of the least magical places in the Empire. It takes a great deal of concentration to cast even the simplest spell here. At least that was true until… ah. I see.'

'Yes,' said Teclis. 'Since the plague of madness, you have found your powers greatly increased. But the risk of spell work has increased as well, and many mages have gone mad. Is this not the case?'

Vogt looked reluctant to speak. The countess spoke for him. 'Ten mages have been put to death in the past week, having succumbed to madness. I have ordered a moratorium on the practice of the art until the crisis has passed.'

Teclis nodded. 'This crater, in which Krugar, chief of the Talabec tribe, founded your city thousands of years ago, was formed thousands of years before that, when a great meteor of pure warpstone struck the earth. My forefathers, whose land this was at that time, placed the waystone above the shattered fragments of the meteor in order to make the land habitable again. There are many such waystones buried around the world, capping similar loci of Chaos energies. The danger when one of these waystones is removed is not just to the land around it, but to the world as a whole. For just as the removal of one link in a shirt of mail weakens it, so the loss of one waystone weakens all others and causes the weave of protection they knit around the world to unravel. If left uncapped, the emanations which poison your city will spread like ripples in a pond, unseating other nearby waystones, which will in turn unseat further waystones until the earth becomes the endless nightmare of madness that it was when the rifts of Chaos first opened, eons ago.' Teclis coughed and touched his chest again. 'And this time, the elves could not contain it, for we are not what we once were.'

The countess and the parliament paled at this vision of apocalypse.

'You are fortunate,' Teclis continued. 'I was near enough to feel the eruption when the stone was dislodged, for only an elf mage with a knowledge of the old lore can reseat the stone. If you had had to send to Ulthuan for assistance I might have come too late.' He turned to the countess. 'I will take the waystone and prepare it. In the meantime, the crypt that held it should be cleared of rubble, and preparations made to seal it once I have reset the stone. Too much time has been wasted already. Men die needlessly as we speak.'

'Yes, Lord Teclis,' said the countess, inclining her head. 'It shall be done. Magister Lord Vogt, escort our guest to your lodge.'

Vogt stood and bowed. 'Yes, countess. Right away.'

'THEY'VE LOST IT!' laughed Manfred as he slammed into the coach and fell back into his seat. 'Half a tonne and as tall as a man and they've lost it!'

Reiner had been sitting in Manfred's coach for the past hour outside the tree shrouded compound of the college of jade magic, waiting while Manfred, Teclis, Magus Nichtladen, and the countess – the only persons the secretive mages would allow in – went with Magister Lord Vogt to retrieve the stone.

'Lost it?' he asked.

'Aye!' chuckled Manfred. 'Mages scurrying around like housemaids looking in cupboards and attics. But it's gone. Stolen most likely.' He rubbed his hands together.

'And you are pleased?'

'Eh?' said Manfred. 'Don't be a fool! Of course I'm pleased. If Vogt had produced it, the Jade college would have got the credit, but now we have as much chance as any to find it. This is a great opportunity.'

'Your concern for the citizens of Talabheim is admirable, m'lord,' said Reiner dryly.

'My concern,' said Manfred, 'is for the Empire as a whole, and if a few must die to ensure its stability over the long term, then I am prepared to take their deaths upon my conscience.'

Reiner smirked. 'Most noble of you.'

WHEN THEY RETURNED to the Law Quarter townhouse the countess had provided for the Reikland legation, they found Lord Danziger, the prim, black-clad exchequer, waiting for Manfred in the drawing room.

'If I might have a word with you in private, lord count?' he asked. His manner was as stiff as his high collar, and his posture as rigid.

'Certainly, Lord Danziger,' said Manfred. 'Hetsau, show his excellency to my quarters.'

When they were settled in Manfred's private rooms and Reiner had served Reikland wine, Danziger spoke.

'As the countess's treasurer,' he said, 'it pains me to see all the funds wasted so far attacking this problem from the wrong end. As you have seen, the parliament is a fractious group, too concerned with casting blame to take decisive action, and though I am loath to say it, I believe some members hope to profit by this trouble. That is why I come to you. You are a confidant of Karl Franz and of the great Teclis. I know you must hold the Empire's interests uppermost, and wish to bring an end to this unpleasantness as quickly as possible.'

'Indeed,' said Manfred, with every appearance of sincerity. 'And if you have some information that may help us to that end, I would be extremely pleased to hear it.'

'I believe I have, sir,' said Danziger. 'I, like most men of means in the city, have volunteered my house guard to assist in the protecting of those neighbourhoods that remain whole. When Teclis spoke of this "waystone" just now, I remembered an incident my captain, Gerde, related to me recently. It seemed nothing at the time. But now...'

'Please go on, m'lord,' said Manfred. Reiner could see him trying to mask his eagerness.

'Gerde was manning the Schwartz Hold barricades,' said Danziger. 'And just after midnight, he saw a group of men carrying a heavy burden into an old granary that had been burned down when the madness began. Gerde dispatched one of his men to follow them and see what they were about.'

'And what did this man discover?' asked Manfred.

'He returned after an hour, saying the thieves had carried their burden through a hole in the granary's cellar to the sewer below it. He trailed them through the sewers and catacombs below Talabheim, until they reached at last a place guarded by well-armed men, and he could follow no further.'

Manfred leaned in. 'This incident was not reported to the city guard?'

'I do not believe so,' said Danziger.

'Then only we know of this?'

'Aye, m'lord. And it would be wise to keep it so.' said Danziger. 'Talabheim is a city of intrigues, and telling one man a confidence is the same as telling a hundred. If we wish to strike swiftly we must remain covert.'

Manfred nodded. 'Very good. Then I will strike tomorrow morning, before sunrise. Send your man to me that he may guide us. Thank you for this information, Lord Danziger.'

'Er, by your leave, sir, if I added my men to yours, I think we would be assured of success.'

Manfred smiled wryly. 'Certainly. Be here tomorrow at the fifth hour and we will see if we can find the stone.'

'Excellent,' said Danziger. 'Tomorrow morning then,' He stood and bowed crisply. Reiner escorted him to the door.

'You don't trust him, m'lord?' he asked, returning.

'As far as I can throw a horse,' said Manfred. 'That is why I ensured that he would accompany us.'

'By implying that you would rather he didn't.'

Manfred nodded. 'He could have meant to send us to our deaths. And had he allowed us to go alone I would have known that was what he intended. Now I know he plays another game.'

'He intends to use us to help capture the stone, and then take it and the credit for himself,' said Reiner. 'Just as you mean to use him for the same purpose.'

'You learn the craft well, Hetsau,' said Manfred.

'But what's to stop him from doing as he intends?' asked Reiner.

Manfred smiled. 'I shall bring Teclis.'

'Ah,' said Reiner. 'And Danziger dare not take the stone from the elf, while you may claim the credit of its recovery for Altdorf and yourself because it was you who brought the fair one here.'

'That is the hoped for outcome, yes,' said Manfred. 'But, just in case, I will have you and your Blackhearts along to make it a certainty.'

Reiner sighed as he collected the wine glasses. 'And you brand *me* rogue,' he said under his breath.

Manfred shot him a sharp look.

FIVE
Will a Fire Unmake It?

'ENJOYING THE HIGH life, captain?' asked Hals, sneering. 'Poncing about with counts and countesses and elves.'

'While we see to the luggage,' said Pavel.

'And the horses,' added Gert.

'And polish the boots,' said Franka.

'You needn't blame me for it,' said Reiner. 'It was Manfred's plan. Not mine.'

Reiner sighed. What would have been jovial banter in the days before Abel Halstieg's death was now in earnest. The poison of suspicion had curdled the Blackhearts' comradeship. He wished he could think of something to say that would make it as it had been, but when he knew one of them was a spy, and would report anything he said to Manfred, he was at a loss for words.

The Blackhearts stood shivering and rubbing their hands in the carriage yard behind the Reiklanders' Law Quarter townhouse. The sun had not yet risen and the morning mist swirling in the torchlight was bitter cold. They were dressed in the livery of Manfred's house guard – black doublet and breastplate painted with his white and gold lion – and armed with swords and daggers in addition to their preferred weapons. Augustus and Rumpolt were stealing curious glances at Franka in her soldier's kit, but said nothing. Darius and Dieter looked more ridiculous as soldiers than they had as surgeons.

Ten of Manfred's Nordbergbruche spearmen stood by them in two neat lines before their captain, a brawny youth named Baerich. They shot dirty looks at the Black-hearts, who slouched and yawned in utter disregard for military discipline.

There was a rap at the back gate and Captain Baerich opened it to admit Danziger and ten swordsmen, all in kit as plain and black as his own.

'We go rabbit hunting with this army?' muttered Hals. 'They'll hear us coming miles away.'

A few minutes later Manfred and Teclis stepped out of the house, followed by Teclis's guard. The elves had exchanged their snow white garb for dark blue surcoats worn over their gleaming armour. Teclis too was dressed for war, with a long, thin sword strapped to his back, though he still walked with his white staff.

Danziger gaped when he saw him. 'Lord… Lord Teclis comes?' he asked Manfred.

Manfred nodded gravely. 'Certainly. The thieves may have magic of their own. It would be foolish to attempt to wrest the waystone from them without a mage.'

Danziger licked his lips. 'Of course, of course.' But he looked suddenly much less enthusiastic about their venture.

Manfred smirked behind his back.

As Captain Baerich's men were opening the gate so that the party could get underway, there came a rumble of running boots from the alley, and the men in the yard went on guard.

Men in green and buff uniforms stopped in the gate, a smaller squad in blue and burgundy behind them.

Reiner peered at them in the darkness and recognised Captain von Pfaltzen with fifteen of the countess's personal guard, and behind them Lord Rodick Untern, the countess's cousin – and Lady Magda's husband – with eight men of his own.

'What is this assembly?' demanded von Pfaltzen, panting from running. 'Where do you go so armed?'

Manfred sighed, annoyed. 'We go, captain, to recover the waystone.'

'You have learned its whereabouts?' von Pfaltzen asked, shocked.

'We follow a rumour.'

'And you neglected to inform the countess?' said Rodick. 'I find that very strange.' He had a high, piercing voice.

'We thought,' said Manfred, 'that the fewer persons party to the secret, the less the chance that those who hold the stone would learn of our coming. Apparently we were not covert enough.' He looked to Teclis for support, but the elf was glaring at them all with equal disgust.

'I think I see more reluctance to include Talabheim in the recovery of the stone,' said von Pfaltzen, 'than any concern for secrecy.'

'Yes,' said Rodick. 'You seek to cheat us of our share of the glory.'

'Am I invisible, sirs?' said Danziger, indignant. 'I am a Talabheim man. The city is represented.'

'Are you, m'lord?' asked Rodick sharply. 'Would not a true Talabheim man have informed his countess had he news of the city's salvation?'

'I must insist this venture not continue unless I and my men are part of it,' said von Pfaltzen.

'And as kin to the countess, I must come as well, in order to represent her interests.'

Manfred frowned. 'This is folly, gentlemen. You impede the great Teclis in his work. The thing requires stealth and swiftness. We are already too many. If your men are added, we will surprise no one.' He turned to Teclis. 'Fair one, can you not say something to make them understand that...'

'I care not who stays or who goes,' said Teclis coldly. 'As long as we go quickly, too much time has been wasted already.'

'Very well,' said Manfred, reluctantly. 'All may come.'

As the companies began organising themselves into marching order, Reiner saw Danziger biting his lip, his eyes darting from one commander to the other, then to the man who was to guide them to the waystone.

Reiner stepped quickly to Manfred and whispered in his ear. 'M'lord, Danziger is not pleased. I don't believe he wishes to recover the stone under these circumstances. Given the chance, he will tell his man to lead us astray.'

'Then he cannot be given the chance,' said Manfred. He crossed to Danziger, speaking loudly. 'So, m'lord. Who is the fellow who will lead us? I would like to meet him.'

He put an arm around Danziger's shoulders, ignoring the exchequer's discomfort, and remained at his side as they, Teclis, von Pfaltzen and Rodick Untern, and the sixty-one men of their combined companies, marched from the townhouse, following the guide through the city under the strangely glowing clouds that capped the crater and hid the dawn.

The Blackhearts marched behind Reiner in surly silence, all but Augustus. 'Glad to see von Pfaltzen with us,' he said cheerfully. 'Didn't seem right, going behind the countess's back. A Talabheim man should lead in Talabheim.'

Danziger did not share Augustus's pleasure at von Pfaltzen's company. 'That's the trouble with men of this city,' Reiner heard him whisper in Manfred's ear. 'They think of nothing but their own advancement!'

'Aye,' agreed Manfred, without a hint of sarcasm. 'It makes it that much harder for honest men such as ourselves to get things done.'

Manfred beckoned to Reiner as Danziger and von Pfaltzen spoke to the chief guard at the Schwartz Hold barricade. 'In the unlikely event this bloated company manages to recover the waystone,' he whispered, 'you are to make sure that only Teclis or your Blackhearts or my Nordbergbruchers comes away with it.'

'Yes, m'lord,' said Reiner. 'Er, are we permitted to use force?'

'Eh? No!' said Manfred. 'We are unwelcome here as it is. Just be in the right place at the right time.'

'Very good, m'lord,' said Reiner, pleased that he managed to keep a straight face.

Manfred returned to Danziger's side before von Pfaltzen left him alone.

The further into the blighted neighbourhood the company went, the more oppressive the clouds above them seemed. A damp wind whimpered around them with an almost human voice. Just as the black curve of Talabheim's crater began to stand out against the grey sky behind it, the men reached the gutted granary. As the Blackhearts waited for the other companies to pick their way down into the wreckage, Reiner saw Dieter squinting over his shoulder.

'What is it?' he asked.

Dieter shot him a sullen look. 'Nothing, jagger.'

'Nothing? Or nothing you care to tell me?'

Dieter glared at him, then shrugged. 'We're being tailed.'

Reiner started to turn.

Dieter stopped him. 'Damn fool! Don't let on! Nothing to see anyway.'

Reiner looked sceptically at the thief. 'You can hear a tail in the midst of this army?'

'Can feel it,' said Dieter. 'Like an itch on the back of my neck.'

'So who is it, then?'

Dieter shrugged. 'Ain't shown himself. Canny cove, and no mistake.'

Reiner shivered and thought back to Jurgen on the road to Talabheim, looking out into the night. He had said the same thing.

IT TOOK A quarter of an hour, but eventually all the soldiers descended into the burned-out cellar and through the black hole into the sewers. The companies lined up in single file on the narrow ledges that flanked the reeking channel, which ran down the centre of the low, barrel-vaulted brick tunnel. In the channel ran a sluggish brown stream, thick with bobbing lumps that Reiner didn't care to identify. It was bridged at regular intervals by granite slabs, and fed by pipes that ran down the walls. Rusting rungs set into the walls disappeared up into chimneys, which led to iron storm grates in the streets above.

Manfred lined up the Blackhearts and his Nordbergbruchers on the left side of the channel behind the elves, while Danziger's men and von Pfaltzen, with the countess's guard, lined up on the right. Rodick's men were somewhere in the darkness at the back. When all were in position, the companies marched forward behind Danziger's guide, who trotted ahead of them like a hound.

Rats scurried away before them, pushed into drainpipes and holes by the light of their torches. And there were other vermin. Fleeing human shadows disappeared down cross tunnels and skulking shapes peered at them from behind fallen rubble. Hunched forms huddled around meagre fires far down long corridors. Some were not quite human. Reiner got fleeting glimpses of twisted limbs, and misshapen heads, and heard distant subhuman growls. None seemed inclined to attack so large and well armed a force.

There were places where holes had been broken through the walls. These opened onto dirt, or shadowed cellars or flooded chambers. From one came a reek of rat so strong that it overpowered the omnipresent stink of the sewer. Reiner and the other Blackhearts exchanged uneasy looks, but said nothing. Some things were better not speculated upon.

At an intersection, above which were painted faded street names, Danziger's guide paused, frowning, as he looked left and right.

Reiner saw Danziger's eyes light up and he stepped forward. 'Er, Elger, did you not tell me you had made a left at Turringstrasse?'

The man blinked back at Danziger. 'Er, no, m'lord. Now that you say it, I believe it was a right.'

'Are you *certain*?' said Danziger, through clenched teeth.

Elger didn't take the hint. 'Yes, m'lord. A right at Turringstrasse. It's come back to me now.' He led the party right as Danziger tried to keep his face calm.

Reiner chuckled. Elger would be receiving a hiding later on, that was certain.

A short while later, they came to another rubble littered hole, and Danziger's swordsman entered it. The companies followed. It opened high in the wall of the cold cellar of an old warehouse. Smashed barrels and terracotta jars littered the floor. Wooden shelves had been propped against the wall under the hole as a ladder, and two of Danziger's men held it steady while the rest climbed gingerly down two at a time.

The storeroom was the first in an odd maze of interconnected basements, corridors, sections of unused sewer, earthen tunnels, crawlways and foundations, all with shattered walls and slumping ceilings propped up with bits of lumber. The company tramped up and down stairways and through knee-deep pools. Some passages were so low the soldiers must bend double, and some so narrow they must turn sideways. Reiner cringed at these choke points. Not the place to be caught if things went wrong.

The black circles of old fires were everywhere, as were broken bottles, half gnawed bones, and piles of stinking waste. Graffiti in several languages was scrawled on the walls. Reiner read, 'The countess is a whore!' and 'Peder, where are you?' and 'Rise and burn!' There were worse things too – evil-looking runes and smeared drawings of unmentionable acts and screaming faces. Withered corpses lay in the shadows, eyeless skulls staring at the soldiers as they passed.

At last, Danziger's guide stopped in an ancient corridor and pointed ahead to a pair of rotten wooden doors that hung off their hinges on the left-hand wall. 'Through them doors,' he said, 'is a big room with a hole in the far wall. Some guards are watching it. That's where they took the stone.'

'We must remove the guards before they raise an alarm,' said Danziger. 'Perhaps two of my–'

'I have a lad who can shoot a pigeon's eye out at fifty paces,' said Manfred, interrupting him. 'He–'

'There is no need,' said Teclis. He signalled two of his elves forward. They strode silently to the doors, nocking arrows on their bowstrings. They peered in, then, so swiftly it was hard to believe they had time to find their targets, they pulled and fired. Then they entered, fresh arrows ready. A moment later, they reappeared in the door and beckoned.

'We may proceed,' said Teclis, starting forward.

The companies followed. Reiner saw a flicker of motion further down the ancient corridor as he stepped through the doors, but there had been timid movements in the shadows all along the way. He ignored it.

The room inside was wide and deep, and reeked like stale beer. The left wall was hidden behind a row of enormous wooden vats. On the right, pyramids of giant hogs heads rose out of the darkness. Not one of them was still whole. Their faces had all been staved in, and dried, sticky puddles of evaporated beer pooled around them.

By the far wall was a small fire, illuminating two bodies which lay beside it, white arrows sticking from their necks. Behind the bodies, the thick stone wall was pierced, like a block of lard that had been impaled by a red-hot poker, with a perfectly circular man-high hole, its curves as shiny as glass. Frozen ripples of rock spread below it like melted wax. Reiner shuddered at the implications of the hole. Who or what had the power to do such a thing? And was the thing that had done it in the next room?

Reiner saw the same thoughts were going though Manfred's mind. Danziger, however, seemed to have no fear. He was urging his men forward eagerly.

'Come along,' he said. 'Before they know we are here.'

Manfred hesitated. 'Er, fair one? Is it–'

'Fear not,' said the elf. 'It is centuries old. The portal and halls beyond it are crudely warded, but I will clear them as we go. Proceed.'

Manfred nodded and signalled the Blackhearts to catch up to Danziger. Von Pfaltzen and Rodick moved their men up as well.

The weird hole opened into an old prison. The air inside smelled of smoke and made hazy halos around the torches. The elves led the way down a cell-lined corridor, Teclis moving his hands and whispering under his breath constantly. The air before him would occasionally shimmer like a soap bubble before popping with a relaxation of pressure Reiner could feel in his chest.

Three times men appeared far down the hall, then turned to run, and three times the elven archers cut them down before they could take a step.

'Might as well have left us at home,' grumbled Hals.

Teclis turned one of the dead men over with a pointed boot and pulled aside his shirt with the tip of his sword. A strange rune had been branded over the man's heart.

'A cultist,' said Teclis. 'This is the mark of the Changer of the Ways.'

Reiner swallowed, and though he was not by nature pious, he made the sign of the hammer. The men around him did the same. Teclis stepped over the corpse and moved on.

The hall ended in a stairwell. The smoke that filled the prison came from the stairs. Teclis and his elves crossed the room and began to descend them. The companies followed, coughing. To Reiner's annoyance, the elves seemed unaffected.

At the bottom was an arched doorway that glowed like the red mouth of hell. The Blackhearts and Danziger's men followed Teclis hesitantly through the door and onto a balcony that overlooked a deep, square pit. The other companies tried to crowd in behind them, but there was no room. The balcony was enclosed in a cage of iron bars. Left and right stairs led down to the pit. These had once had gates, but they had been ripped from their hinges. The smoke was so thick in the pit that at first all Reiner could make out was that an enormous fire blazed in its centre, but as he wiped his eyes he could see men surrounding the fire. They were raising their hands and chanting. A man in blue robes led them.

'The stone!' hissed Franka, pointing. 'They're destroying it!'

Reiner squinted. In the heart of the blaze was a roughly cut oblong menhir, black with soot.

Teclis smiled faintly. 'They may try,' he said. 'But it took a falling temple to unseat it. Will a fire unmake it?'

There was a hoarse shout from below as a chanter noticed the intruders. One of Teclis's elves shot him in the back and he crashed through the men and landed with his head in the blaze. The men at the fire leapt up, grabbing weapons and turning toward the balcony. The robed man began chanting and making elaborate motions with his arms.

The elves fired at him. Their arrows bent away as if pushed by a wind. The cultists charged, roaring, for the two stairways. There were at least fifty of them.

'Nordbergbruchers!' called Captain Baerich, drawing his sword. 'Hold the left!'

'No!' cried Manfred. 'My guard goes first!' He pushed Reiner forward as Baerich glared. 'You must get in ahead,' Manfred whispered. 'Go!'

Reiner grunted and drew his sword. 'Right lads, let's get stuck in.'

'And about time too,' growled Hals.

The Blackhearts charged down the left-hand stair with Manfred and the Nordbergbruchers behind them, as Danziger and his men ran down the right. The cultists met the companies at the bottom, a frenzied mob of frothing degenerates, armed with daggers and clubs, and bare of armour.

Pavel and Hals gutted two with their spears immediately. Reiner hacked at a fellow with purple boils covering his face, then kicked him back into his comrades. Jurgen, the swordmaster, impaled one, then another, and cleaved the skull of a third. Augustus stabbed with his spear from the second row while Rumpolt, having fired his gun, now waved his sword around to no effect. Franka and Gert shot over their shoulders, burying shafts and bolts in unprotected chests and necks.

Behind them, Darius and Dieter did nothing but try to stay out of the way. There was little they could have done anyway, or any room for them to do it. The Blackhearts were in a tactically perfect position; they held the high ground in a narrow, easily defended choke point. All they had to do was hold here and...

Manfred prodded Reiner from behind. 'Go out!' he shouted. 'Get the stone! The spears will hold the stair.'

Reiner groaned. He didn't want to die because of Manfred's political rivalries, but the count's displeasure meant certain death, while wading into a crowd of crazed fanatics was only nearly certain.

'Blackhearts forward!' he called, and pushed into the mob with Jurgen on his left and Pavel and Hals on his right. Gert and Augustus faced out on the flanks. Franka, Dieter and Rumpolt walked backwards, forming the back wall of their small square with the scholar Darius in the centre, eyes wide with fright.

'This is madness,' stuttered the scholar.

'Get used to it,' said Gert as cultists fell all around them. He shot a dirty look back at Manfred, who was calling encouragement from behind his Nordbergbruchers. 'Puttin' his pride before his duty, I'm thinkin'.'

'Seems we might die in a prison after all,' grumbled Hals.

Jurgen decapitated two cultists with a single blow and they were through the throng. Some followed them, but most continued to press for the stairs. Von Pfaltzen's men were pushing onto the balcony from the stairwell and trying to get to the fight. Rodick and his house guards had somehow got in front of them and were fighting down the right-hand stair beside Danziger's swordsmen. Teclis stood at the bars, one fist clenched before him, while his elves shot shaft after shaft into the pit. As Teclis raised his arm the Tzeentch sorcerer jerked into the air above the fire, clawing at his throat as if the high elf's hand was throttling it. Then he dropped and bounced off the waystone into the flames. The way to the waystone was clear.

'Hals, Pavel, Augustus!' called Reiner, as the Blackhearts hurried forwards. 'Get your spearheads under the stone and lever it out of the blaze.'

While Reiner, Jurgen and the others protected them, Hals, Pavel and Augustus thrust their spears into the fire and jammed them under the waystone, then pushed down, using the burning logs as fulcrums.

'All together, lads!' cried Hals.

It was hot work. The waystone was in the centre of the fire, and the spears were only just long enough to reach. The pikemen were instantly drenched in sweat, and Augustus's wild eyebrows were smoking at the ends. It was hot work defending them as well, for the cultists were leaving the stairs to stop them. Reiner, Jurgen, Rumpolt and Dieter stood in a half-circle around Hals, Pavel and

Augustus, protecting their backs from the seething mob, while Franka and Gert shot around them and Darius crouched behind, hiding his head and whimpering.

The cultists' numbers thinned quickly, however, for their retreat from the stairs had allowed the companies to enter the pit, and a sea of colourful uniforms and steel breastplates spilled across the floor to plough into their flanks.

Manfred was just pushing through the press to Reiner and crying 'Well done, boys' when, with a final unison grunt, Hals, Pavel and Augustus at last levered the waystone off the burning lumber. The blackened menhir rolled to the floor on the opposite side of the fire, and rocked to a stop directly in front of the exquisite gold-trimmed boots of Lord Rodick Untern.

The young lord immediately put a foot upon it as if it was a dragon he had just slain and turned to Teclis, who was crossing to them. 'Fair one,' he said, bowing. 'We have the waystone. Please allow the house of Untern, family of our great countess, protector of Talabheim, the honour of carrying it to your quarters.'

Reiner cursed. The boy was quick.

Manfred, Danziger and von Pfaltzen all raised their voices in protest, but Teclis held up a hand. 'To forestall argument,' he said, 'Yes. Carry the stone. Now, let us be gone.'

'Thank you, fair one,' said Rodick as one of his men unstrapped a bundle he carried on his back. It contained four long, sturdy poles and several coils of rope. Rodick had come prepared.

'Bungling fool,' Manfred whispered in Reiner's ear. 'Look what you've done.'

'Yes, m'lord,' said Reiner. 'Very sorry, m'lord.'

Manfred turned away in disgust. 'What sort of Black-heart are you?'

Not a patch on you, you villain, thought Reiner.

Rodick's men were trying to roll the waystone onto the four poles using spears and lengths of lumber.

'You may use your hands,' said Teclis. 'It will be cool to the touch.'

The soldiers didn't appear to believe him. One reached out warily and brushed the stone with his fingers.

'He's right,' he gasped. 'It ain't hot at all.'

The soldiers were not reassured by this unnatural phenomenon, but none-the-less manhandled the stone onto the four poles and lashed it in place with the ropes. Each then took a pole-end and, grunting, lifted it up like a sedan chair.

'So we're done, then?' asked Augustus, as the companies began marching up the stairs and out of the room. 'Weren't as hard as the count made out it would be.'

'Aye,' said Pavel. 'Not really worth getting us out, was it?'

'Beats sitting about in Altdorf on our arses,' said Hals.

The companies wound through the abandoned prison with Rodick's men in the centre, and Danziger, seeming petulant and out of sorts, bringing up the rear.

They had passed out of the prison through the melted portal and were halfway across the vast vat room when Teclis stopped, looking into the shadows. His elves went instantly on guard.

'There are men here,' he said, loud but calm. 'Hidden by magic. We are ambushed.'

Before the words were out of his mouth, a hundred dark forms were swarming from behind the huge vats, waving swords and shrieking, 'The stone! Get the stone!'

Teclis uttered a short phrase and, with a bang, a ball of sun-bright light popped into being above his head, throwing every object in the room into sharp relief. The soldiers of the companies were shocked by this sudden illumination, but their ambushers must have seen something more than light in the ball's radiance, for they cringed away from it, and some turned and fled.

'Blackhearts! Nordbergbruchers!' called Manfred. 'Protect Teclis! Protect the stone!'

Reiner and the others formed a rough square around Teclis and Rodick just as the first wave of attackers hit. Von Pfaltzen and his men encircled them too, but Lord Danziger, caught just coming through the melted hole, fell back to it.

Reiner's mind raced as he fought. Whoever they were, these madmen hadn't been here when the companies first came through the room. Teclis would have sensed them. That meant they had known the companies were coming here to take the stone from the Tzeentchists. And they couldn't have followed them from the granary. Even without Teclis, the companies would have noticed so great a force behind them. Which meant that they had known where the stone was being held. Which meant that someone had eyes in more than one camp.

These attackers were as frenzied as the Tzeentchists, but, unlike them, these men looked not enraged, but enraptured. Their eyes were rolled back in their heads and beatific smiles split their faces as they hacked at the companies. When Reiner slashed one across the arm, he moaned in ecstasy. Nor were these ill-equipped acolytes, caught unawares. These men were well armed and clad in leather and steel.

'Who are these?' cried Rodick, slashing wildly at two slavering men.

'Cultists of the Lord of Pleasure,' said Teclis, then began mouthing another incantation. His elves sent a torrent of white shafts into the attackers. Every one found a mark.

Rumpolt reeled back, clutching his forehead. Reiner's knuckles were shredded from punching a fellow in the teeth. He saw a Nordbergbrucher go down with a hatchet buried in his back, and further down the line, one of the countess's guards toppled, lifeless. But now that their initial confusion at the sudden attack had passed, the discipline of the companies began to show, and more cultists began to fall.

'Forwards, you layabouts!' Manfred cried.

Reiner looked back to see the count pushing Rodick and his men toward the front line. 'You wanted the honour of carrying the stone, then you should welcome the honour of defending it!'

Reiner shook his head in wonder as he parried a sword stroke. Even in the midst of an ambush that they might not survive, Manfred jockeyed for the stone.

Teclis's voice grew louder, and the air around him vibrated with contained energies. He raised his arms and glared out at the ravening horde. Glowing tendrils began to boil from his hands. But just as he began to declaim the last thunderous words of his incantation, a black arrow sped from the darkness and impaled his chest.

SIX
Touch Not The Stone

TECLIS COLLAPSED BACKWARD, falling across the waystone. His guards turned, shocked, but recovered instantly, and flew into action. As five of the elves fired white shafts in the direction from which the black shaft had come, their captain snapped the black arrow nearly flush with Teclis's chest, then picked up the fallen mage in his arms as if he weighed nothing. The others clustered tightly around them, facing out, two with arrows nocked, the others holding swords. Without a word to their human companions they hurried for the exit, cutting down the cultists who got in their way.

'Does he live?' called Manfred after them. 'Does Teclis live?'

The elves did not answer.

As they reached the vat room's broken doors, a flood of deformed mutants poured through them, waving clubs and rusted swords. The elves laid about them furiously, but the mutants seemed uninterested in them, and instead ran directly at the men defending the stone.

'Cowards!' shouted Rodick, shaking his fist as the elves disappeared out the door. 'They've left us to die!'

The horde of mutants broke upon the companies and the Slaaneshi cultists alike, clawing and flailing with misshapen limbs, their eyes glazed. 'The stone,' they moaned. 'Get the stone.'

'We're done for,' whimpered Rumpolt as the Blackhearts fought a swirling chaos of cultists and mutants. 'This is death.'

'Shut yer hole, infant,' growled Hals.

The Slaaneshi attacked the mutants as fiercely as they fought the men, screaming 'Back, foul vermin!' and 'The stone is ours!' The soldiers struck at anything that didn't wear a uniform.

Manfred edged to Reiner, stabbing a cultist in the throat. 'Take up the stone,' he said. 'While our enemies fight each other.'

Reiner nodded, happy to leave the front line. 'Fall back, Blackhearts!'

The Blackhearts disengaged carefully, allowing the other companies to close ranks around them.

'Take up the stone!' Reiner shouted. He stooped to grab a pole-end as the others found their places and did the same.

'What's this?' cried Rodick, turning and ducking a sword as the Blackhearts lifted the waystone by the poles. 'We were told to carry the stone!'

'And you shall again,' said Manfred. 'But my men already have it up. To the corridor! We are too exposed here.'

'This is underhanded, sir,' said Rodick, as the Blackhearts started forward. 'I protest!'

'Protest if we live,' said Manfred.

The waystone was lighter than Reiner expected, and the Blackhearts made good time to the door, walking it in the centre of a moving island of soldiers, who were in turn surrounded by a boiling surf of screeching mutants and cultists. The floor underfoot was slick with blood.

Seeing that his colleagues were leaving him behind, Lord Danziger and his men left the safety of the melted portal and fought across the room after them. The mutants in particular seemed to offend Danziger's sense of propriety. 'Disgusting perversions!' he bellowed. 'Unclean vermin! Touch not the stone!'

Reiner, freed from the fight, at last had time to wonder at the black arrow that had felled Teclis. Who had shot it, and why? And what dread power must he have to pierce Teclis's wards and armour as if they were nothing? Close on those questions came another. Why had the mutants, who had before cowered away from the companies, suddenly attacked so savagely, and with such singleness of purpose? And how did they also know of the stone?

The island of men reached the door, and the Blackhearts squeezed through, surrounded by Manfred's spearmen and Rodick's house guard. Danziger's men pushed in behind them as von Pfaltzen's troops stayed in the door, penning in the majority of the mutants and cultists.

'Go,' cried von Pfaltzen, waving a hand. 'We will hold them. Get the stone to the countess!'

Manfred saluted him. 'Courage, captain,' he called, then motioned the Blackhearts down the hall with the Nordbergbruchers and Rodick's and Danziger's men guarding them.

Reiner looked back at von Pfaltzen. It was possible, he thought, that the captain was the only man in this whole enterprise who cared more for the security of Talabheim than his personal advancement.

Danziger's men took the rear as the companies ran through the maze of cellars and catacombs, while Rodick's men scouted the way ahead. The Blackhearts sloshed across flooded chambers and ducked through stifling crawlways. The waystone soon felt twice as heavy as when they had picked it up, and they sweated through their shirts.

As they trotted through a series of looted crypts and mausoleums, Rodick dropped back to Manfred.

'You have held the waystone long enough,' he said. 'We will take it again.'

Manfred sneered. 'Your ambition is showing, Untern. No matter who carries it, it goes to Teclis in the end.'

'And what of your ambition?' asked Rodick.

'I have no ambition but to serve the Empire and my Emperor,' huffed Manfred.

Their argument was interrupted by a shrieking swarm of mutants that poured from another corridor. They crashed into Danziger's men, tearing at them with bare hands and bashing them with bricks and stones. The swordsmen hacked and kicked at them, shouting with anger and surprise. Mutants died by the score, but more came behind them.

Reiner looked back, baffled. 'Where do they all come from? How do they find us?'

Manfred smirked. 'Don't look a gift horse in the mouth.' He waved the Blackhearts on. 'Hurry. While they're engaged.'

'But Lord Danziger will be left behind,' said Augustus.

'Precisely.' said Manfred. 'Hold them, Danziger!' he called. 'And fear not. We will get the waystone to Teclis!'

'Curse you, Valdenheim!' shouted Danziger. 'Come back!'

Manfred sighed as the Blackhearts followed Rodick's men and the Nordberbruchers around a corner. 'What has become of the spirit of noble sacrifice that made this Empire great?'

Rodick giggled. Reiner held his tongue.

More mutants followed them, pacing the party like wolves. They kept their distance, but Reiner could hear them murmuring, 'Get the stone. Get the stone,' in monotonous unison.

The Blackhearts gasped and stumbled under the weight of the thing. Gert's round face was as red as a steak. Franka's eyes were glassy. Reiner's legs ached and his arms shook. The carrying pole was slipping in his sweaty grip. He cursed Manfred for denying Rodick's men their turn to carry it. He would have been happy to give it up.

At last they reached the abandoned cold cellar that led up to the sewers. The Blackhearts staggered wearily to the tilted shelves that served as a ladder to the hole, Rodick's men and Manfred's Nordbergbruchers trotting around them.

'Down! Put it down!' choked Reiner.

The Blackhearts gratefully eased the stone to the ground as the party looked back. Lurching and shambling across the floor came the mutants. There were scores of them, some already bloody and limping from the earlier melees. Reiner didn't understand what drove them. Many cried out in pain at every step, yet they came on, still mumbling their endless refrain, 'Get the stone. Get the stone.'

Reiner took stock of Manfred and Rodick's forces. Baerich and five spears were all that survived of the Nordbergbruchers. Rodick had lost only one man – proof they had indeed hung back in the fighting. The Blackhearts had all their number, though they were neither whole nor hearty. Reiner could barely lift his arms.

'Up, men,' said Rodick, and clambered up the tilted shelves and over the rubble that littered the lip of the hole with his men behind him. 'Hurry,' he called from the top. 'Before they reach us. Pass up the stone!'

'Come down, curse you,' barked Manfred. 'Take the defence. Your men are untouched.'

'But my men are already up, and there is no time to change,' said Rodick, mimicking Manfred.

'Do you mock me, sir?' Manfred looked back. The mutants were nearly upon them. He grunted with frustration. 'Death of Sigmar! Spearmen, hold them off! Blackhearts, pass up the stone.'

'Aye, m'lord,' said Reiner. 'Lift away, lads. Frank... Franz, guide us up.'

As Baerich and the remaining Nordbergbruchers spread out in a meagre half circle, Reiner and the

Blackhearts took up their poles and lifted the stone.
Behind him, Reiner heard the mutants hit the thin line of
spears. He cringed. He could feel daggers and swords
striking for his back. He could feel foetid breath on his
neck.

The shelves creaked ominously as Hals and Pavel
stepped up onto them with the stone carried between
them. Two of Rodick's men stepped through the hole
and put feet on the top shelf to brace it. One of the men
had his back foot on a heavy chunk of granite. It rocked
and he nearly fell.

'Careful,' called Rodick.

Reiner heard a scream of agony behind him, and Manfred cursing.

'Hurry, you sluggards!' bellowed the count. 'They overwhelm us!'

The Blackhearts took another step. The shelves flexed
beneath them. The howling of the mutants and the cursing of the spearmen filled Reiner's ears.

'Step!' he called.

The shelves groaned as they took more weight. The
sides bowed. The stone slid back alarmingly, and the
ropes that tied it to the poles creaked. Rodick's men
reached down toward them. Rodick had joined them,
stretching out his hands.

'Now pass it up,' said Reiner.

With grunts of effort, the Blackhearts passed the four
stone-laden poles hand to hand up the shelves. At the
top, Pavel and Hals handed the first pole to Rodick's men
and took the second from Dieter and Rumpolt. Jurgen
and Augustus, having passed the last to Reiner and Gert,
stepped to the sides of the shelves and pushed against
them, trying to hold them together.

Rodick's men took each of the poles in turn, and the
shelves groaned in relief as they were relieved of the
weight. Finally, Rodick took the fourth pole from Pavel,
bracing his foot on the unsteady granite boulder. As he
lifted, his foot slipped and the boulder toppled down,

smashing through the shelves and glancing off Jurgen's right shoulder, knocking him to the floor. The other Blackhearts crashed down in a rain of splintering wood as the shelves disintegrated.

Rodick gasped. 'Count! Forgive me! What an unfortunate accident.'

'Accident my arse,' growled Hals, picking himself up. A horned mutant threw itself at him. Hals elbowed him in the eye, groping for his spear. Reiner drew his sword and stepped between two of the spearmen, cutting and thrusting. There were only three Nordbergbruchers left, and they were sorely pressed. Manfred was bleeding from a dozen small wounds.

'Blackhearts, hold the line!' Reiner shouted.

The others caught up their weapons and faced out, limping – all but Darius, who cowered against the wall as usual, and Jurgen, who sat dazed, his right arm limp at his side.

The count snarled up at Rodick. 'You did that deliberately.'

Rodick saluted him as he lifted the stone with his men. 'Hold them, Valdenheim! And fear not. We will get the waystone to Teclis!'

'Curse you, Untern!' shouted Manfred, as the young lord and his men disappeared into the sewer with the stone. A mutant gashed Manfred's arm with its claws and he turned back to the fight, hacking left and right. 'Hetsau,' he said. 'We must get after him. Get us out of this hole.'

'Aye, m'lord.' Reiner backed out of the line and looked around. One of the side panels from the shelves was still whole. He propped it against the wall under the hole, next to where Darius was examining Jurgen's useless sword arm.

'Up you go,' said Reiner. 'Both of you.'

Darius tottered up first as Reiner braced the plank with his shoulder, then Jurgen. Reiner grunted under his weight.

'Ready to retire, m'lord!' he called.

Manfred glanced back. 'Very good, Hetsau. Bows and guns back to cover the rest.'

Franka, Gert and Rumpolt dropped out of the line and clambered up the plank. When they reached the hole. Gert and Franka turned and fired down into the mutants while Rumpolt loaded his gun.

'Baerich, Nordbergbruchers!' said Manfred. 'Fall back.'

The captain and his last two spearmen stepped back from the fight, grateful, and pulled themselves wearily up the plank.

Now only Pavel, Hals, Augustus, Dieter and Manfred stood against the horde, and the mutants were beginning to edge around them toward Reiner.

'The rest will have to run back all at once, m'lord,' called Reiner. He hacked down a mutant who pawed at the plank.

'On your command, then,' said the count.

Reiner cut down another mutant, then waved up at the others, watching anxiously from the hole. 'Pull up the plank and hold down your hands!'

Darius hauled up the plank, then got on his belly with Jurgen, Rumpolt, Baerich and the Nordbergbruchers, and stretched down his arms, while Franka and Gert continued to fire at the mutants.

'Now, m'lord!' said Reiner.

'Fall back!' shouted Manfred.

Reiner had to give Manfred credit. Conniving manipulator he might be, but coward he was not. He was last to turn from the mutants, slashing about wildly to protect the others while they disengaged, then running and springing for the wall like a man half his age.

The men in the hole caught the hands of the men on the ground and pulled for all they were worth, and Hals, Pavel and Augustus scrabbled with their toes. Dieter needed no help. He flew up the wall like a cat, then turned and added his arm to Darius's and dragged Manfred into the sewer tunnel.

Reiner had caught Jurgen's left hand and he could see the swordsman's grim face turn white with agony as he braced himself with his wounded arm. Franka dropped her bow and grabbed Reiner's other hand. The fear for him that he saw in her eyes sent a thrill through him. Maybe he hadn't lost her after all.

Claws grabbed Reiner's ankles. He screamed, thrashing and kicking his leg. 'Pull, curse you!'

Jurgen and Franka redoubled their efforts and Reiner inched up, then came up all at once as he caught the mutant who held him in the teeth and it let go. Reiner landed face first on the rubble-strewn sewer ledge and rolled away, panting as Pavel, Rumpolt and Dieter hurled stones down at the leaping mass of mutants and stomped on their fingers.

Manfred brushed himself off and looked in the direction Rodick had gone. 'Enough. We must catch Untern,' he said. 'The pup needs a lesson.'

The Blackhearts and the Nordbergbruchers backed away from the hole, then lit fresh torches and followed Manfred down the hall, limping and groaning.

Reiner fell in beside Franka. 'Franka...'

Her face hardened as she caught the look in his eyes. 'Yes, captain?' she said, loud. 'You wish to speak with me, captain?'

Reiner cringed. 'Never mind, never mind.' Damn the girl.

They reached an intersection of tunnels. There was no torchlight in any direction.

Manfred cursed. 'Where has he got to? Did he fly?'

Dieter took a torch and examined the floor and walls around each of the four corners. 'This way,' he said at last, pointing to a scrape on the bricks of the right-hand passage. 'They touched the wall with the stone.'

'Excellent work,' said Manfred. 'Lead on. Is this the way we came?'

'Aye,' said Dieter, and started down the tunnel, eyes on the ground. But as the others followed, Jurgen looked behind them.

'Captain,' he said to Reiner. 'They come again.'

Manfred heard and cursed. 'Double time, trailbreaker.'

Dieter grunted, but picked up his pace. After a bend, the tunnel straightened out.

Manfred shook his head when he saw no torchlight before them. 'How could they have got so far ahead?'

Fifty yards along, Dieter stopped abruptly. 'Hang on,' he said. He turned back, looking at the floor, then paused at an iron ladder bolted into the brick wall. He examined the rungs, then looked up into a dark chimney. 'They went up.'

'Up?' asked Manfred, incredulous. 'With the stone?'

'Aye,' said Dieter, pointing. 'Scrapes on the rungs. Rope strands. Footprints.'

'Then we must go after them,' said Manfred. 'Come.' He mounted the ladder and began to climb. A black arrow whistled out of the dark and glanced off the wall next to his face. Manfred flinched back with a cry.

'Climb another rung and the next will find your heart,' said a voice.

Everyone turned. Limping out of the shadows, surrounded by a crowd of blank-eyed mutants, was a tall, pale-skinned elf, a black longbow in his left hand, an arrow on the string.

Reiner heard shuffling behind him and looked behind. More mutants were pushing into the torchlight from that direction as well. They were surrounded.

SEVEN
The Hand of Malekith

AT FIRST REINER thought the elf was one of Teclis's guard, for he had the same proud, cold features and regal bearing, but he wore no armour, and his beautifully made doublet and leggings were black, not blue. It was in his glittering dark eyes, however, that the difference was most evident. Though they were as distant and alien as those of Teclis and his guard, there was a malevolence there that went beyond mere uncaring indifference to the fates of lesser beings.

'I am grieved to hear,' he said in a pleasant voice, 'that the stone has eluded me. But at least I have you, and that may yet win me the stone. Surrender your weapons to my slaves and come with me.'

Manfred sneered. 'We have beat back your "slaves" before, sir. We can again.'

A black shaft sprouted from Captain Baerich's chest and he collapsed at Manfred's feet. The arrow pierced his breastplate and stuck out his back. Reiner hadn't seen the elf move, and yet he was laying another arrow on his

76

string. The other Nordbergbruchers cried out and started forward, spears lowered. They were dead before they had taken a step.

'It isn't my slaves you should fear.' the elf said, coolly. 'They are only to keep you from running. Now, need more die?'

Manfred looked down at the corpses of Baerich and his men, his face pale. At last he licked his lips and looked up. 'Surrender your weapons,' he said.

'M'lord!' protested Augustus.

'Obey my orders,' barked Manfred.

The Blackhearts reluctantly handed their swords and spears and bows to the drooling mutants, who then hemmed in their prisoners in a stinking wall of diseased flesh. Reiner was in full agreement with Manfred. Surrender was the only option, but to give in to such pitiful foes felt wrong, even to a Blackheart.

'Now, my slaves,' said the elf to the mutants, 'Take me to your deepest, most fortified hole. I require a residence.'

He limped forward with a wince, and Reiner noted for the first time that the elf had the broken-off shaft of a white arrow sticking out of his jerkin, a handbreadth above his left hip-bone.

'We will move slowly,' he said. 'For while Teclis's guard are poor archers, they are extremely lucky.'

THE MUTANTS LED them down into the earth by means of abandoned cellars, airshafts, and what appeared to be an ancient tin mine, until they reached natural caverns, the walls of which glittered in the torchlight as if they were embedded with glass. There was a faint roaring in Reiner's head as they entered, which he first thought was air moving through the caves, but when he focussed on it he wasn't sure it was a sound after all, more a babble of random thoughts bubbling beneath the surface of his consciousness, like a fly buzzing inside his skull. He fought the urge to swat it. He could see that the others were affected as well, shaking their heads and twitching. Darius had his hands to his temples, moaning.

'All right, scholar?' asked Reiner.

'Fine. I'm fine,' Darius snapped.

Reiner wasn't so sure.

They came at last to an enormous, roughly circular cave, its walls encrusted with pitiful rag-and-stick tents, out of which crawled more mutants, even more twisted than those who held them. It soon became obvious, however, that the mutants were not the first visitors to this underworld. A massive arch was carved into the wall to the left of the main entrance, and straight ahead, where a deep chasm cut through the floor, a stone bridge had been built, beyond which Reiner could see more tunnels in the far wall. Both arch and bridge were aeons old, their geometric designs nearly worn away by time.

The elf limped through the stone arch, the mutants following with the captives. Inside was a high, round chamber, in the centre of which was a circle of black stones, twice the height of a man, surrounding a flat, round altar. Cut into the walls around the stone circle were a score of iron-barred cells.

The elf nodded approvingly. 'An aspect of Khaine was worshipped here. A more fitting home for a son of Naggaroth than a sewer.'

Manfred's eyes went wide. 'You are a dark elf?'

'I am Druchii,' said the elf, raising his chin. 'That other name is a slander invented by our treacherous cousins. Now listen well. Today is a great day. The despised Teclis is dead, and one of Ulthuan's precious waystones is within my–'

'How can you be certain Teclis is dead?' interrupted Manfred.

The elf turned cold eyes on the count. 'Because,' he hissed. 'I struck him with an arrow poisoned, diseased, and enchanted with magics created just for his murder. My dear mother may have named me Valaris, but I am nothing but Teclis's death. I have trained since my birth, seven hundred years ago, to do one thing and one thing only – kill the great mage of Ulthuan. It was said that no assassin could defeat Teclis's magics, and no mage could penetrate his defences, so I was made to be both. I learned the ways of the slayer at the knee of the master of shadows, and spent a hundred years in servitude to the sisterhood of Khaine to be allowed to study their mysteries, all that I might defeat the "fair one"'. He snorted. 'And so that he is dead, I care not whether I survive. I am but the hand of Malekith. My death – my pain – means nothing.'

Reiner stared at the elf. He had been told that Teclis was thousands of years old, but the knowledge had the quality of myth about it, and was hard to think of as a reality. Here was a being who had lived fourteen human generations in the pursuit of a single goal.

Valaris eased his weight to his unwounded side. 'However,' he said, 'with a chance to destroy a waystone and undermine the foundations of our treacherous cousins' stranglehold on the world within my reach, I am thankful I was spared, though I am frustrated that my wound makes it impossible for me to accomplish the task myself.' He sighed. 'At least I have a tool that will do what I cannot.'

'You speak of us?' asked Manfred. 'We are not your slaves.'

'And I am glad of it,' said Valaris, looking around at the mutants. 'They would be unsuited to the task. The warpstone taint has destroyed their minds, making it possible for me to control them. But it also makes them unable to think for themselves. And I have no doubt it will take cunning to win the stone.'

'And what makes ye think we'll do what ye want, y'chalk-faced twig?' said Hals.

Valaris raised an eyebrow. 'Hark, hark. The dogs do bark.'

A mutant behind Hals raised a cudgel and bashed the pikeman on the back of the head. Hals clutched his head and cursed.

'You will do what I want,' continued the elf as if nothing had happened, 'because I will hold the count hostage, and will kill him if you fail to bring the stone to me in three days.'

Reiner's heart jumped. By Ranald! Was this the chance for which the Blackhearts had waited so long? The dark elf might be able to control the minds of the mutants, but it was clear he couldn't read thoughts. He had no idea that Reiner and the others would leave Manfred to die in a heartbeat – all but the spy, of course. Reiner grunted. Always it was the spy who ruined every chance. But if they could discover and kill him while Manfred was still Valaris's prisoner, they might escape the count's insidious poison at last.

Reiner saw Manfred had come to the same realisation. His face was nearly as white as the elf's. 'Sir,' he cried, trying to look noble, though his brow was wet with sweat. 'If you think such a scheme will work, then you do not know the men of the Empire. The restoration of the stone is the salvation of our land, and my men know that I would gladly sacrifice my worthless life to that end. If you send them on this errand, they will not return, and I will applaud them for it.'

The elf smiled. 'I believe I know the men of the Empire well enough. Did I not just see them leaving each other to die in order to appear the hero that rescued the stone? I believe, count, that you try to trick me into letting you go. You are too fond of your life, and your position, and your wealth, to make so noble a sacrifice, and your men are no doubt greedy animals like all their kind, and will bring the stone back to me for the rewards you will heap upon them for your salvation.'

Reiner rejoiced in silence. The dark elf's prejudices were going to free them. They would walk out of the catacombs and, once they found the traitor, they would walk out of Talabheim and disappear into the world with no one left alive to order the poison loosed into their veins.

Manfred pursed his lips. 'Then send them and you will see. But I ask a small mercy of you. That if they do not return, you grant me a few moments to pray.' The count said, turning cunning eyes on Reiner. 'Blessings for the brave men who join me in sacrificing their lives for the good of the Empire.'

The elf looked up, his eyes darting from Manfred to Reiner. 'Blessings you say?'

He frowned, then stepped to Reiner and took his wrist, circling his left hand over it. A throbbing pain pulsed through Reiner's arm and he tried to jerk away.

Valaris held him in an iron grip, then let him go laughing. 'I have underestimated the cunning of men,' he said. 'This is almost Druchii. Bound by poison.' He smiled at Manfred. 'You shall be allowed your prayers. Now,' Valaris waved a hand at the mutants and they herded the men toward the cages in the wall. 'I have gifts I must prepare for you. I will return.'

He turned away and limped out of the room as the mutants pushed the men into one cramped cage.

As the mutants locked them in, Reiner turned to Manfred. 'So, m'lord. It is your wish that we do not return for you, and do not bring the stone to the dark elf? Your sacrifice is truly worthy of the great heroes of the Empire's golden age.'

'Don't be an ass, Hetsau,' said the count. 'If you fail to bring the stone here in three days, you will not see a fourth.'

Reiner gasped, feigning shock. 'But m'lord. Do you mean that you lied? That you are not willing to sacrifice your life for the good of the land? Do you fear death?'

'I fear nothing,' spat Manfred. 'And if it would save the land, I would welcome death, but the Empire needs me, Hetsau, as much as it needs the waystone. Even more, now that Teclis is dead. For with him gone, the waystone is useless until another elven mage can be brought from Ulthuan to reseat it. I will be needed to keep order and negotiate with the elves. I must stay alive, you see?'

Reiner saw that Manfred *was* afraid. Strange that a man who showed no fear in battle would prove such a coward in captivity. Perhaps it was that a man with a sword in his hand always felt there was a chance, while a caged man felt powerless. Whatever the reason, Reiner had seen mercenaries and engineers face their fates with more heart.

'I see, m'lord,' Reiner said. He didn't bother to hide his sneer. 'But your humble servants have many fewer reasons to live. In fact they grow weary of life under the yoke, and might feel that the Empire would be better off keeping the waystone and getting rid of you, and would be willing to sacrifice their lives to that end.'

Franka's eyes went wide as Reiner's words sank in, and the others stared at him.

Manfred went pale. 'What are you suggesting?'

'Nothing, m'lord,' said Reiner. 'Except that the threat of death begins to lose its force if one's life isn't worth living. So, if you truly wish us to steal the waystone from the Empire, and bring it to a sworn enemy of mankind at the risk of our lives, and against all natural inclinations, perhaps you would consider adding an incentive in addition to the usual intimidation.'

'And what would that be?' asked Manfred, sneering in his turn. 'Gold? Better quarters? Harlots at your beck and call?'

'Freedom.'

The Blackhearts looked at Reiner, hope glittering in their eyes.

'Let this be the Blackhearts' last mission,' Reiner continued. 'Promise us that if we free you, you will free us. A simple trade.'

Manfred raised a sceptical eyebrow. 'And you say you are willing to die if I do not agree to this?'

Reiner looked around at the others questioningly. He hoped he had gauged their temper correctly.

'Aye,' said Hals, nodding. 'This is no life.'

'Might as well kill us now and save us the trouble,' said Pavel.

Franka stuck out her chin. 'I am ready.'

'And I,' said Jurgen without looking up.

Gert just glared at Manfred, arms crossed.

The newer men didn't look so certain, but they didn't disagree.

Manfred hesitated, looking around at them all, then sighed. 'Very well. You have given me good service, and though it saddens me that brave men would turn away from their duty to protect their homeland, I will release you if you succeed in getting me to safety.'

The Blackhearts let out tense breaths.

'We have your word?' asked Reiner.

'You have my word as a gentleman and a representative of the Empire of Karl Franz.'

Being born of the gentle class himself, Reiner knew what the word of a gentleman was worth, but he was in no position to force any other guarantee from the count. 'Very well,' he said. 'Then we will recover the stone and free you.'

'In three days,' said Manfred.

'Three days,' agreed Reiner.

There was a disturbance among the mutants and the men looked up. Valaris was returning.

'I have a gift for each of you,' he said, looking at them through the bars. 'And another for the leader of the men who will go.' He opened a small square of cloth, revealing what appeared to slivers of blue glass. 'While Teclis lived, you were protected by his spells against the effects of Talabheim's warpstone. Now he is dead, that protection is removed. I care nothing for your welfare, but you must be sane to be useful, so I have chipped shards from a crystal I wear. Placed under your skin, they will ward off the emanations.'

'Under the skin?' asked Manfred.

'Yes,' the elf grabbed Rumpolt through the bars and pulled him close with casual strength. 'Like so.' He rucked Rumpolt's sleeve up and, selecting one of the crystal slivers, he pushed it under the boy's skin so that it lay like a cyst just beneath the surface. Rumpolt squealed and jerked his arm away. Blood ran freely from the wound.

Valaris curled his lip. 'Do you flinch from your salvation? Pathetic.' He held the cloth out. 'Come, take them. I do not care to touch more of you.'

Manfred, Reiner and the others stepped forward and took slivers from the box. Reiner jabbed his shard in swiftly, so he didn't have time to think about it. The murmuring that had cluttered the back of his brain since he had entered the glittering caves receded almost to nothing. The others slid their crystals in too, grunting or hissing. Darius sighed, seemingly relieved. Only Franka hesitated.

Reiner stepped to her. 'Do you want me to do it?'

She looked up at him and her face hardened. 'No. You have cut me once already.' She shoved the splinter vehemently into her arm and stifled a cry as it went too deep.

'Franka!' Reiner hissed.

She turned away from him, wiping her eyes with the back of her hand.

'Now,' said Valaris. 'Who leads the rescuers?'

Reiner reluctantly turned to the elf. 'I do.'

'Then come, and bare your chest.'

Reiner stepped to the bars, unbuckling his breastplate, then pulling open his doublet and shirt. Valaris drew a black-bladed dagger and, eyes closed, chanted under his breath in his own tongue. Faint curls of smoke rose off the blade and Reiner could smell the scent of hot iron. The tip of the dagger glowed a dull red.

Reiner wanted to run and hide from the smouldering knife, but the prospect of being dragged from the cage by filthy mutants and held down while Valaris did what he intended anyway made him decide that gripping the bars and holding still was the better option.

The elf finished his incantation and opened his eyes. 'Hold steady,' he said. 'If I mar it, I will have to start again in a new place.'

He pressed the blade into Reiner's flesh, just below his right collar bone and began cutting a curving line. The pain was indescribable, a bright line of agony that seemed to grow worse after the blade tip had passed. Reiner flushed with a cold sweat. His palms slipped on the bars, slick. His knees shook.

'Steady, fool.' said Valaris. He moved to Reiner's left side, sketching quickly but precisely with the smoking blade. Reiner's hands squeezed the bars so tightly he felt he might bend them. He closed his eyes. Explosions of colour burst across his eyelids. His head spun and he thought he might be falling. He opened his eyes again, terrified that he had moved and that Valaris would repeat the torture from the beginning. He couldn't do it twice.

'Done,' said the elf, stepping back.

Reiner sank to his knees, moaning. Through swimming eyes he looked down at himself. High on his chest were bubbling red lines in the shape of a complex elf rune.

'I am no fool,' said the elf. 'I know you will seek to betray me. The younger races have no honour. This is my safeguard. While these wounds are fresh, what you see and hear, I will see and hear. So if you intend to bring the countess's army with you when you return the stone, or if you conceive some other treachery, I will know it, and the count will die.' He smirked. 'After, of course, he has said his prayers.'

He turned to the mutants. 'Now, come slaves, return to these noble warriors their weapons and let them be on their way. And may the blessings of Sigmar be upon them.' He laughed darkly.

Reiner groaned and got to his feet as the mutants opened the cage door. Franka was looking at him, biting her lip, but she turned away when he tried to meet his eyes.

EIGHT
The Countess Demands An Explanation

AFTER A LONG, weary walk back up through the catacombs to the sewers, then across the mad city under blood-red late afternoon clouds, Reiner stopped the Blackhearts just before they reached the back gate of the Reiklander legation's town house.

'Hold a moment,' he said, groaning. The sweat seeping into Valaris's knife work made it burn like it was still on fire. 'It just came to me. Without Manfred, we are in a difficult position. If we return without him, we will be questioned about his disappearance, and quite possibly arrested.'

'So we don't go in?' asked Pavel.

'How are we to get the stone if we don't?' Reiner asked. 'A gang of masterless ruffians will not be allowed to get anywhere near the stone. We need Manfred's influence to reach it.'

'So we're sunk before we begin,' said Hals.

'No,' said Reiner, thinking. 'No, we take Manfred in with us.'

'Eh?' said Rumpolt. 'But Count Manfred is in the cave with–'

'Not at all,' said Reiner, grinning suddenly. He looked around, sizing up the Blackhearts. 'Darius, give Jurgen your cloak. Jurgen, pull the hood well forward and keep your head down. Good. Now, an arm over my shoulder and one over Dieter's, and see if you can manage a limp. Excellent.' He looked at the others. 'When we go in, we will disperse and don our servant's garb again. See to your wounds as best you can. I will send Franka with word when I learn where the stone is held and contrive a plan for its recovery. Now, onward.'

'Open the gate,' Reiner cried as they reached it. 'Open the gate for Count Manfred!'

A Nordbergbruche bowman looked out, then threw open the back gate when he saw them.

'Is the count hurt?' he asked, concerned.

'Yes, he's hurt, blast you,' said Reiner. 'Now go before us and clear the way!'

'Where is Captain Baerich?'

'Dead. Now go.'

The bowman paled, but led Reiner, Dieter and Jurgen toward the house as servants ran before them, crying the news. The other Blackhearts turned toward the servants' quarters. Reiner, Dieter, Jurgen and Franka followed the bowman through the stableyard and the kitchen unmolested, but as they reached Manfred's second floor suite, the other members of the Reikland legation spilled into the hall, all calling to Manfred and demanding to know where he had been.

'Darius,' said Reiner, slipping out from under Jurgen's arm. 'Take him inside. Bowman, return to your post.'

Reiner threw open Manfred's door, then stepped toward the jabbering lords and clerics, as the others hurried Jurgen into the count's room.

'M'lords, please!' called Reiner. 'Quiet yourselves! Count Valdenheim is grievously wounded and must take to his bed. He is too hurt to speak.'

'But he must!' cried Lord Boellengen, looking like a flustered goose. 'He has embarrassed us all with this skullduggery! The countess demands an explanation!'

'As do we,' puffed Grand Master Raichskell. 'Why were we not informed of this morning's undertaking? It is outrageous that Knights of the Order were not included.'

'Nor were my Hammer Bearers!' cried Father Totkrieg.

'There is some mystery here,' said Magus Nichtladen.

'If Valdenheim has done something to dishonour the Emperor's name,' said Lord Schott, 'he will answer to me!'

'My lords,' said Reiner. 'I cannot speak for the count, but I will communicate your questions to him and bring you his answers. Now, if you will excuse me.'

'We do not excuse you,' piped Lord Boellengen imperiously. 'We must speak to Count Valdenheim regardless of his condition. Countess Elise has called an emergency meeting of the parliament. He must attend.'

Reiner sighed and opened Manfred's door. 'Enter if you must, m'lords. But Count Valdenheim is incapable of speech. He was cut with an unclean blade, and his mouth and throat are choked with boils. His physician fears they may be infectious. Some sort of Chaos pox, it might be.'

The lords recoiled, hands going instinctively to their mouths.

'He... he is ill?' asked Raichskell.

'So it seems, m'lord,' said Reiner.

'But he must attend,' said Boellengen, backing away. 'The countess will expel the legation if she is not given an explanation of the morning's occurrence.'

Reiner paused, pretending to think. 'Perhaps it would be permissible for me to appear in the count's place, and give his explanation?'

'You?' sneered Boellengen. 'A clerk?'

'The countess may find my presence more palatable than Count Manfred's, m'lord,' said Reiner. 'He is a bit... unpleasant to behold.'

The lords grimaced, then muttered together for a long moment. At last Boellengen turned back to Reiner. 'Very well. The parliament meets in an hour. Make yourself presentable.'

'Certainly, m'lord.' Reiner bowed, then slipped through the door and locked it behind him, breathing a sigh of relief. Darius had his physician's kit unrolled and was tending to Dieter, Jurgen and Franka, who sat on Manfred's enormous canopied bed.

'Will we live, scholar?' asked Reiner.

Darius shrugged. 'Nothing appears mortal, sir, but I have limited skills as a physician.'

'How's your arm, Rohmner?'

The swordmaster had his shirt off, massaging his thickly muscled shoulder. It was black and blue. 'Numb and stiff, captain. But it will pass, I think.'

'That's a mercy.' Reiner turned to Manfred's wardrobe. 'While I'm gone all of you must keep the door locked and let no one in, no matter what they say or who they are. Is that clear?'

'Aye, captain,' said Franka.

The others nodded.

'I,' he said, taking a fresh shirt from the wardrobe, 'must go speak to the countess and her parliament.' He sighed. 'I'd sooner face the mutants again.'

'WHEN THE REIKLAND legation came to us yesterday,' said Countess Elise from her chair at the northernmost point of the parliament's U-shaped table, 'we were cautious. But Count Manfred promised co-operation. He promised the help of the great mage Teclis. Yet, not ten hours after he speaks these words, he attempts to recover the waystone without informing any official of Talabheim, and–'

'I was there, countess,' piped up Danziger.

His face was mottled with bruises, and his left hand thickly bandaged. Von Pfaltzen was in attendance as well, a cut over his left eye. Reiner was surprised to see them.

When he had left them, their situations had seemed desperate.

'Without my authority!' the countess snapped at Danziger. 'And with knowledge you should have shared with the parliament. And what comes of this unsanctioned undertaking? The stone lost as soon as it is found. Nearly thirty men dead. Count Manfred and Lord Teclis wounded near unto death...'

Reiner choked, and then was caught with a fit of coughing. The stone lost? Teclis alive? Was this good news or bad? He patted his chest and nearly screamed in agony. He had forgotten Valaris's knife cuts. Valaris! He groaned. Now the dark elf knew Teclis lived. At least he hadn't cut a mouth into Reiner's chest. He couldn't order him to kill the high elf.

Reiner looked up to see the countess and the parliament glaring at him. He ducked his head. 'Forgive me, countess, members of the assembly, but the count sent me immediately from his side to be with you. We had heard no news, of Teclis or the waystone.'

'Then let me inform you,' said the countess dryly, 'so that you may inform the count. The noble Teclis lives, though barely. At his request we house him in a secret location, so he may tend to his healing without fear of further attempts on his life. And our cousin Rodick has informed us that he was robbed of the stone by cultists as he left the sewers. It is therefore with great anticipation,' she said, turning cold eyes on Reiner, 'that we wait to hear Count Valdenheim's mouthpiece explain his master's reasons for attempting the action.'

Reiner stood and bowed. 'Countess, the count thanks you for your courtesy, and answers that he moved in secret in order to catch those that held the stone unawares. He further says that, though he made his plans known only to Teclis and his own men, Lord Rodick and Captain von Pfaltzen knew of it by morning. He is wounded to think that his noble hosts might have had him under surveillance.'

'And did he not prove the necessity of our caution by his actions?' asked von Pfaltzen.

'Count Valdenheim also finds it disturbing that agents of the ruinous powers knew of the mission almost as soon as Captain von Pfaltzen and Lord Untern did,' continued Reiner. 'He will undoubtedly be more displeased when he learns of the theft of the stone after he took such great personal risks in order to recover it.'

'Does he suggest,' cried the countess, 'that the parliament of Talabheim colludes with cultists?'

'I do not know what he suggests, countess,' said Reiner. 'Only what he says.'

'It appears that Talabheim has more spies and informers than it has trees,' sniffed Lord Boellengen, who sat with the rest of the Reikland legation along the wall.

The parliament erupted at this, with every member shouting at the Reiklanders and the Reiklanders shouting back, turning the chamber into an echoing cacophony of insults.

In the midst of this tumult, a page came in and whispered in the countess's ear. She listened at first with confusion and then with surprise, then called for order. When this failed to quiet the room, she pounded the table with her mace of office, and at last the members of parliament and the representatives from the Reikland turned and fell silent.

'Noble visitors and learned colleagues,' she said with unconcealed sarcasm. 'It may be that all our recriminations are for naught, for I have been told that one waits without who has knowledge of the stone's whereabouts and wishes to speak to this assembly. Do you wish to hear her?'

A few voices questioned who 'her' might be, but most said 'aye,' and the countess signalled for the chamber's doors to be opened. Reiner and the others craned their necks to see who the visitor might be. Reiner's heart jolted as he saw that it was Lady Magda Bandauer – or rather Lady Untern now – who entered, wearing a tightly ruffed satin dress in her husband's colours of blue and burgundy. Her face was as composed and serene as a statue's. She looked as if she ruled here instead of the countess. *And if she has her way,* thought Reiner, *she will.*

The lords eyed Magda solemnly as she curtsied deeply to the countess, then stood demurely, waiting to be spoken to.

'Lady Magda,' said the countess. 'Wife of my dear cousin, Rodick. Welcome. We are told you have some new knowledge of the waystone?'

'I do, countess,' said Magda. 'And I thank you for allowing me entry to these hallowed halls. It is a great honour.' She curtsied again and continued. 'As you know, my husband, your cousin, has not rested since the masked villains robbed him of the stone earlier today. He has hunted them high and low, and offered bounties for information, and sent men of our house into the most dangerous, unsavoury quarters of Talabheim looking for news of it, and at last he has had some success. He believes he knows, almost to a certainty, where the stone is, and who possesses it.'

'Yes?' said the countess. 'And who is this person? Where do they hold it?'

Lady Magda lowered her eyes. 'That I do not know, countess, for Rodick would not tell me.'

The countess's eyes flared. 'Then... then why are you here? Have you come to tease us? I do not understand.'

'I apologise, countess,' said Magda. 'I did not mean to appear coy.' She raised her head, jaw set. 'The difficulty is that Rodick believes that the person who holds the waystone is so highly placed, and so powerful, that he dare not reveal his name until he has irrefutable proof of his guilt. Unfortunately, Rodick's ability to gather this proof is hampered by his powerlessness and his lack of men.'

The countess raised an eyebrow as the parliament began to rumble with whispers. She sat back in her chair. 'Rodick is hardly powerless, lady,' she said. 'He is a knight of the realm, and if he has need of men he has only to ask. I am his cousin after all.'

'And he is grateful for your charity, countess,' said Magda. 'But Rodick fears retaliations even you may not be able to protect him from. What if my husband recovers the stone without succeeding in gathering enough evidence against he who holds it? That person could strike back at him, and without a more prominent position and a force of men to call his own, Rodick might be murdered for his bravery. This should not be the reward of the man who saves Talabheim and the Empire.'

The countess smiled, as if a question had been answered. 'And what measures does my dear cousin feel will ensure his safety?'

'Countess,' said Magda. 'In order to further his investigations, and to ensure that he has an official voice to counter any accusations after he has recovered the stone, Rodick asks that he be made Hunter Lord Commander of the Talabheim city guard, and be given the seat in Parliament that comes with the position.'

The parliament erupted, the voice of Detlef Keinholtz, the current commander of the city guard, louder than all the others. 'It's nothing but blackmail!' he shouted.

'Rodick has recovered the stone already!' said Lord Scharnholt. 'There is no highly placed villain.'

'Recovered it?' cried the bakers' guild master. 'Don't be a fool! He never lost it!'

'It's all a ruse!' said Arch Lector Farador. 'A play for a seat in the parliament. And he risks the safety of the city to do it!'

The countess banged her mace for order and the hubbub slowly subsided. She turned a pleasant smile on Magda. Only the sparkle of her eyes revealed her fury. 'So, if we grant him this appointment, Rodick will guarantee the recovery of the stone?'

Magda nodded. 'There are no guarantees in life, countess. But it will certainly make his task much easier.'

'No doubt,' said the countess. 'Particularly if he already has the waystone in his possession.'

'My lady,' said Magda, looking hurt. 'I cannot say how deeply it pains me to find such distrust in the hearts of such noble men and women. If you must search my lord's house in order to satisfy your suspicions...'

'We would certainly find nothing, of course,' said the countess, dryly. 'And the reason that my cousin does not make his case in person has nothing to do with the fact that, if he were here, I could order him to turn over the stone and imprison him if he did not, but only because he is even now on the trail of the waystone and cannot break away from the hunt.'

'Why yes,' said Lady Magda. 'That is exactly the reason, countess.'

There was more uproar at this. The countess leaned forward and conferred with those beside her. Reiner stared at Magda. What a woman! What aplomb! He was torn between wanting to bow to her mastery, and wanting to strangle her with his bare hands.

The countess raised her hand. 'Lady Magda, we thank you for bringing this news to our attention and for making our cousin's wishes known to us. We require a little time to consider his terms and ask that you return to us in three days' time to hear our answer.'

'Thank you, countess,' said Magda. 'We await your pleasure. Though I remind you that the plague of madness grows daily worse, and much tragedy may befall in three days.'

'Thank you, lady,' said the countess, drawing herself up haughtily. 'We need no reminders of the city's troubles. You are dismissed.'

Lady Magda curtsied low, then turned and walked to the exit with unhurried grace. Reiner looked around at the members of the parliament. If looks could kill, Lady Magda would have been a red smear on the chamber's polished floor.

NINE
In My Heart I Know It

IT WAS NEAR midnight before Reiner returned to the Reikland legation's residence and climbed the stairs to Manfred's suite of rooms. He knocked on the door.

'Can't come in,' came Franka's sleepy voice.

'It's Reiner.'

There was a clacking of locks and the door opened. Franka blinked out at him, rubbing her face. He stepped past her and she locked them in.

'At least you are unaccompanied by bailiffs,' she said, yawning.

'No,' said Reiner. 'We are not arrested. The parliament was distracted from our villainy by greater villainy.'

'Oh?'

'Magda.'

'Ah.'

'She and Rodick hold the waystone hostage with the job of chief constable and a seat in the parliament as ransom,' said Reiner, sitting wearily on the bed and pulling off his boots. 'Where are Jurgen and Dieter and Darius?'

Franka jerked a thumb at the adjoining valet's quarters. 'Sleeping.'

'Any trouble?'

'No.'

Reiner nodded, then looked shyly at Franka. He opened his mouth, then shut it again. Valaris was eavesdropping. He would hear everything Reiner wanted to say to Franka. Reiner flushed. It was like being on stage. Then he shrugged. What did Valaris care about their lives? He only wanted the stone. He couldn't wait to speak until after the dark elf had freed them. They might be dead before then.

'Er... er, Franka.'

'Captain?'

Reiner sighed. 'Less of the "captain" if you don't mind. It's Reiner to you and you know it.'

'Do you order me to call you that?' asked Franka, stiffly.

Reiner kicked his boots across the room. 'Curse it, girl,' he said. 'I know I am a fool, but can you not forgive it? Can you not understand?'

Franka shrugged. 'I can understand the reasons you think I might be a spy, but can I forgive it? No.'

Reiner flopped back angrily on the bed and hissed as he jolted his inflamed chest.

Franka looked down at him, pain creasing her forehead. 'Reiner, only say it. Say that you know I am not the spy.'

'But I do know you are not the spy!' he cried. 'In my heart I know it.'

'But only in your heart?' asked Franka, fixing him with shining eyes.

Reiner held her gaze for a long moment, trying to will himself to say what she wanted him to say, to lie to her as he had lied to so many in his life. It would be so easy. But...

He looked away, ashamed, and heard a sob in her throat. He threw himself off the bed and stood, straightening his doublet. 'Summon the others, archer. Get them all up.'

'Now?' asked Franka, sniffing.

'Now.'

THE BLACKHEARTS STUMBLED, sleepy and surly, into Manfred's rooms, and sprawled on the available furniture, scratching and yawning. Reiner stood in the centre of them, arms crossed, feeling hard as stone, and hoping he looked that way.

'I have good news,' he said, when they had all settled themselves.

'Manfred's died of the gout and we're all free men?' asked Hals.

'Stow it, pikeman,' snapped Reiner. 'I'm not in the mood.'

Hals's eyes widened. 'Beg pardon, captain.'

'The first bit of good news,' Reiner said, starting again, 'is that Teclis lives.'

The Blackhearts brightened at this.

'Good old chalkie,' said Gert. 'Tougher than he looks.'

'The second piece is that Rodick and Magda hold the waystone ransom and refuse to give it up to the countess unless Rodick is made chief constable.'

'This is good news?' asked Pavel.

'It gives us an even chance,' said Reiner. 'Had Rodick given the stone to the countess, it would be locked away in her manor behind ten score guards and Sigmar knows what locks and wards. Clever as they are, Magda and Rodick haven't those resources. So it is only a matter of finding where they've hidden it.'

'We'll have some company there, I'm guessing,' said Hals.

'Aye,' said Reiner. 'The countess asked Magda for three days to consider her offer, and you can be certain it wasn't so she might confer with her cabinet. If she hasn't already sent von Pfaltzen and his men and the whole of the Talabheim city guard out sniffing for the stone I'll be very surprised.'

'Magda must know this,' said Franka.

Reiner nodded. 'She practically dared the countess to search her house, so she's hidden it well. Fortunately,' he said smirking, 'being thieves, tricksters and villains, I hold out some hope for our success.' He sighed. 'Only remember this. If we fail, and the waystone is returned to the countess, our job becomes that much harder.'

The Blackhearts nodded and began to rise.

Reiner held up his hand. 'There... there is one other thing.'

The Blackhearts settled back again, but Reiner only chewed his lip, staring at the Araby carpet.

At last he looked up. 'This should have been spoken of long ago, and it has hurt us that it hasn't.' He laughed bitterly. 'It might hurt me to say it now. Might kill me. But I can stand it no longer.' He looked around at them all. 'One of us is a spy for Manfred.'

They looked back at him levelly, but said nothing.

'I see this comes as no surprise to you,' he said. 'I didn't think it would. Ever since Abel's poisoning, we have been treating each other like lepers, and I have been the worst of all. I have suspected even those I... I have known longest.' Reiner forced himself not to look at Franka. 'I don't blame Manfred for wishing to spy on us. We are Blackhearts after all. I might have done the same.' He sighed. 'Unfortunately, since Abel's death, the presence of the spy has had an unexpected consequence. It has destroyed the camaraderie and the trust that are essential to a fighting company. We have been lucky so far, but if we can't depend upon one another, it will eventually kill us, and I don't know about the rest of you, but I want to live to see my freedom.'

The Blackhearts still said nothing, but Reiner could see them thinking it through.

'So here it is,' Reiner continued, letting out a shaky breath. 'Now that Manfred has agreed to free us if we can free him, we are all on the same side. There is no longer any need for secrets. In fact there is more need for us all to be honest and above board with each other so that we can better work together for Manfred's salvation.' He swallowed. 'Therefore, I ask the spy to reveal himself, so that the poison of suspicion will stop eating away at us and we can rely upon one another again.'

The Blackhearts looked around expectantly, waiting for someone to speak up. Reiner's heart thudded. His nails bit into his palms. No one spoke. No one stood. No one raised their hand or attacked them. They only continued to glance around, waiting for someone else to do something.

Reiner's fists clenched. 'No?' he asked. 'You haven't the courage? My arguments did not convince you?'

'Maybe there isn't a spy,' said Gert.

'Of course there is a spy!' spat Reiner. 'Beard of Sigmar! There may be two! A new one among our new recruits to keep an eye on the old one! Or maybe three! Manfred could have turned one of us first four to watch the others! Maybe you are *all* spies! Or maybe I am the spy! Maybe...' He caught himself – a little too late perhaps, for the others were looking at him warily – and dropped his arms abruptly to his sides.

'Get out,' he said through clenched teeth. 'Go. Assemble at dawn in the coach yard. Dress to hunt.'

The Blackhearts stood and filed out silently, keeping their eyes fixed on the floor. Reiner watched after Franka as she turned into the hall. Her face was drawn and pale, her eyes troubled. She didn't look back.

REINER LAY AWAKE in Manfred's luxurious bed. He couldn't sleep. Thoughts of Franka and her stubbornness rattled unceasingly in his head like dice in a cup. The cuts in his chest kept him awake too, their dull throb spiking to agony every time he turned. He needed something to kill the pain, both pains. He needed... he needed to get drunk. He didn't want to leave the room and hunt for the pantry. Boellengen or one the others might corner him with questions. Maybe Manfred had a bottle.

He got out of bed and opened the armoire, pushing Manfred's clothes aside, and opened a valise, burrowing through shirts and ruffs and combs and perfumes. Nothing drinkable. He tried another. At the bottom, under Hern's *Histories and Families of Talabec*, was a small leather-bound book. Reiner flipped it open idly then stopped. It was a journal, written in Manfred's hand. The entry he had opened to was from two years previous. It read, 'The Emperor has learned of Holgrin's "treachery" through a third party. He will be hanged tomorrow. All goes as planned.'

Reiner's blood ran cold. Sigmar's balls! What had he stumbled upon? He flipped forward to the last entry, dated only two days ago.

'Our recovery of the waystone is paramount. It must be proved that Talabheim cannot rescue itself. And if "evidence" could be found that the countess was behind the stone's disappearance, so much the better. (Put Reiner's lot to work on this?) The Emperor has expressed a wish that Talabecland develop closer ties to the Reikland, and what better way to achieve that than have a Reiklander rule Talabecland's greatest city, and then soon the duchy itself. With Elector Count Feuerbach missing, there is no better time to strike. I have languished too long in the shadows. It is time to step into the sun.'

Reiner stared slack-jawed at the words. He had known Manfred to be manipulative and unscrupulous in his dealings with his underlings and those he considered traitors, but this ambition was something Reiner hadn't noted before. And his willingness to destroy the innocent as well as the guilty if they stood in his way was, well, criminal. Reiner forgot about drinking and returned to bed. He turned up the lamp and read long into the morning.

'WE'RE NOT ALONE, that's certain,' said Gert, poking a spyglass through the curtains in the chilly second storey room of an abanadoned manor house across the Avenue of Heroes from Lord Rodick Untern's palatial residence where Reiner was attempting to spy on Lady Magda's movements.

It had been surprisingly easy to find a deserted house nearby. Many noble families had fled the crisis in Talabheim for the less affected areas of Crater Lake and Dankerood. They had had their pick of three.

Reiner peeked from the room's other window, surveying the street. 'No,' he said. 'Those three on the corner, dressed as Taalist brethren. Isn't the heavy fellow one of von Pfaltzen's lieutenants?'

'Aye,' chuckled Gert. 'I can see his breastplate under his robes.' He pointed to the left. 'And the young knight who has been fussing with his horse's bridle for the last hour. He was one of Lord Danziger's men, who fought beside us in the sewers.'

'So he is,' said Reiner. 'See, he has a bandage on the fingers of his right hand.'

'And the two dandies walking past Magda's door?' asked Gert. 'They are certainly someone's spies.'

'In the mustard and violet?' asked Reiner. 'Aye, I've seen those colours before. Lord Scharnholt's I believe. These Talabheimers do not seem to care to work together.'

'Aye,' said Gert. 'Just like yesterday. None of 'em wants to share the glory.'

'A seven-legged beetle,' muttered Darius from the far corner of the room. He held up something that squirmed in the tweezers from his surgeon's kit. 'Even the insects are affected.'

Reiner looked around. 'Put it down, scholar,' he said. 'Sigmar knows what it might do to you.'

Darius sighed and tossed the thing away. 'What is my reason for being here?' he said glumly. 'You don't need a scholar. I am of no use in a fight. I have no skills helpful in espionage. I am not the witch you think me. I cannot make light or fire with a word. If you wanted me to deduce the genus of a plant from its leaves or root structure I could do it in an eye blink, but somehow I doubt it will come up.'

'Would you rather be back in prison, with the noose waiting for you at dawn?' asked Reiner.

Darius shrugged. 'As you said to m'lord Valdenheim yesterday, the threat of death loses its force if one's life isn't worth living.'

There were footsteps in the hall and Hals pushed in, dressed in a peasant's smock and straw hat. Reiner raised a questioning eyebrow.

Hals shook his head. 'Nothing, captain. I took that barrow of leeks and squash we stole around to the kitchen gate like ye asked, and chatted up the cook when she come out, but she don't know nothing.' He tossed the hat on a chair and wiped the sweat from his bald head. 'The mistress ain't at home. The master is out fighting the madmen. Ain't cook's business to ask their business.' He fished a silver coin from his pouch, grinning. 'Sold her six leeks and two squash at least, so we've some profit from it.'

'Hmmm,' said Reiner. 'That's something, though. She doesn't feed a company of men with six leeks and two squash, so Magda didn't lie about Rodick being away. Magda's home however, no matter what the cook says. We've seen her in the upper windows.'

The door opened again and Franka, Pavel and Dieter came in.

'Well?' Reiner asked.

Pavel shrugged. 'I followed that footman to the boot maker, the draper, a bookseller, and the houses of three different lords. Two of 'em he gave letters at the front door. At the third he sneaks around back and plays kissing games with the chambermaid.'

'What were the names of the lords to whom he delivered notes?' asked Reiner.

'I didn't hear the names, but I can lead you back,' said Pavel.

'Good,' said Reiner. 'Franka?'

'The scullery maid and lady's maid went together to the market, to a dressmaker, a chandler and a sweetmeat shop, then returned. They spoke to no one but tradesmen.'

Reiner laughed. 'The rest of the city may be in flames, but m'lady must have her sweets.' He turned to Dieter. 'And you, master shadow?'

Dieter put his feet up on a decorative table. 'I got in. Climbed up to the roof, then jimmied a dormer. Cased the shack from attic to cellar.' He smirked. 'Tiptoed behind the lady's back three times. The stone ain't there. Nor is Rodick or his men. She's alone but for the servants and the guards.' He made a face. 'And rats. Needs to set some traps in her cellar.'

'Captain,' said Hals, eyes glowing. 'What a chance! We can–'

Reiner shook his head. 'No. We daren't. Not until the stone's found.'

'We could twist it out of her,' said Franka coldly. 'And then kill her. She deserves that and more.'

'Aye, we could,' said Reiner. 'But this close to freedom, I don't care to be torturing and killing the wives of cousins of countesses. It would be just like Manfred to free us from his poison only to turn us over to the hangman for crimes done in his service.'

'But, captain–' said Pavel, but he was interrupted by voices coming from the hall.

'Stand downwind, curse you,' came Augustus's bellow. 'Y'reek like a beggar's kip.'

'And so might you,' Rumpolt whined. 'If I'd pushed you.'

The door opened and Jurgen ducked in, a pained expression on his usually stolid features. He was followed by Augustus and Rumpolt. The young handgunner was covered in wet brown slime, and the room was filled with an overpowering faecal stench. The Blackhearts retched and covered their faces.

'What in Sigmar's name?' asked Reiner, coughing.

'The clumsy infant fell in the sewer,' said Augustus, laughing.

'You pushed me!' bleated Rumpolt.

'I tried to catch you, fool!'

'Shut up, the both of you,' cried Reiner, standing. 'Rumpolt, go wash yourself in the trough! Curse you, why did you come up here in the first place?'

'Because I knew he was going to lie about–'

'Never mind! Just go!' shouted Reiner. 'Run.'

Rumpolt pouted, but turned and hurried back out the door.

Gert made a face. 'Augh! Sigmar's death. He's left footprints!'

'Come on,' said Reiner. 'Let's adjourn to the dining room. I'm not cleaning that up.'

When they had resettled themselves around an oval dining table two floors down, Reiner turned to Augustus. 'So, anything below?'

Augustus shook his head. 'Nothing. No secret ways into the house. No holes. No hidden vaults or crypts. We even fished in the channel, which was when moon-cow fell in. He didn't find anything.'

The others chuckled.

'I found no hidden doors inside either,' said Dieter.

Reiner sighed. 'Curse the woman. Where has she hidden it? We'll have to check the lords she sent notes to, though I doubt she'd be so incautious.'

'You blame her and not her husband?' asked Darius. 'He seemed a devious little brat.'

Reiner smiled. 'You don't know the Lady Magda as some of us do. She is more devious than ten Rodicks. In fact, it is she more than anyone who's to blame for us being under Manfred's thumb. If she hadn't filled Manfred's younger brother Albrecht with evil ambition, he wouldn't have recruited us to fetch that cursed banner for him, and we wouldn't have run to Manfred asking for protection.'

'And Manfred wouldn't have done his brother one better by poisoning us,' said Franka bitterly.

Hals spat over his shoulder. 'I knew she was a bad'un, even before she turned on us at the convent.'

'You didn't!' said Pavel. 'Or we would have heard you go on about it all the way there. You were as fooled as the rest–'

'The convent!' cried Reiner, interrupting him. 'Sigmar bless you, pikeman. The Shallyan convent!'

Everyone turned and looked at him, confused.

Reiner tipped back in his chair. 'Lady Magda doesn't appear to have told anyone in Talabheim that she was once a sister of Shallya. She no longer wears the robes – not even a dove-wing necklace. None would think she had any connection to the faith. None but us.' He turned to Augustus. 'Kolbein, this is your city. Where is the temple of Shallya?'

Augustus frowned. 'Er, there's the sanitarium and the big temple in the City of the Gods, and some kind of mission down in the Tallows. Don't know any other.'

Reiner nodded. 'Well, the Tallows are overrun, yes? It would have to be the big temple then.' He stood. 'Come. Let us go speak to the sisters before the walls pass along our words and all of Talabheim joins us.'

The others rose with a scraping of chairs and turned towards the door, but just then Rumpolt appeared in it, panting. He was dripping wet, his boots leaking streams of water.

'Why did you move? Were you hiding from me?' he asked accusingly.

'Don't be an ass, Rumpolt,' said Reiner. 'Now turn about. We're going.'

Rumpolt sidled aside to let the others through. 'You needn't be mean about it,' he muttered.

THE BLACKHEARTS HURRIED through the broad, deserted avenues of the City of the Gods, passing temples and shrines to Taal, Sigmar, Myrmidia and Ulric, and then up the wide marble steps of the Shallyan temple, a low, modest building of white stone almost hidden in the looming shadow of the gleaming marble sanatorium attached to it. They ran under the carving of outstretched dove's wings above the lintel, and into the cool stone interior. But the usual air of soothing calm one expected in the Lady of Mercy's temple was distinctly absent. Grey-robed sisters ran this way and that, and cries and moans came from the corridors beyond the main chapel.

The temple's abbess ran toward them, wimple trembling in agitation. 'Thank Shallya you've come!' she said. 'They have overwhelmed our guards and are breaking into...' She paused. 'But you are not the city guard. I sent Sister Kirsten...'

'We are not the guard, Mother,' said Reiner. 'But we will help. Who is attacking you?'

'Hooded men,' said the abbess, pointing to a door in the left wall. 'They came up through a hole in the floor of the catacombs. They break into the vault as we speak.'

'Wait here for the guard,' said Reiner. 'We will see what we can do.'

'Shallya bless you, my son,' said the abbess as they raced across the chapel.

The door led to a stairway that wound down to the catacombs. Screams and crashes echoed up to them as they clattered down it.

'Someone's got in ahead of us,' growled Hals.

'But how did they know?' asked Reiner, taking a torch from a bracket and starting down the stairs. 'I don't understand it.'

Reiner tripped over the corpse of a sister at the base of the stairs. More dead sisters were strewn about the corridor, as well as three dead guards, swords clutched tight in their bloody hands. The Blackhearts leapt the bodies as they hurried forward. Rats scurried into the shadows at their approach.

A heavy door lay torn from its hinges. The Blackhearts looked through it into the temple's vault. Statues and paintings and piles of books and scroll tubes cluttered it. A sister wept in a corner, her grey cassock spattered with red. Blood made interesting patterns as it flowed across the decorative tile floor away from three bodies. Two were guards. The third was a hooded figure in brown robes with a burlap bag covering his face. Reiner shivered as he saw it, and prayed it wasn't what he thought it was.

The wounded sister groaned and pointed behind the Blackhearts. 'Stop them! They've stolen Lady Magda's gift!'

'Eh?' said Reiner. 'What gift?'

'A beautiful statue of Shallya, taller than a man. She only bequeathed it to us yesterday and already it's gone!'

Reiner exchanged looks with Pavel and Hals. 'Poor Lady Magda,' he said.

'There!' called Franka, pointing to a cross-corridor.

The Blackhearts ran to the intersection. Down the right corridor, a cluster of hooded figures was manoeuvring a heavy object through a door.

'Come on, lads,' said Reiner.

They charged down the corridor, swords out. The hooded men redoubled their speed. Jurgen sprinted ahead, but before he could reach them, the thieves had squeezed the white statue through the door and slammed it in his face. Reiner heard bolts slide home as he skidded to a stop.

'Bash it in!' he cried.

Gert drew his hatchet and started chopping at the sturdy panels while Jurgen stabbed it with the tip of his sword and began prying away splinters.

'Silly fools,' said Dieter. 'Let me.'

He pushed forward and knelt by the keyhole, taking a ring of strangely shaped tools from his pouch. Gert and Jurgen watched as he pushed his picks into the hole and twisted. Almost before he had begun he had finished, and pulled the door open. 'There,' he said.

The Blackhearts rushed into the room. Rats skittered into the shadows. It was a store room, filled with medical supplies and trundle beds. A rough hole yawned in the floor, surrounded by heaps of cracked flagstones and moist earth. A length of rough hawser dropped down into it. Reiner and the others ran to it and looked down. The sluggish flow of the sewer channel glimmered in the light of Reiner's torch. The reek of sewage was mixed with a rank animal musk.

Franka recoiled at the smell, trembling. 'Myrmidia's shield, no. Not again.'

The others cursed and wrinkled their noses.

'Maybe it's only rats,' said Pavel, but it didn't sound like he believed it.

'Aye. Like Magda had in her cellar,' said Reiner grimly. 'Come on. Down we go.'

They took more torches from the hall, then climbed down the rope one at a time, Jurgen first, and looked up and down the dark, curving tunnel. The waystone thieves were out of sight.

'This way,' said Dieter, examining the floor.

They ran in the direction he indicated and after a short while saw flutters of movement far ahead of them as the thieves ran under a sunlit grate.

'How fast they move,' said Rumpolt, panting. 'We couldn't carry it half that fast.'

'They are twice as many,' said Augustus.

The Blackhearts hurried on, trying to keep up with the fleeing figures, but the thieves carried no torches so it was hard to tell how far ahead they were.

'How do they see?' asked Darius. 'It's black as pitch down here.'

Reiner kept his theories to himself.

After a long stretch where they saw no sign of the robed men, Dieter skidded to a stop.

'Wait!' he barked, turning and studying the ground. 'They've turned.'

The rest watched him as he trotted back along the ledge, frowning. He stopped at one of the granite slabs that bridged the channel. 'Crossed over.'

The Blackhearts followed as he stepped across and turned down a side corridor, then paused a dozen yards in, scratching his head. 'Tracks stop here. They... ah!' He began to examine the wall closely, running his hands lightly over the crumbling bricks. 'There must be...' he mumbled to himself, then, 'Aye, here's the... So where...? Ha!'

With a grin of triumph Dieter pulled a brick from its place high on the wall and reached into the gap, digging about with his fingers. A muted clatter of gears came from under their feet, and a section of the wall sank inward a few inches. Dieter pushed on the wall. It swung in, revealing a cobweb-choked corridor that sloped away from them into darkness. The dust on the floor had been lately disturbed by many feet. Reiner didn't care for the smallness of the prints, nor their unusual outline.

The Blackhearts hurried on, following Dieter's lead through another confusing maze of cellars, forgotten catacombs, collapsed tunnels and buried temples. From time to time Reiner thought he heard the scurrying of feet in front of them, but it was difficult to be certain above all their own gasping and creaking. He continued to look ahead, though it was impossible to see beyond the light of their torches.

After half an hour, they entered the strangest place Reiner had yet seen in Talabheim's underground. It appeared to be a city street, complete with tall tenements and shops on either side and cobbles underfoot, except that the ground was tilted at such a drastic angle that it was difficult to walk, and that the third floors of all the buildings disappeared into a hard-packed earth ceiling above. It looked as if the street had been dug out after some great avalanche of mud had buried it. Slanting shafts of weak sunlight shot down from narrow chimneys bored in the roof. Burning torches jammed into broken brick walls and the smell of meat smoke spoke of current habitation, but the Blackhearts saw no one as Dieter led them around corners and down side streets, his head down like a wolfhound on the hunt.

As Dieter turned down an alley, Reiner put a hand on his shoulder, for there was movement in the darkness at the end of it. The thieves were lowering the statue of Shallya into a gaping rift in the alley floor. Shallya's shoulders disappeared as they watched. It looked like the goddess was sinking in a sea of earth.

'Now's our chance, lads,' said Reiner. 'On them!'

As the Blackhearts raced forwards, Franka hopped onto a pile of rubble and loosed a shaft at the thieves. One squealed and fell with an arrow in its chest. The rest looked up and the statue dropped abruptly through the rift. Reiner felt a thud of impact through his feet. The thieves crowded into the ragged hole after her, their long robes flapping.

Jurgen caught the last few and slashed left and right. They pitched into the hole, their severed limbs spinning down after them. Reiner looked down into the rift. It was as black as the void. The Blackhearts gathered around him, staring down warily.

'Captain,' said Franka, behind them.

Reiner and the others turned. Franka crouched over the thief she had slain with her arrow. She held its burlap leper's mask in her hand.

The thief had the head of a rat.

TEN
This is Not My Home

'A RATMAN!' SAID Pavel.

Hals spit over his shoulder.

'Not again,' said Gert.

Reiner groaned. He had known it in his heart since he had smelled the rat stench in the cellar of the Shallyan temple, but having his fears confirmed made him sick.

'Don't be daft,' said Augustus. 'Ratmen are a myth. They don't exist.'

'Well, this one don't,' said Hals. 'Not any more. Nice shooting lass.'

Rumpolt backed away, making the sign of the hammer. Dieter crossed his fingers. Darius stepped closer, eyes glittering.

'Vindication!' he said. 'The professors said the outlawed books I read were wrong, the scribblings of a warped brain. Another example of their close-minded, reactionary ignorance.' He looked up at Reiner. 'Can we take it with us?'

'We've other things to worry about at the moment, scholar,' said Reiner, looking down into the hole.

'You're not going down there?' wailed Rumpolt. 'There were twenty of the things at least.'

'Oh, there'll be more than that, laddie,' said Hals. 'Hundreds.'

'Thousands,' said Pavel.

'But have we a choice?' asked Augustus. 'We have to recover the stone. The elf will kill us if we don't.'

'And the ratmen will kill us if we do,' said Franka.

'The executioner's joke,' laughed Gert, and put on a highbrow accent. 'Will you have the noose or the axe, m'lord?'

A rattle of pebbles made them look up. Creeping into the alley from both ends was a throng of mutants. Reiner grimaced. These were more deformed than the poor broken men they had fought yesterday. There were many with extra limbs or eyes. Some were only barely recognisable as human. One walked on stork-like legs that sprouted from his back, while his human legs dangled, shrivelled and useless below him. A little girl with an angelic face had tree-stump arms and legs, crusted in rocky scabs. A woman whose face had no features groped forward with hands that had eyes on each fingertip. A man limped forward on stubs of legs that ended in ever-bleeding orifices. He wore the remains of a Talabheim guardsman's uniform.

But no matter how pathetic the mutants appeared, their eyes shone with hunger and hatred, and they clutched bones, stones, clubs and swords in their twisted hands.

'Kill them!' said a gaunt giant with translucent skin. 'Kill them before they bring soldiers and kill us all.' Reiner could see the man's tongue working through his glassine teeth.

The mutants howled and charged. The Blackhearts turned out to face them, slashing wildly. Reiner chopped through the stork-man's spindly bird-shanks like they were matchwood and he fell. Hals buried his spear in a man whose entire body seemed one giant boil. He popped, splashing pus everywhere.

'Into the hole!' shrieked Rumpolt. 'Into the hole! It's our only chance!'

'No!' bellowed Reiner. 'And be trapped twixt these fiends and the rats? Are you mad?' He looked around, then pointed to the back of a looming tenement. 'Through that door!'

Gert threw his bulk against a rotten wood door, caving it in, and the Blackhearts backed through, keeping the horrors at bay with swift spear and sword work.

Inside was a filthy, plaster-walled hall, knee-deep in rubbish, which opened out into a small central court – little more than an air shaft – ringed at each floor by balconies that accessed the apartments. An open stairwell rose into the earth ceiling on the far side, a door to the street beyond it. More mutants goggled down at them from the upper floors before flinching back out of sight.

'Dieter,' called Reiner. 'Can you lead us back out of this hell hole?'

'Aye,' said the thief. 'If we can get through these... things.'

'Wait, captain,' said Franka. 'There's a wind coming down. Fresh air.'

Reiner raised his head and sniffed. Blowing down from the stairwell was a faint breeze with a distinct hint of outdoors on it.

'Up then!' he said.

They struggled across the court, elbowing through mounds of smashed furniture, broken crockery, rotting vegetables, rotting corpses, and pig bones. As the Blackhearts left the hallway the mutants spread out, clambering over the rubbish and trying to surround them. Reiner drove his sword through the neck – at least he thought it was its neck – of a thing whose entire skin was a carpet of writhing pink tendrils. Augustus speared a boy with batwing membranes between arms and ribs.

Rumpolt tripped over the corpse of an old woman as he swung his handgun wildly by the barrel. Franka stabbed the transparent man in the groin and he fell back wailing and gushing blood that looked like water.

'Now up!' shouted Reiner. 'But 'ware above!'

He pushed Jurgen forward and the swordsman took the lead, two steps at a time. The others ran up after him, Hals, Pavel and Augustus coming last and walking backwards, spears levelled.

A man with veins on the outside of his skin shouted up to the storeys above. 'Don't let 'em get away! They'll bring the guards! Stop them!'

Mutated hands reached through the rails to grab legs and ankles. Reiner and the others stomped and slashed, leaving severed hands and tentacles twitching in their wake. A cresting wave of horrors clambered and leaped over the banister. Gert caught one in mid air and hurled it down into his fellows, a length of railing crashing to the floor below in a rain of tinder and falling mutants. More came from above, but only in ones and twos, and Jurgen's flashing sword quickly dispatched them.

When they had reached the second flight and the mutants were thinning around them, Reiner shoved Rumpolt's face into the wall.

The handgunner looked around, eyes wide, a smear of dust on one cheek. 'What was that for?'

'I give the orders,' said Reiner, pushing him up the stairs as he spoke. 'No. "Into the hole", or "Retreat" from you, you understand?'

'But–'

'I'm a reluctant leader,' Reiner carried on, ignoring him, 'as the lads will tell you. But in battle, there's one voice. And it certainly ain't yours!'

'But I was only…'

Reiner shoved him again. 'You aren't listening! One voice, you hear me, gunner? One!'

'Aye, captain,' said Rumpolt, thrusting out his lower lip.

Reiner turned away from him, disgusted, and the company continued up the stairs.

Three storeys up, the stairway rose up into the earth ceiling. The chill wind the Blackhearts were following whistled down from the darkness. There were no more mutants above them, but the mob that swarmed up the stairs had swelled to a hundred or more. The stairs ended at an open door, black as night. Reiner stopped and thrust his torch in, revealing a peak-roofed attic, low and cramped. The Blackhearts halted behind him.

'Are y'certain there's a way out?' asked Gert, uneasy.

'There must be,' said Reiner. 'Or they wouldn't be trying to stop us.'

The first rank of mutants were being pressed into the pikemen's spears as the rest pushed up behind them. The stairs creaked ominously.

'They'll be climbin' over us soon, captain!' called Hals, over his shoulder. An axe blade missed him by a hair's breadth.

Franka stabbed between them and opened up a gash in a mutant's belly. Rumpolt picked up a loose brick and hurled it, and hit Pavel in the back of the head.

'Rumpolt!' Reiner roared.

Pavel stumbled forward, grunting, and a sword blade skidded across his breastplate and plunged into his arm. He thrust back reflexively and spat at the mutant who had struck him, but he was unsteady on his feet. 'Who threw that paver?' he shouted, furious.

Rumpolt ducked his head guiltily, but Pavel saw him. 'I'll be having words with you, laddie!'

'Less of it, pikeman,' shouted Reiner. 'Hold the door 'til we find the way out.'

'No trouble, captain,' Pavel said. 'If the infant doesn't kill us first.' He kicked a mutant in one of its faces and gutted another. Three more thrust at him.

Reiner entered the attic. 'Hafner, with me. Take this torch. And don't throw anything.' Reiner hurried forward with Rumpolt, Gert and Jurgen, crouching low beneath the slanting roof. Franka, Dieter and Darius filed in behind them. Pavel, Hals and Augustus stayed in the door and set their spears.

Filthy blankets and piles of straw were tucked under the eaves where the roof touched the floor. Scraps of food and bits of candle littered the planks, and roaches scuttled everywhere. Something marginally human backed away from their torchlight, its eyes glowing like a cat's. The low room bent at a right angle. The cold breeze blew in Reiner's face as he turned into it.

'There,' said Jurgen, pointing ahead.

Reiner followed his gaze. Ten paces on, the planks and slates of the roof had been torn out, leaving a ragged hole a yard high and just as wide. A rough tunnel slanted up from it. Reiner stepped forward and looked in. Only a few yards above, bars of golden light shone down through a grate.

'Franka,' said Reiner. 'Up there and have a look.'

'Aye, captain.' She clambered up on fingers and toes and peered up through the grate.

'All I can see is sky, captain.' she called back.

'Sky,' said Gert. 'Thought I'd never see it again.'

'We'll have to risk it,' said Reiner. 'Up you go Gert, and be ready to raise the grate on my command.' He turned to the others. 'The rest of you in behind him.'

Dieter, Jurgen, Rumpolt and Darius began ducking into the hole as Reiner ran back to the corner. In the doorway, Hals, Pavel and Augustus were bathed in sweat and blood. Dead mutants were piled at the top of the stairs as high as Pavel's belt, and more clawed over them, stabbing madly at the three pikemen with swords and staffs.

'Now, Gert!' called Reiner to his left, then, 'Fall back, pikes! Run!' to his right.

There was a second's pause, then Reiner heard a muffled clang from the tunnel, and Darius, who stood outside the hole staring at Rumpolt's backside, followed the handgunner in and disappeared.

The three pikemen jumped back from the door and turned, running in a crouch. The mutants tumbled through the door behind them, crawling over the pile of their dead.

Reiner pointed the pikemen at the hole. 'In boys, in!'

Hals dived in head-first and Pavel and Augustus followed. Reiner took one look back at the swarming mutants, then shot in after them, his skin crawling, but though he heard the things scrabbling and slobbering behind him, he reached the grate unscathed and was lifted out bodily by Hals and Augustus, who set him on his feet. They were in a burned out cellar, open to the sky. The blackened beams of the upper floors lay like dragon bones across the ash covered flags of the floor.

'The grate, quick!'

Jurgen and Gert muscled it to the hole, and dropped it with a clang, smashing heads and crushing forearms as the mutants surged up. But there were too many behind the first wave and the grate began to rise. Gert and Jurgen jumped on it, trying to hold it down with their weight, but they rocked and teetered like men standing in a shallow boat.

Reiner looked around. One end of a massive roof beam rested precariously at the very end of a crumbling brick wall next to the grate.

'Lads! The beam!'

All the Blackhearts but Jurgen and Gert ran to it and began pushing at its side. It wouldn't budge. They grunted and strained to no effect as Jurgen and Gert stabbed down through the bucking grate.

'Not the beam!' said Pavel. 'The wall!' And to illustrate, he began jabbing at the powdery bricks below the beam.

'Good thinking!' said Reiner. 'Everybody at it!'

The Blackhearts began hacking and chopping at the end of the wall with their spears and swords. Reiner stepped to Gert and took his hatchet from his belt, then hammered on the wall with the back of it. Bricks smashed and fell out of the dry mortar like hail until it looked like a giant had taken a bite from the wall.

Suddenly, with a groan and a popping of exploding bricks, the beam's weight finished the job, crushing the unsupported bricks below it and sliding toward the edge.

'Gert! Jurgen!'

The swordsman and the crossbowman leapt clear of the grate as the beam crashed to the flags with a deafening boom. The grate lifted, the mutants welling up under it, but the beam bounced once and mashed it back down, pinning their arms and fingers and necks beneath it. Horrible muffled screams came from below it.

Reiner slapped Pavel on the back while the others caught their breath. 'Well done, lad. Now let's away.'

Reiner led them up a stone stairway and they spilled through a door onto the street, and froze in shock. The neighbourhood had become a jungle.

The Blackhearts stood at the base of the crater wall, the street rising rapidly to their right into the cluttered vertical slum of shacks that clung to its inner curve. But though there were buildings all around them, it hardly seemed they were in a city at all.

Talabheim had been long known throughout the Empire as the city of gardens. Its parks were famed for their beauty. Trees lined most streets, and even the poorest hovels had flowers at every window, but now the trees and flowers had consumed everything. Mutant ivy poured down the crater wall like a green waterfall. Once stately oaks and beeches had grown into twisted monstrosities, sprouting gnarled, questing branches that had smashed through walls and pushed down buildings. To the left was a hulking, black-leafed giant that might once have been a larch. Fat purple fruit hung from its branches. The fruit screamed through gaping sphincters.

The structures that still stood were wreathed in matted vegetation. Some were choked by pale, pulsing lianas that sprouted wet pink flowers. Others were hung with torso-thick black vines that bristled with thorns as long as daggers. Burned tenements rose out of this under-brush like tottering matchstick giants. The vines that covered the lower storeys of one were hung all over with bodies. Reiner cringed as he saw that the vines had grown through the corpses like curved spears. Blood-red grass grew between the cobbles, coarse and sharp.

Hideous mutants crept through this jungle like wild beasts, travelling in packs for safety and eyeing each other warily. Reiner watched a man with a parrot beak for a mouth led what might have been his family across the street and into a shattered bakery. Before they were all in, the branch of an oak tree twitched down and snatched up one of his children.

The parrot man turned and beat the branch savagely with his staff, until with a rustle of leaves, it dropped the boy to the ground. The man grabbed him and ran inside with his four-armed wife.

'Shade of Sigmar,' said Reiner softly. 'Where are we?'

'Hell,' said Gert hollowly. 'This is hell.'

'It is the Tallows,' said Augustus. 'At least... Oh, Father Taal! What have we done to you?' he cried suddenly, turning away and covering his eyes. 'This is not my home,' he mumbled. 'This is not my home.'

Franka too was moved. Tears streamed down her cheeks. 'Captain,' she said, choking. 'Reiner, this cannot be the fate of the Empire! We cannot allow this to happen! Look at them, the poor horrible things! They could be my mother and father. They could be...' She firmed her jaw. 'We cannot give the stone to that... elf. I care not what he does to us! We must bring it back to Teclis. We must put everything right!'

'Quiet, you little fool,' said Reiner, tapping his chest meaningfully though it was agony to do it. 'Of course we will bring the stone to the Druchii. We made a bargain with him and we will honour it.'

The others looked at him sullenly. He ignored them and turned to Augustus. 'Right, Kolbein. You know this place. Lead us back to civilization.'

'Aye, captain,' Augustus said dully. He looked around at the horizon. 'The Street of the Emperor's Grace is… this way.' He pointed left down the street, then started marching stolidly through the long red grass. The others fell in behind him, weapons out.

The journey was quite literally a nightmare. Here they saw a man hacking off his fur-covered left hand with an axe. There was a thing with a head like a bobbing bouquet of eyeballs. Here was a dog dragging itself by its front paws, its back half a scaly fish tail. There walked a naked woman with fangs down to her chin trying to nurse her dead baby at her breast.

Fortunately, most of the denizens seemed too concerned with their own affairs to bother with the well-armed Blackhearts. Reiner hoped they reached their destination soon, however, for the sun was setting quickly and the thought of travelling though this place at night made his blood run cold.

As they walked, Hals examined the blood matted hair at the back of Pavel's head while Pavel wrapped the gash in his arm with linen from Darius's kit.

'Not to worry, lad,' said Hals. 'He ain't knocked yer brains out. Ain't even a hole.'

'I'd knock his brains out,' said Pavel, giving Rumpolt a dirty look. 'If he had any.'

'It was an accident!' cried Rumpolt. 'I meant to throw it at the mutants.'

'And if y'hadn't thrown it at all,' said Hals, 'there'd ha' been no accident.'

'Y'owe Voss a pint of blood, infant,' said Augustus.

'I was only trying to help.'

'Aye,' said Pavel. 'Help. It's no wonder the lads of yer company sent ye to the gallows. They were trying to save their lives.'

'Have ye no common sense?' asked Hals. 'Were ye not trained?'

'Trained?' laughed Augustus. 'He's hardly weaned!'

The pikemen laughed, as did Dieter and Gert.

Rumpolt looked close to tears. 'Captain, will you let them mock me so?'

'I'm waiting for them to say something that isn't the truth,' said Reiner dryly.

'You side with them?' said Rumpolt, disbelieving. 'When they abuse me for a mistake?'

'I side with them because they are proven men,' he said. 'You'll have to prove yourself their equal before I think of siding with you. And you've a long way to go, laddie. A long way.' Of course one of the others is a spy, Reiner added gloomily to himself, but at least they could handle themselves in a fight.

Rumpolt lowered his head. His hands gripped his gun barrel as if he were trying to choke it.

Reiner grunted. Curse the boy. He seemed to invite insult by his mere presence. He was trying to think of something encouraging to say when a yelp from behind made them all turn.

Thirty paces back, Darius was being dragged into an alley by an obese, toad-like woman with a mouth that opened to her navel. The scholar had a knife in one hand and a clump of writhing vines in the other.

'Hie!' cried Reiner. 'Leave off!'

The Blackhearts ran back, shouting and waving their weapons. The toad-woman dropped Darius, terrified, and bounded with surprising speed into the shadows.

Reiner pulled Darius up roughly by the arm. 'Are you mad? What are you doing falling back?'

'I… I'm sorry,' said Darius. 'I was taking cuttings.'

'Cuttings?'

'Aye. Look.' Darius held up the wriggling plants. 'The mutations are fascinating. I want to plant the seeds and see if they breed true away from the influence of the warpstone. Imagine what might be learned from–'

Reiner dashed the stalks from his hands. 'Fool! They're diseased. Do you want to spread this madness?'

Darius glared at him. 'I am a man of method. I would not let that occur.'

'You certainly won't,' said Reiner. 'Because you're leaving them behind.' He shoved Darius forward and the Blackhearts marched on.

As THEY PASSED through the barricades at the border of Old Market and the company began to march wearily through the only marginally less lunatic merchant quarter, a crushing depression settled upon Reiner. With every step, the futility of continuing their quest was more apparent. The ratmen had the waystone. And by tomorrow morning, if the fables of the beasts' globe-spanning tunnels were true, it might be anywhere in the world. The Blackhearts' chances of recovering it were worse than a mark's chance of winning at dice in a rigged game.

Giving up would be such a relief. All he had to do was lie down and do nothing for three days and then Manfred would kill them before the dark elf killed him. It would all be over – all the struggle, all the confusion with Franka. Nothing but blissful oblivion.

But the faint, flickering hope of freedom floated ahead of him like a will-o-the-wisp drifting across a swamp, and try as he might, he couldn't let it go. It was so tantalisingly close. Only an army of vermin stood in the way.

'Right, lads,' he said as they reached the townhouse's back gate. 'We'll carry on as before, and make another try for the stone tomorrow, after I have thought of a way to get it away from the ratmen.'

That none of them laughed at that foolish statement was proof of their weariness. They only nodded and wandered off to their various quarters. Reiner, Jurgen, Darius and Franka climbed the stairs to the second floor, then stopped as they saw the nobles of the Reikland legation in full armour milling around Count Manfred's quarters, all talking at once. Manfred's door was open.

'Hetsau,' called Lord Boellengen, his chinless face livid with outrage. 'What is the meaning of this? Where is Count Manfred?'

ELEVEN
Beasts and Vermin

REINER GROANED. HE was not ready to be clever. All he wanted to do was close his eyes. He took a deep breath and stepped forwards, looking as earnest and concerned as he could manage.

'M'lords, I apologise if we have caused you any concern. I would have informed you of events earlier but, as you can see, we have had a trying day ourselves and are only just returning from the most desperate adventure.'

'Do not try to oil your way out of this, rogue,' said Lord Schott, sneering. 'Where is Count Manfred?'

'I am endeavouring to tell you, m'lords,' said Reiner. 'There was an attempt on the count's life early this morning, in this very house. Strange assassins breached the locks of his room by unknown means, and only the skill of Jurgen here held them off. Afterwards, for his safety, the count felt he should be moved, like Teclis, to an undisclosed location, and this we have done.'

'What nonsense is this?' rumbled Grand Master Raichskell. 'We heard no attack. We did not see the count leave.'

'The assassins were very silent m'lord,' said Reiner. 'And we removed Manfred as quietly as possible, so as not to alert any spies among the household staff.'

'I see,' said Boellengen, sceptically. 'And where is the count now?'

'Er, forgive me, m'lords,' said Reiner. 'But the count has asked that I keep his new quarters a secret, even from his allies. He has reason not to trust the walls of Talabheim with the knowledge.'

Boellengen and Schott and the others exchanged looks. Boellengen said something to an attendant, who hurried away, then he turned back to Reiner. 'We begin to suspect, Hetsau,' he sniffed, 'that you have abducted Count Manfred. You and these others will turn over your weapons and surrender to our custody.'

'M'lord,' said Reiner. 'I assure you, we have done nothing to Lord Manfred. We are, in fact, entirely concerned with his safety.'

'Be that as it may,' said Boellengen, 'we will hold you until you agree to bring us to Count Manfred and he tells us that all these peculiarities were by his command.'

'But, m'lord...' said Reiner, desperately. Sigmar! If they were locked up, it was over. The dark elf's deadline would pass and they would be found in their cells twisted and dead by Manfred's poison. His foolish wish to end it all would come true.

Boellengen interrupted him. 'I am disappointed that we cannot question you immediately, but a crisis has arisen that requires our immediate action, and we must go.'

Men in Boellengen's colours appeared at his shoulder. More men came up behind them on the back stairs. Jurgen put his hand on his hilt.

Reiner shook his head. 'Save it, lad. We'll end up fighting the whole Empire.'

'Shaffer, Lock them and the rest of Manfred's "servants" in the cellar,' said Boellengen. 'And place a guard, for these are cunning men. Then join us at the Shallyan temple. We must go.'

Reiner's heart jumped. 'The Shallyan temple, m'lord?' he said as a soldier laid a hand on his shoulder. 'So you discovered Lady Magda's trick too? And know that the waystone has been stolen again?'

Boellengen turned back sharply. 'What do you know of this?'

'We saw the thieves take the stone, m'lord,' said Reiner. 'We pursued them.'

Lord Schott stepped forward. 'You are the men the sisters spoke of? Who came before the city guard? You know of the... creatures?'

'The ratmen, m'lord?' said Reiner. 'Aye. We had learned of Lady Magda's treacherous attempt to hide the stone, and went to recover it, but the vermin were there before us. We tried to stop them, but alas–'

'Never mind your excuses,' said Boellengen. 'Did you pursue them to their lair? Do you know where it lies?'

'We followed them to its entrance, m'lord,' said Reiner. 'But were attacked by mutants and were forced to retire. I could lead you to the spot.'

'Lord Boellengen,' said Raichskell, aghast. 'You would trust this villain?'

'With a rope around his neck and a sword at his back?' said Boellengen. 'Aye.' He gestured to his captain. 'Collect the rest of his companions and make them ready to depart. I want them before us, to spring any traps they might lead us into.'

As HE WAITED with the Blackhearts in the courtyard of the barracks of the Talabheim city guard while the Reikland and Talabheim companies assembled for a massive expedition into the ratmen's domain, Reiner pieced together from scraps of overheard conversation the events that had led to it. Shortly after the Blackhearts had followed the ratmen out of the Shallyan temple, the city guard had arrived. They had lost the trail, but found the bodies of ratmen in the vault. These bodies and the story of the theft of Lady Magda's 'gift' were eventually brought to the countess, who quickly added two and two together and ordered a full scale search for the waystone in Talabheim's underground.

Five hours had passed while the various parties had wrangled over who should go and who should stay, but the grand coalition was now nearly ready to get under way. Seven hundred armed men stood in ordered rows waiting for the signal to march, each company carrying coils of stout rope, lanterns and ladders. In addition, Magus Nichtladen had provided each company with a mage, charged with keeping the emanations of the warpstone from affecting its men.

From the Reikland came Lord Schott's greatswords and Lord Boellengen's handgunners, as well as Grand Master Raichskell's Templars, augmented with Manfred's Nordbergbruche Knights, and Father Totkrieg's Hammerbearers. From Talabheim came Hunter Lord Detlef Keinholtz, leading four hundred Talabheim city guard, von Pfaltzen with forty of the countess's personal guard, as well as companies of swordsmen from both Lord Danziger and Lord Scharnholt. They filled the barracks courtyard from wall to wall, waiting for their masters to finish arguing.

'I fail to see,' Lord Scharnholt was saying, 'why m'lord Danziger is allowed to join us.' The minister of trade was outfitted in a brilliantly polished breastplate that might once have fit him, but now could barely contain his overflowing figure. Reiner wondered if he could even reach across his belly to draw his sword.

'It was not I who stole the stone, but Lord Untern,' said Lord Danziger, haughtily. 'I wonder why the Minister of Trade, who hasn't seen fit to step onto the field of battle in fifteen years decides to join us. Not even the invasion of the Kurgan was enough to stir him from the dinner table.'

'Battles are won not only on the field, Danziger,' said Scharnholt. 'I stayed behind to ensure the provisioning of the troops.'

'Ha!' barked Danziger. 'Perhaps that is why half of them starved on the return from Kislev.'

'And where is Lord Untern?' asked Lord Boellengen, his skinny neck sprouting from his breastplate like an asparagus from a flowerpot. 'And Lady Magda, his wife? Have they been apprehended?'

'We intend to find them directly after the waystone has been recovered,' said von Pfaltzen, then shot a cold glance at Reiner. 'Now, if m'lord's terrier is ready to lead us to the rat hole, we will get underway.'

'He is ready,' said Boellengen. 'Wither away, ratter?'

Reiner bowed his head, hiding fury behind a mask of servility. 'To the Tallows gate, m'lord. I will direct you from there.'

Von Pfaltzen signalled, and the companies got underway.

Despite Boellengen's threat, Reiner hadn't a rope around his neck, but his breastplate had been removed, and his wrists were securely bound together and two of Boellengen's men walked behind him with drawn swords. The other Blackhearts hadn't been bound, but their weapons and armour had been taken, and each had a minder watching their every move. Reiner felt less like a ratter than a piece of cheese before a rat-hole.

The small army marched through the dark streets of the city, the weird twisting aurora in the sky above the crater casting odd highlights on their weapons and helms. Reiner shuffled forwards in a fog of fatigue. The other Blackhearts were no better. They had been up before dawn, and chasing ratmen and fighting mutants ever since.

When they reached the Tallows barricade, the massive logs were walked aside, and the army streamed through. Reiner shivered as he stepped once again into that nightmare realm. He almost wished Boellengen had blindfolded him as well as bound his wrists, so he wouldn't have to see it again. Mercifully, he was spared. Though fires flickered in the broken windows of some of the tree tangled tenements, and shadows shambled in the distance, the denizens of the lunatic quarter had enough sense still to stay well away from so large a force of men. The army met no one on its way to the collapsed building under the lee of the crater wall.

Reiner led Boellengen and von Pfaltzen and the other lords into the blackened cellar and pointed to the beam that lay over the grate in the floor. 'There is a narrow tunnel leading down from here to the attic of a buried tenement. There are several blocks of buried streets down there, m'lord. Dug out like tunnels. The rift the ratmen went into is in an alley.'

'Buried streets?' Boellengen scoffed. 'What tale is this?'

'He speaks true, m'lord,' said von Pfaltzen. 'A century ago there was a mudslide after a heavy rain. A portion of the crater wall broke away and an entire neighbourhood disappeared. Thousands died. It was decided that it would be too expensive to dig out, so it was built over.'

'It was only tenements,' said Scharnholt.

'A callous thing to say, sir,' said Danziger, drawing himself up. 'My grandfather owned those tenements. He lost five years' rent to that disaster. Not to mention the expense of building new structures.'

After a detail of thirty men had lifted away the beam and cleared the bodies of the trapped mutants, Reiner led the way into the slanting tunnel to the attic, then down the tenement's spiralling stair, stumbling and falling against the walls because Boellengen refused to untie his wrists. Reiner saw nothing but fleeing shadows as they descended.

It took more than an hour for all seven hundred troops to march down the stairs and then form up in the buried street, then Reiner took Boellengen and the other lords into the alley behind the tenement and showed them the rift in the ground. 'They went down there m'lord, but we were attacked by the mutants and could not follow. I know nothing beyond here.'

Boellengen took a torch and dropped it into the dark hole. It bounced down a vertical chimney for a few yards then spun through open space to land a way below that. 'Then you shall explore,' he said. He turned to Reiner's minders. 'Put a rope down there, and another around his neck.' He smiled smugly at Reiner. 'If all is clear, give one tug. If you are in trouble, give two, and we'll pull you out.'

'By the neck, m'lord?' asked Reiner. 'That will end my troubles indeed.'

'Oh, we'll free your hands. You look strong enough to hold yourself up.'

'Your confidence in my abilities is inspiring, m'lord.'

Reiner's minders secured two lengths of rope to a gate post. One threw one coil down the hole, while the other, who must have been a hangman in his spare time, made a very competent noose with the second.

He grinned as he snugged it around Reiner's neck. 'Don't let yerself down too fast. Y'might come up short.'

He untied Reiner's hands. Reiner took up the first rope and began to back down into the hole, bracing himself with his feet against the rough walls. Two body-lengths down, the chimney ended in open space and he had to lower himself hand under hand. He looked down, half-expecting to see a sea of ratmen looking up at him, fangs gleaming, but the area illuminated by the torch was empty – a narrow, sandy-floored tunnel with dark, glittering walls.

When his feet touched he picked up the torch. The shattered remains of the statue of Shallya lay around them. It had been hollow, as he suspected. The ratmen's footprints led left into darkness. Reiner walked a little way in each direction, making sure there were no hidden dangers, then tugged the rope once.

Three more ropes dropped down, but the rope around his neck began to pull taut and he went up on his toes to keep from choking.

'All clear, curse you!' he shouted. 'All clear!'

'Aye, we heard,' came Boellengen's voice from above. 'Just don't want you getting any ideas about slipping your leash.' He giggled.

Reiner cursed silently as his toes cramped and his throat constricted – arrogant coward. Did he truly think Reiner would run in this labyrinth of horrors?

Boellengen's captain and three of his men slid down and faced the darkness, swords out.

'Come ahead,' called the captain, then turned grinning to Reiner. 'Practising yer hangman's hornpipe, villain?'

'I'm practising dancing on your grave, whore-son.'

The captain kicked him in the stomach and Reiner swung, gagging and clutching at the rope, before his toes found the floor again.

'That'll learn ye,' said the captain, chuckling, and undid the noose, but not before he had retied Reiner's hands.

Reiner added him to the list.

The Blackhearts followed Boellengen's men down the ropes, and then came all the other companies, four men at a time. They lined up three abreast down the tunnel in the direction the ratmen had taken. It took another hour and a half. If there were any ratmen in the vicinity they would have decamped long ago, thought Reiner, or attacked.

At last they got underway, the long snake of men twisting away into darkness. The tunnel was a long-dry riverbed, at some points so narrow the company had to go single file, at others so steep they had to use ropes to descend.

After a time it levelled off, and the walls showed signs of having been widened.

Shortly after this, Franka shivered. 'The light,' she said.

Reiner looked around him. It was almost invisible in the blaze of the company's torches but he could see it in the shadows; the weird purple light that lit the ratmen's world. Reiner shivered too, memories of the ratmen's filthy encampment under the gold mine, their terrifying weapons, the vivisectionist ratman in his surgery where

Reiner and Giano had found Franka caged and lost to all hope. It must strike Franka even worse than he, he thought, and reached out unconsciously and squeezed her hand.

She squeezed back, then, realising what she was doing, took her hand away.

They rounded a curve in the tunnel and came upon the source of the light, a glowing purple globe set high in the wall. More lit the tunnel into the distance.

'What is that?' asked Scharnholt, pointing.

'A rat-lantern,' said Reiner.

'Eh? They make them?' asked Lord Schott.

'Aye, m'lord.'

'Impossible,' said Danziger. 'They are beasts. Vermin. It must be some natural phenomenon.'

'These are the least of their marvels, m'lord,' said Reiner.

'And you know everything about them, do you, mountebank?' sneered Raichskell.

Reiner shrugged. 'I have fought them before.'

Boellengen brayed a laugh. 'Ha! Myths are but mundanities to him. He is a teller of tales, friends. Pay him no mind.'

A distant clashing and screeching made them look ahead. A cluster of hunching figures dressed in scab-brown jerkins ran across the tunnel from a passage fifty yards away. Long furred snouts poked from brass helmets and curved swords dangled from scaly claws. A shot boomed and one fell sprawling as his fellows raced on. Another mob of ratmen, these in jerkins of greyish green, were hot on their heels. Two knelt and fired long-barrelled guns after the first group, then hopped up and ran on, reloading on the fly.

'Beasts and vermin, m'lords?' said Reiner as Boellengen and the others gaped at the disappearing ratmen.

'But... but...' Boellengen stuttered.

'They seem to me to have all the trappings of civilization,' Reiner said dryly. 'Weapons, uniforms, they fight amongst themselves.'

A little further on Reiner began to hear a sound rising over the tramp and jingle of the companies. At first he couldn't make out what it was – just an echoing cacophony like people shouting over the roar of a waterfall. Then he began to make out individual clashes and screams and bangs. It was a battle, and not a small one, and it was nearby.

Reiner looked at Boellengen and Schott. They had heard it too, and their eyes darted around, searching for the source.

Von Pfaltzen pushed up to the lords. 'What is that?' he asked. 'Is that a battle? Where is it?'

Lord Boellengen licked his lips. 'Ahead of us, I think.'

Von Pfaltzen sent scouts forward and they came back white-faced and shaking. Reiner couldn't hear what they told von Pfaltzen, but the captain paled as well. He and the Talabheim and Reikland commanders clustered together, arguing over strategy. Reiner caught only scraps of it.

'...thousands of them...' from von Pfaltzen.

'...protect the rear...' from Scharnholt.

'...this blasphemy cannot be allowed...' from Father Totkrieg.

'...return with more men...' from Boellengen.

At last a strategy was agreed upon, and the companies edged around each other in the cramped tunnel, rearranging their order of march, then started forwards again. Reiner and the Blackhearts travelled with Boellengen's men, now nearly at the rear. Only a hundred paces on, the tunnel made a right turn and opened out into a vast chamber from which the sounds of battle rang sharp and clear.

The companies edged out onto a broad plateau that looked down into a wide, fan-shaped valley over which soared a stalactite studded ceiling. But as big as the cavern was, it seemed hardly large enough to contain the swirling mass of ratmen that warred within it.

TWELVE
Great Magic is Done Here

Two GREAT ARMIES fought each other in the cavern valley, though the action was so fierce it was difficult to tell them apart. There seemed no order to the conflict, just hordes of spearmen – spear-rats, Reiner corrected himself – fighting hordes of sword-rats, while teams of rats from both armies wandered through the mayhem, shooting flame from brass hand cannons. Explosions of green smoke erupted from all parts of the field, causing all the ratmen near them to collapse, choking. An enormous rat-ogre, like the one Reiner and the Blackhearts had fought at Gutzmann's fort, waded through a cluster of spear-rats, swinging an axe with a blade as large as a knight's shield. It left broken bodies and rivers of blood in his wake.

Just below the Talabheimers and Reiklanders, on the slope that descended from the plateau to the valley – so close Reiner could pick out their scars – ranks of brown-clad rat-long gunners fired into the melee. On the far side of the chamber, gunners in green did the same. Ratmen by the score died on every part of the battlefield, but more poured from half a dozen tunnels and passages to join both sides.

Most of the chamber was made from the same glittering stone as the rest of the caves, but the right wall was different. It was glossy black, with a greenish sheen, and when Reiner looked at it, it seemed the mind-whispers that Valaris's crystal slivers had dampened grew louder again. Darius trembled as he stared at it. Rickety scaffolding covered it, from which hung wooden ladders and ropes and pulleys and buckets. On the floor before it mine carts sat upon iron rails that disappeared into tunnels and further chambers. Neither the green army or the brown army was using the scaffolding to fire from, nor were they damaging it.

'Hoped I'd never see them nasty little buggers again,' said Gert, wrinkling his nose. 'Why do they fight, d'y'-suppose?'

Reiner chuckled. 'For the waystone? Cursed thing seems to sow discord wherever it goes.'

'But why?' asked Franka.

Reiner shrugged.

Lord Boellengen cowered behind von Pfaltzen, staring at the sea of ratmen. 'Sigmar! We are outnumbered ten to one.'

Von Pfaltzen trembled with righteous indignation. 'This cannot be allowed. They must be exterminated. This cannot happen under the streets of Talabheim.'

'Nor anywhere in the Empire!' said Father Totkrieg.

'But perhaps we should return with more troops,' said Danziger, chewing his lip.

'And artillery,' said Scharnholt.

'You overestimate them,' said Schott. 'Look how easily they die. We will drive them before us.'

A huge rat-ogre lumbered out of a side tunnel onto the plateau, its handlers whipping it toward the rear of the rat-handgunners on the slope. Boellengen's handgunners fired at it in a panic. It roared, then crushed one of its handlers as it fell, riddled with bullets. The other handlers ran back into the tunnel.

Von Pfaltzen and Schott cursed.

Schott turned on Boellengen. 'M'lord, control your troops.'

The damage was done. The rat-gunners had heard the firing and were looking up the slope. They saw the companies and pointed, squealing. Some fired, dropping a few of the Talabheim guard, but most ran toward the battle, chittering warnings.

'Lord Keinholtz,' von Pfaltzen called. 'Form your spears in a triple line four paces back from the crest of the slope. Be sure you cannot be seen from below. Place your bowmen to the right. Lord Boellengen, you will take your handgunners to the left. Bows and guns will catch the enemy in an enfilade as they top the rise. Lord Schott, you will protect Boellengen's gunners on the left. I will protect those on the right. Father Totkrieg's hammers will flank the enemy's left once they are engaged. Master Raichskell's knights will do the same on the right. Lord Danziger, hold your men behind the Talabheimers and fill in as necessary. Lord Scharnholt, watch the tunnel mouth behind us for an attack from the rear.'

The companies scrambled to obey his orders, running this way and that, as below, the rats did the same, both green and brown armies shifting to address this new threat, their own squabble temporarily forgotten. They advanced on the hill as one, squealing for human blood.

Reiner looked around. No one was paying any attention to the Blackhearts. Lord Boellengen and his company were getting into position and priming their guns, their duty as the Blackhearts' minders forgotten.

'This is our chance, lads,' said Reiner softly. 'Back up to the tunnel the rat-monster came from, as if you were defending it.'

They edged away and pretended to stand on-guard at the side tunnel even though they had no weapons. Jurgen crossed to where the crushed handler was still struggling to crawl out from under the rat-ogre. It snapped at him. Jurgen kicked it unconscious, then took its dagger and cut its throat.

He returned to Reiner. 'Your hands, captain.'

Reiner held out his wrists and Jurgen cut his ropes with a single stroke. 'Thankee, swordmaster.' He looked around. Scharnholt's men were to the right, guarding the mouth of the wide tunnel. They were still being ignored. All the other companies faced the slope, bracing themselves for the ratmen's charge.

'Right then,' said Reiner. 'Let's find this blasted rock.'

As they stepped into the narrow passage Reiner heard a shout behind him and froze, thinking they had been seen, but it was only a command to fire, quickly followed by a rattle of gunfire and the squeal of dying ratmen. Reiner let out a breath and motioned the others on. A few yards along the passage split, one branch curving left toward the main tunnel, the other a ramp that dropped sharply down and back. They took the ramp and saw, as they reached the bottom, a triangular opening at the end through which they could see the big chamber. Before the opening were drifts of furred corpses – the remains of some side conflict.

'Arm yourselves, lads,' said Reiner.

The Blackhearts picked through the corpses reluctantly. The ratmen's weapons were strangely shaped, and sticky with slime and filth.

Hals and Pavel sneered as they tested spears with serrated tips.

'Flimsy twigs,' said Hals. 'Snap if y'look at 'em hard.'

Franka and Gert sought in vain for bows, but the ratmen didn't seem to use them. Franka settled for a curved short sword, Gert a longsword. Dieter found a pair of saw-toothed daggers.

As Reiner fixed a sword and dagger to his belt, he noticed a handful of egg-sized glass spheres spilling from a ratman's satchel. The ratmen's smoke grenades! He had been victim of one the last time the Blackhearts had encountered the walking vermin. They had kidnapped Franka out from under his nose in a cloud of smoke. He scooped up three and stuffed them in his belt pouch. Jurgen selected the biggest sword he could find. Rumpolt pulled a long-barrelled gun from the bottom of the pile.

Reiner shook his head. 'No, lad. Take a sword.'

Rumpolt looked insulted. 'You don't trust me with a gun now?'

Reiner suppressed a growl. 'It ain't that. It's too dangerous. The bullets are poison.'

'Fine.' Rumpolt threw down the gun.

It fired with a deafening bang and the bullet ricocheted off the walls. Everyone jumped, then turned on the boy.

'Idiot!' snapped Hals.

'What d'ye think yer doing?' shouted Pavel.

'Y'mad infant!' said Augustus. 'D'ye mean to kill us?'

Reiner hissed. 'Quiet!' He looked around at the others. 'Anyone hit? No? Then carry on.'

They continued to the triangular opening and looked out into the chamber. The horde of ratmen was surging up the slope, squealing and shaking their weapons in fanatical rage. At the crest, Boellengen's handgunners disappeared in white smoke as they fired their third volley. The lead ratmen flew back, twisting and screaming. Their comrades leapt at their bodies, uncaring, and charged, crashing ten-deep into the Talabheim front line.

The spearmen held, though they were pushed back several steps, and began stabbing into the wall of fur before them. Totkrieg and Raichskell's companies swept into the rat army's flanks, swords and hammers rising and falling like threshers.

'Good lads,' said Augustus approvingly.

'They can't last, though,' said Pavel, surveying the seething mass of rats on the slope. 'Look at 'em all.'

'Ain't there ever an end to 'em?' snarled Hals.

'At least they won't be looking our way,' said Reiner. 'Edge round to that wide tunnel there.' He pointed to a dark mouth, near the scaffolded black wall.

The Blackhearts crept out, hugging the cavern wall, keeping as much as possible behind stalagmites and jutting boulders.

As they got closer to the black wall, the whispering in Reiner's brain got louder, and his skin began to tingle as if he stood too close to a fire. He noticed the others were twitching and frowning as well. Hals waggled a finger in his ear. Darius winced like he was in pain.

'Warpstone,' Reiner said, looking at the wall amazed. 'The vermin are mining warpstone.'

'How do they stand it?' said Darius.

Dieter looked at his arm, rubbing the lump caused by the dark elf's shard of crystal. 'Ain't this supposed to protect us? I can hear the buzzing again.'

'It's too much, perhaps,' said Darius. 'The shards can only do so much.'

'Then let's find the stone and get out,' said Hals. 'I've all the arms and legs I need, thankee.'

'I could use another eye,' said Pavel, touching his eye-patch as they continued on.

Gert grunted. 'Not in the middle of yer forehead.'

An outcropping of towering boulders stuck out from the wall. They began slipping around it when Franka, who had taken point, pulled up short.

'Hold,' she said. 'More rats, guarding a tunnel.'

Reiner and Hals edged forward and looked beyond a big rock. There were twelve tall, black-furred ratmen in gleaming bronze armour standing on their toes in front of a low opening, trying to see over the boulders to the battle. A flickering purple glow came from the tunnel behind them. Reiner and Hals eased back.

'The black'uns,' said Hals grimly. 'I remember them. Hard villains. Not like the rest of these scrawny runts.'

Reiner nodded, remembering the ten vicious vermin in Gutzmann's gold mine who had nearly been his death, as well as Franka's. 'Nonetheless, I've the feeling what we seek is behind them. They must guard something important, or they would be in the battle.' He looked around at the Blackhearts. 'We'll need to take 'em out all at once, so they can't raise any alarm. Can we do it?'

'Wish I had a bow,' said Franka.

'Or armour,' said Augustus.

Rumpolt muttered, 'Or that gun.'

The others nodded.

'Right then,' Reiner said. 'We'll wait for the next hand-gun volley. The noise will mask our bootsteps. Weapons ready.'

The Blackhearts held their weapons at their shoulders and gathered behind the rock, listening to the clashing and cries of battle behind them.

Boellengen's quavering voice rose above the clamour. 'Fire!'

'Now!' whispered Reiner.

The Blackhearts surged around the rock as stuttering gunfire echoed through the chamber. For an instant the vermin didn't see them coming, and it was their undo-ing. The Blackhearts were upon them before they could draw, Jurgen in the lead. He cleaved through the leader's skull as it cleared its sword, then spun and cut another's arm off before facing two others. If the swordmaster was thrown off by the short length and light weight of his stolen weapon he didn't show it. He still fought like any three of the others.

Pavel, Hals and Augustus fought in a line like the pike-men they were, and forced back three ratmen. One of them screamed, Hals's spear in his ribs, but the spear-head snapped off as the ratman fell.

Hals cursed. 'Y'see?' He began laying about him with the butt end.

Gert hacked at one, but he was no swordsman, and made little headway. Rumpolt fought another, flinching away from the ratman's attacks and making none of his own. Darius hid and did nothing, but by now, no one expected him to. Dieter seemed to have disappeared.

Reiner fenced two vermin, the curved rat-sword twisting awkwardly in his hand. Franka hovered at his shoulder, and as one of the ratmen lunged at Reiner's chest, she darted in and gashed its wrist. It barked, surprised, and Reiner impaled it, then dodged a thrust from his second opponent.

A second rat fell before Pavel, Hals and Augustus and they pressed the third, who leapt back, squealing. Rumpolt echoed that squeal and fell, rolling, as his rat slashed down at him. Jurgen, two more black ratmen falling away from his crimson blade, turned at Rumpolt's cry and leapt to knock his attacker's blade aside.

Dieter appeared behind the ratman Gert fought and stabbed him in both sides with his serrated daggers. The ratman screeched and tried to turn, and Gert ran it through the heart.

Reiner and Franka cut down Reiner's second opponent, and looked around. The others stood over the dead ratmen, panting and wiping their blades.

Rumpolt rolled on the ground, holding his foot. 'I'm murdered,' he moaned. 'Murdered.'

Reiner motioned to Darius, who was coming out from behind a rock. 'See to him, scholar.'

Jurgen picked up one of the black vermin's longswords and tested it, then nodded.

'Better?' asked Reiner, taking one for himself.

'A little,' said Jurgen.

The others followed Jurgen's example.

Hals stayed with his broken spear. 'Never got the hang of them toothpicks,' he said.

'I haven't my kit,' said Darius, looking at Rumpolt's foot. 'Fortunately, it isn't much of a cut.'

'But it hurts!' Rumpolt whined.

The melee had not been noticed. The battle on the slope raged on behind them, and the purple light flickered unabated from the tunnel.

'Right,' said Reiner, starting toward it. 'On your guard. Get up, Rumpolt.'

'But I'm hurt,' said Rumpolt.

'Up!'

Rumpolt pouted, but pulled himself up and hobbled after the others as they entered the tunnel.

Darius flinched back, hissing.

'What is it, scholar?' asked Reiner.

'Great magic is done here,' Darius said. His eyes were wide. 'Dangerous magic.'

The Blackhearts slowed, uneasy. Hals and Pavel made the sign of the hammer. Augustus touched his legs, chest and arms in the Taalist 'roots, trunk and branches' gesture. Gert spat. They continued on at a crawl, wary as cats, the purple light growing brighter with every step.

As they rounded a curve the end of the tunnel came into view – a glowing purple gash in the gloom, flickering with lightning flashes. Reiner could feel the hair rising on his head and his forearms. A rushing, like that of a wind storm, filled their ears, and under it, a weird, sibilant chanting.

'We shouldn't be here,' said Rumpolt. His sword shook in his hand.

'Aye,' said Hals. 'We should all be in a taproom somewhere, having a pint, but we ain't.'

'If ye want to go,' said Augustus, 'we won't miss you.'

'That's enough, pikeman,' said Reiner. 'Come on.'

They pressed on, though it felt to Reiner like they were chest deep in a river and pushing against the current, and at last reached the glowing opening. Within was a roughly oval chamber that tapered to a point far above like an enormous tent. The walls were pierced by several entrances. The floor was a shallow bowl polished smooth by water.

In the centre of the bowl was the waystone, set upon an eldritch symbol inscribed in the floor in blood. Glowing purple rocks pulsed in six bronze braziers placed at regular intervals around it. Lavender mist rose from these. Between each brazier a snow-white ratman in long grey robes faced into the circle, shaking and clawing at the air as it chanted hissing syllables. It seemed to Reiner that the vermin were pulling the purple mist from the air and pushing it with great effort toward the centre of the circle, where it whirled like a tornado around the waystone. Purple lightning flickered in the mist and danced around the white rat-mages, who shook as they fought to contain the power they manipulated. Their fur ruffled and their robes whipped around them. Reiner shivered. For despite all the whirling motion and noise, there was no wind, only a strange, still pressure that pushed on his chest and made him want to pop his ears.

'What are they doing?' he whispered. 'Do they seek to destroy it?'

'I… I think not,' said Darius, hesitantly.

'Then what?' asked Reiner.

The scholar frowned, squinting at the lightning. 'I think… I think they mean to reset it.'

THIRTEEN
I Am Not An Infant

'RESET IT?' ASKED Reiner. 'You mean, er, make it work again?'

'Aye, I think so,' said Darius.

Reiner looked back at the chamber, where the rat-mages' chanting was rising in pitch and the shaking of their bodies grew more violent. 'How can you tell?'

'Er, well, their ceremony seems to mimic a ritual of binding, and the symbol on the floor looks like an elf rune.'

Everyone turned to stare at him.

'So, you are a mage,' said Reiner.

'No, no!' Darius shook his head. 'I've told you. These are things I've studied in books. I cannot make use of them.'

The others looked sceptical.

'But why would they want to fix it?' asked Reiner at last.

Darius shrugged.

Reiner turned back to the oval chamber, chewing his lip. 'Have you any idea how to stop them?'

'Stop them?' said Darius, alarmed. 'That would be very dangerous.'

Suddenly, the pressure got much worse. It felt like a giant was crushing Reiner's chest. Darius cried out and staggered, clutching his head. The rat-mages began screeching their litany while the vortex of mist whirled faster and lightning kissed the walls. The roaring was deafening. The Blackhearts backed away.

Reiner shook Darius. 'What's happening?' he shouted.

'I think they are losing control of the energies they have summoned,' said Darius, his face contorted. 'We must run!'

'Run?'

'If the energies escape...' Darius struggled to find words. 'Anything might happen!'

'Fall back!' Reiner cried.

The Blackhearts didn't have to be told twice. They bolted down the passage as the arcane wind rose to a scream and the desperate chanting of the rat-mages dissolved into frenzied chittering. Lightning chased them, licking down the tunnel. They leapt over the bodies of the black-furred vermin.

'Behind the rocks!' cried Darius.

The Blackhearts sprinted for the outcropping and dived behind it.

There was a deafening thunder crack and a blinding purple flash that knocked them flat. Dust and rocks rained down upon them. The great chamber glowed so brightly it seemed a purple sun had appeared in it. The shadow of the Blackhearts' rocky refuge was as sharply defined as an ink spill on white paper. Lightning played across the ceiling and shot into the warpstone wall as if drawn to it like a magnet. Reiner's brain felt like it was being collapsed to the size of an acorn. Strange voices screamed in his ears and his skin felt on fire. Though he could feel the ground under him, it seemed as if he was falling.

Through half-blinded eyes he could see ratmen running everywhere, clawing at their eyes and ears. Many lay dead, long faces twisted in agony. Many more were falling. Their putrid animal musk filled the chamber. Their squealing was pitiful.

Then the light faded and the lightning ceased, leaving the cavern in almost total darkness. The ratmen's purple lights had gone out. Only the Blackhearts' torches and those of the men upon the plateau remained. There wasn't a living ratman left in the chamber.

The Blackhearts writhed on the ground, clutching their forearms and crying out. Reiner frowned at this strange phenomenon, then suddenly he was doing it himself. His arm burned as if it had been touched with a brand. He looked down and saw a bright blue glow coming from beneath his skin. Valaris's crystal shard! It was hot as an ember.

'Make it stop!' cried Rumpolt. 'Cut it out! It burns!'

The boy drew his dagger, but before he could slit his skin the shards began to dim and cool.

Reiner sat up, head swimming, his hair dusted with dirt and pebbles. The others did the same. Only Darius remained on his back, his head buried in his arms, whispering under his breath.

'All whole?' asked Reiner. 'All in our right minds?'

'Ain't been in my right mind since I took Albrecht's brand,' grumbled Hals as the rest nodded.

Reiner shook Darius. 'Scholar?'

Darius slowly unfolded. His nose was bleeding. 'Is... is it over?'

'You would know better than I.'

Darius blinked around, shivering. 'The... the energies have dissipated, but there is still much residue.'

'Is it safe to go back?'

Darius shrugged. 'As safe as it is here.'

'Go back?' barked Augustus. 'Are you mad? I'll fight any man, beast or monster alive, but what can a spear do against that?'

'But not going back will *certainly* be our death,' said Franka.

'Maybe it's better to die by Manfred's poison,' said Augustus.

'No,' said Reiner, remembering Abel Halstieg's twisted body and rictus grimace. 'No, it isn't.' He got to his feet and looked up to the plateau where the Talabheim guard and the other companies were dazedly recovering themselves. The rats on the slope below them had fled. The rats on the floor of the cavern had died. It was strewn with their carcasses. 'Come. We haven't much time.'

The Blackhearts picked up their weapons and their torches and followed him around the boulders – and stopped again, staring. The side of the outcropping facing the tunnel to the invocation chamber reflected their torches like glass. Indeed, every surface on that side of the cavern looked like it had been polished in a furnace. Once jagged rocks were as smooth as beach pebbles. The sandy, rubble-strewn floor had fused into a slick lumpy slab. The tunnel had melted like hot wax, and shone with a faint internal luminescence.

'Sigmar!' said Pavel. 'Had we been caught in that…'

Jurgen pointed silently to the dead black ratmen. They were but bones, and the bones glowed purple.

Though Reiner was as reluctant as any of them, he pushed ahead. If it was still intact, the waystone was only twenty paces away. He couldn't hesitate now.

The tunnel walls were as smooth and phosphorescent as the intestine of some deep sea leviathan. Purple light pulsed down them, turning the Blackhearts' skin an unhealthy grey. Reiner could hear hissing and popping as if from cooling rock, though the tunnel was as cold as the rest of the caves.

The walls of the invocation chamber were melted to a glowing, glassine sheen. Of the blood daubed rune on the shallow bowl-like floor there was no sign, but the copper braziers were now copper puddles. The rat-mages had been vaporised, but their shadows remained – long grey silhouettes that stretched away from the centre to the walls. Reiner scuffed one with the toe of his boot. It was burned into the rock.

The stone pedestal on which the ratmen had placed the waystone slumped to one side like a collapsed layer cake, but the waystone itself, though it had fallen on its side, was entirely untouched, as white and clean as a tooth.

'The thing's uncanny,' breathed Gert.

'Well,' said Darius. 'Precisely.'

'Come on,' said Reiner. 'Let's get it up.'

'Wait,' said Dieter. 'Company.' He pointed to a tunnel on the far side of the chamber.

The Blackhearts listened. There were voices – human voices – coming from it.

Reiner cursed. 'Douse torches. Quick.'

The company ground their torches out on the floor and backed out of the chamber. There was still light to see by. The walls radiated purple.

As Reiner watched, men stepped cautiously into the chamber – Lord Scharnholt and his house guard.

Scharnholt's eyes lit up when he saw the waystone. 'Ha!' he cried. 'Excellent.' He strode forward, puffing a little, with his men trailing more cautiously behind him. 'Come, all of you. Before the others come. They'll have been put off by that blast, but not for long.'

'Another opportunist,' muttered Franka, disgusted. 'Only out for himself.'

'This will be a great victory for our master Tzeentch!' said Scharnholt as his men began laying poles next to the waystone. 'All praise the Changer of the Ways for returning the stone to us!'

'All praise Tzeentch!' murmured his men.

'Father Taal, preserve us,' murmured Augustus.

The others made warding signs and spat over their shoulders.

'At least,' said Reiner dryly, 'he isn't thinking only of himself.'

Hals glared at him. 'Y'cannot joke about this, captain. We cannot let this daemon lover live.'

'No.' Reiner drew his vermin sword. The others readied themselves. 'Particularly not when he has our stone. But wait until they've lifted it before we attack. We don't–'

'Ah!' came a voice behind him.

Rumpolt was hopping on one foot and glaring at Augustus. 'You oaf! You've trod on my hurt foot!' he hissed.

'What was that?' said Scharnholt, looking up.

Reiner turned back to the chamber, and locked eyes with the lord.

'Valdenheim's villains,' Scharnholt cried. 'Kill them!'

'Curse it!' said Reiner. 'Right, lads, in we go.'

'Now look what you've done! Y'damned infant!' spat Augustus. He shoved Rumpolt to the floor, then turned and raced after the others as they charged forward to meet Scharnholt's men.

'I am not an infant!'

The two sides slammed together. Reiner angled for Scharnholt, but the podgy lord backed behind two of his men, muttering and waving his bejewelled fingers. Reiner parried the thrust of the first and ducked the second's swing, then slashed him across his forward leg. His sword sliced open the man's breeks, but didn't even scratch his skin. Reiner frowned. Augustus thrust his spear between his opponent's breastplate and shoulder guard, stopping him short, but the man only grunted and knocked it away, and Augustus had to spring back desperately to avoid his counter-thrust. Jurgen brought his sword down on his man's unprotected forearm so hard that the man dropped his blade, but the blow made not a mark in his flesh.

Hals stepped back, blood leaking from a shallow cut on his neck, his broken spear hacked and splintered. 'Die, ye filth! Why won't ye bleed?'

Reiner looked at Scharnholt. His fingers inscribed a cage in the air. 'Rohmner. On Scharnholt. It's his doing.'

Jurgen nodded and began hacking and shoving his way toward the lord. Before he got far, Reiner saw movement behind them.

It was Rumpolt, charging Augustus's back, tears in his eyes. 'I am not an infant!' he shrieked.

Augustus fought two men, and didn't hear. Rumpolt slashed him across the back, blooding him. Augustus yelped and stumbled forward. The pommel of his right-hand opponent's sword cracked him in the temple. He dropped like a sack of flour.

'Rumpolt!' Reiner cried, trying to back out of his fight.

Jurgen jumped in front of Augustus to protect him from the Tzeentchists, his sword everywhere at once. Hals, Pavel and Gert spread out instinctively to hold the rest at bay.

Franka screamed at Rumpolt over her shoulder. 'What are you doing, you fool!'

'Stop shouting at me!' screeched Rumpolt. He swiped a backhand at her.

Franka ducked sideways, nearly stepping into her opponent's thrust. She twisted desperately. Rumpolt raised his sword at her back.

'No!' Reiner leapt away from his two adversaries, taking a cut on the calf, and blocked Rumpolt's strike. 'Calm yourself, you madman, or we'll all die!'

Rumpolt was beyond reason. 'Why does everyone shout at me?' He swung clumsily at Reiner, weeping. Reiner parried easily and ran the boy through the heart.

Rumpolt's eyes went wide with surprise. 'It... it isn't my fault.' He clutched at Reiner as he slid off his sword, tearing open his doublet.

Reiner kicked him away and turned to block his opponents, who had followed him. There was no time for anger or remorse. Scharnholt's men had taken advantage of the confusion and pressed the Blackhearts on all sides as they stood over Augustus. They laughed as the Blackhearts' blades glanced off them. Pavel took a gash in the shoulder. Even Jurgen bled – a cut across his left palm. He tried to push for Scharnholt again, but the Tzeentchists knew his goal now, and blocked him.

'Darius,' said Reiner. 'Can you counter his magic?'

'Why won't you listen to me?' wailed Darius. 'I am not a witch. I am a scholar.'

'Sod magic,' said Hals, and spun his broken spear-end at Scharnholt.

It caught Scharnholt on the ear and he cried out, his fingers pausing in their pattern.

Three of his men went down instantly, surprised as their invulnerability vanished.

'Ha!' barked Hals, snatching up Rumpolt's sword. 'Come, ye cowards! Now we'll see!'

But before another blow could be struck, a loud voice bellowed behind them. 'What is this? Cease this melee at once!'

Reiner looked back. Boellengen, Danziger and von Pfaltzen were entering with their companies and fifty Talabheimers. Reiner heard Scharnholt curse, and Reiner echoed him. A few moments more and they might have been away with the stone.

'M'lords,' cried Reiner, springing back from the fight. 'Thank Sigmar you've come! We have just found Lord Scharnholt stealing the stone and claiming it for his master, Tzeentch!'

'Madness!' shouted Scharnholt. 'He lies!'

The two sides backed apart, eyeing each other warily.

'He used magic against us, m'lords!' continued Reiner. 'Our swords could not cut the flesh of his men! Arrest him as a traitor to Talabheim and the Empire!'

'What madness is this?' asked von Pfaltzen. 'You accuse a lord and member of the parliament of Talabheim of such a heinous crime? Have you any evidence?'

'There can be no doubt he is marked, captain,' said Reiner. 'No follower of the Ruinous Powers so adept as Lord Scharnholt could remain unblemished by his master's touch. If you were to remove his breastplate and...'

'Don't be ridiculous!' said Scharnholt. 'How can you listen to this proven rascal, m'lords?'

'So you claim his story false, m'lord?' asked von Pfaltzen. He actually seemed to be weighing the case.

'No,' said Scharnholt, causing gasps from the lords. 'It is true in every particular, except that it was *he* who *I* came upon trying to steal the stone. And he who used foul sorcery to protect his men.' He pointed to his dead men. 'Look at my poor fellows. His men are barely scratched, but for the brave fellow who refused his evil orders and was killed for it. Naught but sorcery could allow such rabble to prevail over my trained troops.'

'Ye want another go?' growled Hals.

Reiner shot him a sharp look. 'M'lords, please,' he said. 'Did I not bring you to this place as promised? Have you not found everything I said you would find? Is the stone not at your feet? Why would I lie now?'

'Because you hoped to take it for your evil ends while we fought the vermin,' said Boellengen.

'M'lord,' Reiner pled, inwardly cursing Boellengen for hitting upon the truth. 'You know not who you aid with this argument. If you would only ask him–'

'I will not open my...' interrupted Scharnholt.

Lord Boellengen held up his hand and turned on Reiner. 'Hetsau, there is one way to prove yourself credible and make us take seriously your accusations against Lord Scharnholt.'

'Anything, m'lord,' said Reiner. 'Only name it.'

'Bring us to Count Manfred,' said Boellengen. 'Show us that he is safe and we will listen to you.'

Reiner balled his fists, his stomach sinking. He couldn't do it. He couldn't even lie and say he would, for the dark elf would be listening. 'M'lord, I have made a vow to Count Manfred not to reveal his whereabouts under any circumstances. I will not break that vow, though I die for it.'

Scharnholt laughed. 'Just the sort of thing he would say had he killed the count.'

Boellengen sneered. 'If that is your answer, then you *will* die, but slowly, on the rack, having told us long before what we wish to know.'

Snakes of fear crawled up Reiner's spine. He was terrified of torture, but he was equally terrified of Manfred's poison, and the hope, faint though it might be, that he might yet escape before they brought him to the rack, refused to die. He swallowed. 'I will not betray Count Manfred,' he said.

Boellengen sighed. 'Very well.' He waved at hand at von Pfaltzen. 'Captain, I ask you to arrest this man and his cohorts for attempting to steal the waystone and dooming the city of Talabheim to madness and Chaos.'

Von Pfaltzen nodded. 'With pleasure.'

'Wait!' said Scharnholt, pointing at Reiner. 'What is that on his chest?'

Reiner looked down. His torn doublet had fallen open, revealing a part of Valaris's knife work. He put a hand up to close it, but Danziger stepped forward and ripped it open, revealing the symbol the dark elf had carved in his chest.

Boellengen recoiled, horrified. 'A mark of Chaos!'

The lords and their men made the sign of the hammer and muttered prayers under their breath.

Von Pfaltzen drew his sword, his face cold and set. 'Cultists are not arrested. They are executed.'

FOURTEEN
All We Must Do Is Nothing

REINER CHOKED. 'My lords… I can explain.'

Von Pfaltzen turned to the Talabheim Guard. 'Take their weapons and have them kneel. My men will take their heads.'

The Blackhearts backed up, pressing into a wary clump as a score of Talabheim archers aimed at them.

'Ye daft fools!' said Gert. 'We ain't daemon lovers! Y'have it wrong!'

'Y've a plan, captain?' whispered Pavel hopefully.

Reiner shook his head, lost. His hands dropped to his sides. He froze. His left was touching his belt pouch. There were three hard lumps within it. His heart leapt. He looked behind him. Only a few Talabheimers stood between them and the tunnel Scharnholt had entered from.

'Lay down your weapons, dogs,' said the Talabheimer captain.

'Do as he says,' murmured Reiner. 'Then join hands and be ready for smoke.'

'Smoke?' said Darius.

As the Blackhearts threw their swords and daggers to the ground, Reiner slipped his right hand into his pouch and raised his voice. 'Join hands, brothers! We will face this martyrdom together, as we have faced all other wrongs prosecuted against us!' He took Franka's hand with his left and raised his right as the others grasped hands.

Von Pfaltzen and the others stared, puzzled at this strange outburst.

'We'll show it our heels,' said Reiner, and smashed the two glass orbs he had palmed on the ground. Instantly great clouds of thick black smoke billowed up and enveloped them.

'To the back tunnel!' Reiner hissed, and ran, dragging Franka with him.

'What in Taal's name!' choked Augustus, but he ran with the others.

Shouts echoed through the musk. An arrow thrummed past Reiner's ear. He flinched and continued running. His eyes were burning and he couldn't stop coughing. The Blackhearts hacked and wheezed around him, bumping into each other and stumbling over their feet in the spreading cloud. Reiner's outstretched hand touched the glassy wall and he felt left and right in a panic. If they didn't find the tunnel this would all be a black joke. There! He pushed forward into shadow and the smoke dissipated. He looked back. The Blackhearts stumbled into the tunnel behind him, coming out of the oily smoke with eyes shut and tears on their cheeks.

'Now run!' he said. 'We haven't bought much time.'

They ran. Though they had no torches, the residue of the rat-mages' magical blast still lit the tunnel in a dim purple glow, so they were not entirely blind. Sounds of pursuit came from behind them – running boots, men shouting orders. They sped up, but almost immediately they heard noises ahead of them as well.

'The rats!' said Franka. 'They're coming back!'

Reiner looked around. The purple glow was fading as they travelled beyond the radius of the explosion. In the darkness Reiner saw a blacker darkness, low on the right wall. Beyond it, a steady purple light was bobbing closer.

'In there!' Reiner hissed.

The Blackhearts dived into the low hole, pushing down it as fast as they could.

Then Pavel jerked to a stop. 'Waugh!' he said. 'What is that stink?'

A horrific death stench overwhelmed them. All the Blackhearts choked and retched and swore.

Reiner covered his mouth. He had only smelled something so foul once before – the last time he had travelled in the ratmen's domain. 'It's… it's a vermin rubbish tip.'

'Back out!' said Darius. 'Find another place!'

'Ah!' cried Franka. 'What did I put my hand in?'

'We can't stay here, captain,' said Augustus. 'It's foul!'

'Shhh, curse you!'

The ratmen were right outside the hole, passing by, squeaking excitedly. The Blackhearts held their breath. Suddenly the vermin's voices rose and Reiner thought they had been discovered, but then, beyond the chittering, they heard the shouting of men.

'Fall back! There's too many!' came one voice.

'Ratties must have got 'em,' came another. 'Back to Boellengen.'

Though Reiner couldn't understand their gibbering, it sounded to him as if the vermin were similarly reluctant to engage. They backed past the rubbish hole again, squealing, then turned and ran. The passage fell silent, though they could hear shouting and movement in the distance.

'They've gone,' said Pavel. 'Let's get out of this midden.'

'No,' said Reiner. 'We'll wait here until things have settled a bit.'

'But, captain!' said Augustus. 'The smell–'

'The smell will keep anyone from looking here, won't it?' said Reiner. 'When it's quiet, we'll follow the army back out, and see if we can make a try for the stone along the way.'

'You think you can take it from five hundred men?' asked Darius.

'Easier than stealing it from the countess's manor house.'

They sat silent for a moment, the buzzing of flies and the skittering of roaches growing loud in their ears. Reiner's fatigue, which he had kept at bay while moving, caught up to him, and his limbs felt like lead.

'What was that smoke?' asked Dieter at last.

'An invention of the ratmen,' said Reiner. 'A grenade of sorts, but it makes only smoke.'

'Great trick,' said Dieter. 'Come in handy in my line of work.'

A party of men went by the hole and they froze. The party's reflected torchlight illuminated the Blackhearts' surroundings. Reiner wished it hadn't. They sat hunched against a mound of rat-corpses, rotting grain, gnawed bones, offal, and broken machinery. The place crawled with rats and roaches. The Blackhearts grimaced, then the party passed and darkness fell again.

'Nice work with Rumpolt, captain,' said Hals after a moment. 'Only wish it had happened sooner.'

Reiner swallowed. He'd nearly forgotten. The boy's shocked, dying face flashed before his eyes.

'A minute sooner would have suited me,' said Augustus. 'Mad infant cut me worse than them daemon-lovers did.'

Reiner sighed. 'Damned fool boy. He left me no choice.'

'I've no pity for him,' said Pavel. 'We might have the stone but for him. Trouble from the beginning, he was.' He snorted.

'Aye,' said Gert. 'Manfred made a mistake with that one, certain.'

'He had no business being a soldier,' said Franka. 'Let alone a spy.'

There was another silence, then Hals chuckled. 'The look on Pavel's face when he bashed 'im with that brick.'

Pavel laughed. 'Woulda' gutted him there and then if my hands hadn't been full.'

'And when he fell in the sewers?' guffawed Augustus.

'What a reek!' said Gert.

'We shouldn't mock the dead,' said Franka, but she giggled too.

They fell silent again.

Reiner put his head down on his knees, just to rest his eyes. 'We'll go in a moment,' he mumbled. 'Once we catch our breath.'

REINER'S HEAD SNAPPED up and he opened his eyes. Or had he? It was as dark with them open as closed.

Where was he? His hand went to his sword. It scraped on the ground. The noise was greeted by grunts and snorts.

'Who's there?' mumbled Pavel.

'Are we ready to go?' Franka yawned.

A horrid odour assaulted Reiner's nose and he remembered where he was – and what he was meant to be doing.

'The companies!' He leapt up and cracked his head on the midden's low ceiling. 'Ow! Curse it! We've... Ow! We've slept! They've gone!' He crouched again, rubbing the top of his head. 'Let's have a light, someone.'

'Aye, captain,' said Pavel. 'Hang on.'

There followed a stretch of grunting and cursing and scrabbling, then a flare of tinder and finally the orange, brightening glow of a torch. The Blackhearts were sitting up and yawning and rubbing their eyes.

Franka shrieked. She was covered with roaches. They all were. They brushed at them furiously.

'Out! Out!' said Reiner.

The Blackhearts scrambled out of the hole, cursing and choking, then recovered themselves in the passage. Reiner looked down it in both directions. There was no sound or light.

'How long have we slept?' asked Franka.

'I'll tell you next time I see the sun,' growled Augustus.

'I think a good while, curse it,' said Reiner. 'The companies must have removed the waystone long ago.'

'Y'don't think the ratties got it back?' asked Hals.

Reiner shook his head. 'I doubt it. Too scattered. Which means that the cursed stone is... is in the countess's manor house.'

As the enormity of that truth hit him, Reiner groaned and slumped against the wall, then slid down to squat on the ground. The waystone was in the manor, guarded by thick walls and iron gates and a hundred guards. How could they get it out? They couldn't. It was impossible. 'Curse it,' he muttered. 'Curse everything. I'm too tired. I don't care anymore.' He looked down at his chest and pulled open his shirt, revealing the dark elf's raw red cuts. 'Valaris, you corpse-skinned sneak, do you hear me? I'm finished. Let Manfred say his prayers and put us out of our misery. I'm done with this poxy life. There's not a thing in the world worth living...'

He stopped as he saw Franka gaping at him. They locked eyes. His heart thudded. She was furious. He knew her expressions well enough to see that – angry that he was giving up, angry that he was selfishly killing them all because he felt he couldn't go on. But suddenly her angry face was the most beautiful thing in the world. He would gladly take a scolding from her. Happy or sad, mischievous or sullen or sulky, he loved her, and realising this – that he did have something worth living for – he knew he had to go on. He had no idea how he was going to do it, but as long as Franka lived and cared enough about him to be angry with him, he would keep trying to find his way to the end of this nightmare.

'Er,' he said, then forced a light-hearted laugh which sounded to his ears like somebody strangling a cat. 'A joke, Lord Valaris. A joke, born of weariness. But I do not give up. I do not wish to die, and we will recover the stone if every knight in the Empire stands in our way, never fear.'

The Blackhearts stood motionless, eyes darting around as if expecting Manfred's doom to come winging out of the darkness. When nothing happened they relaxed.

'Captain,' said Hals, exhaling. 'Captain–'

Reiner held up a hand. 'I know, and I apologise. I'd no right to include you in my little… joke. I'll… we'll have a vote next time, eh?'

Hals stared at him for a long moment, then guffawed and turned away, shaking his head. 'Mad. He's mad.'

Pavel snorted. 'And what does that make us?'

The others chuckled nervously – all but Jurgen, and Franka who looked at Reiner with big, baffled eyes.

'Well,' said Reiner, tearing his eyes from her with difficulty. 'We better go back and see what they've done with it. Then we'll see what we can do about getting it back.'

'Er, captain,' said Augustus as the others began to gather themselves together. 'Being a good Talabheim man, I'm wondering…' He paused, uncomfortable. 'If it might not be the right thing to do… to do what you meant to just now.'

'Eh?' said Reiner, confused. 'What do you say, pikeman?'

'Well, everything's as we'd want it, ain't it?' said Augustus, slowly. 'Er, if it weren't for the count and the poison and all. The countess has the stone and Teclis will fix it. All we must do is nothing and all will be put right, aye?'

Reiner's stomach turned. 'Are you suggesting that we should sacrifice our lives for the good of the Empire? That we should betray Lord Valaris and die so that others might live?'

Augustus nodded. 'Aye, I suppose that's what I mean. Aye.'

Reiner sighed. From the moment Manfred had made his bargain with Valaris, Reiner had been trying to discover a way to defeat it – to deliver the stone to the dark elf, free Manfred, then bring the might of Teclis and the Empire down on the dark elf before he destroyed it. But with Valaris eavesdropping on every word anyone said in

Reiner's presence, he couldn't tell the others his plans. He hoped his old comrades knew him well enough to guess what he had in mind, but there was no way for Reiner to reassure Augustus of his intentions. Instead he had to reassure Valaris that Augustus's wishes were not his own.

'Pikeman,' Reiner said, 'there is a reason that Count Manfred has named us his Blackhearts. It is because we have no honour. We are criminals over whose heads he holds a noose. We do his bidding because we value our lives more than we value any friendships or loyalties to country, race or family. I don't like what happens to Talabheim, but if I must choose between Talabheim and my own skin, I will choose my skin, and drink to Talabheim's memory when once again we return to Altdorf. Do you understand me?'

Augustus blinked at him for a moment, blank faced, then lowered his head, his jaw clenching. 'Aye, I begin to. I guess I thought ye might have more honour than that backstabbing jagger.'

'More honour than a count of the Empire? Don't be ridiculous,' laughed Reiner. 'We're gallows birds. Now,' he said, turning to the others, 'enough of this. Let's be off.'

The others were looking at him with the same sullen stares Augustus had turned on him.

He snarled. 'What? Does it pain you to hear it put so baldly? We are villains! Now, onward.'

THE BLACKHEARTS SKIRTED the mine chamber, taking side tunnels and hiding from the ratmen patrols, until they found their way back to the top of the plateau where the army of men had formed their line. They stayed low and well back from the slope, for below them, in the fan-shaped valley, the ratmen were regrouping and returning to work. Soldiers of the green army were shackling their brown rivals into long coffles, then turning them over to whip-wielding overseers, who put them to work digging at the warpstone workface and carrying the stuff to the waiting carts.

The army of men must have retreated with the way-stone in a hurry, for they had left their dead where they had fallen and the plateau was thick with them – men of every company, staring through sightless eyes, blood staining their colourful uniforms. The Blackhearts robbed the corpses of their gear and their gold, happy to strap on human weapons and armour again, as well as stuffing themselves with the scraps of food they found in the dead men's belt pouches and taking tinderboxes and torches. Reiner wolfed down a half-eaten chicken leg and some mouldy bread. He was so hungry he didn't care.

Hals ground the butt of a tall oak-shafted spear and pushed against it. It hardly flexed. 'That's more like it,' he said. 'That'll take a knight's charge.'

Franka found a bow and Gert a crossbow and they filled their quivers with arrows and bolts plucked from the bodies of dead ratmen.

Once they were all kitted out, Reiner signalled them again, and they began the long walk up through the sandy tunnels.

IT WAS MID-MORNING when they at last returned to the surface and began making their way again through the Tallows. Again, the denizens of the corrupted ward seemed more interested in fighting each other than preying on the Blackhearts, and they passed through it, unmolested, the roiling clouds and strange glowing aurora churning unceasingly above them.

As they made their wary way, Reiner motioned for Franka to fall back a bit.

'Yes, captain?' she said, stiff.

'Aye,' said Reiner quietly. 'I know you're none too pleased with me at the moment. My little tantrum was uncalled for, and I apologise. But I want to tell you what it was that called me back from the brink. For I think I might have gone through with it – killed us all out of peevish misery, but when I saw your face...' He blushed.

It sounded mawkish and juvenile to him now, but it was the truth. 'Well, I no longer cared to die.'

Franka looked at the ground. She held the pommel of her sword very tightly. 'I see.'

'I've been an idiot,' Reiner continued. 'Not trusting you, I mean. I've let my suspicious nature rule me. I know one of us is Manfred's spy. But I also know – I've always known, really – that it isn't you. I just haven't let my head trust my heart. They… they are now of one accord.'

'And so you expect me to forgive you?' she asked.

Reiner's heart sank. 'No, I suppose not. I should never have mistrusted you in the first place. The original crime cannot be undone, and I would not blame you if you never forgave me, no matter how much that would grieve me.'

'Ask me again,' she said coolly, 'when once again we return to Altdorf and drink a toast to Talabheim's memory.'

Reiner stared at her. 'You, er… When…? Do you mean that…?'

She turned and poked him in the chest, directly on top of one of Valaris's cuts. Reiner hissed in pain.

'You'll have no further answer from me until then, captain,' she said, and turned away.

Reiner rubbed his chest, wincing. His heart pounded in excitement and confusion. What had she said? Did she mean that she forgave him? Or did she mean she believed him the villain he had told Augustus he was? She couldn't believe that, could she? Surely she knew him better than that? Surely… He caught himself. The little witch! She had turned the tables on him and no mistake. She was showing him how she had felt when he hadn't trusted her. Unless she truly didn't trust him. Could she be so blind?

All the long way back to the Tallows barricade his mind turned in tight circles of worry, and at the end he was no more reassured than when he started.

FIFTEEN
We Have Tonight

REINER TURNED A sausage over the small fire Jurgen had made in the cellar of an abandoned cooperage in the merchant district. Bloody light filtered down through the caved-in floor above. Reiner, Franka, Jurgen, Augustus and Darius sat in the fire's red glow, making a meal of sausages, black bread and beer, for which they had paid ten times the normal fare. Reiner didn't mind the price. He'd paid for it with dead men's gold. At least they had found food to buy. That was getting harder as the farmers outside the city were staying away out of fear of the madness, and the looting and robbery in the neighbourhoods got worse.

Reiner looked around at his companions and chuckled mirthlessly. This was the band of brave adventurers who were going to storm the countess's manor and steal the waystone out from under the noses of a hundred guards? Franka stared into the fire with glazed eyes. The fingers of Jurgen's cut left hand were so swollen he could barely make a fist. Dieter rotated his head around like he had a

163

kink in his neck. Augustus was as silent as Jurgen. Darius muttered under his breath. No one seemed inclined to conversation.

Unsteady boot steps clunked on the floorboards above. They looked up. Hals's voice reached them.

'Izzis the one?' he slurred. 'All look alike t'me.'

'Think so,' came Pavel's voice. 'I 'member the barrels.'

The boots moved to the stairs.

'Don't matter if it ain't,' said Gert loudly. 'We can lick any beasties might be hiding in th' shadows. We're 'ard men, we are.'

The three pikemen stumbled down the stairs and cheered loudly as they saw the others.

'Here we are, lads!' cried Gert.

'Told ye it were the place,' said Pavel.

'Long live the Blackhearts!' crowed Hals.

'Quiet you pie-eyed fools!' whispered Reiner. 'Have you drunk the city dry?'

Hals put his finger to his lips and the other two giggled. They found places around the fire.

'Shorry, captain,' said Hals. 'Took a bit of drinking to get mouths moving. These Talabheimers can put it away a bit.'

'Hope they told ye nothing,' muttered Augustus.

'No no, they tol' us,' said Pavel. 'But izz bad news.'

'Aye, very bad,' said Gert. 'Very bad.'

'How bad?' asked Reiner, grimly.

'Well,' said Hals, sticking a sausage on a stick and holding it over the fire. 'Met a few of von Pfaltzen's lads at the Oak and Acorn. Just come from eight hours in the deeps under the countess's manor, guarding they didn't know what in her treasury vault.'

'Secret ain't out to the common soldiers,' said Pavel. 'But they knew something was up. All the jaggers been grinning ear to ear and patting themselves on the back about some great victory.'

'An' we know what that is, don't we?' said Gert, winking.

'So it's locked in a treasure vault?' asked Reiner.

'Aye,' said Hals. 'Vault's three floors down under the old barrel keep, below the kitchens and the store rooms, by the dungeons. Guard's been doubled at the vault, and at the gate up the head of the dungeon stairs.'

'That ain't th' bad part,' said Pavel. 'Th' bad part is that the vault has three locks. And the three keys for the three locks are held by three different captains on three different watches.'

Reiner held up four fingers. 'So, we've the Manor district gate, the gate to the countess's manor, the gate to the dungeon, and the door of the vault to get through, and out of, carrying a half tonne block of stone. Lovely.'

'And ye can't just waltz through the house, neither,' said Pavel. 'There are guards and servants everywhere. Someone would be sure to notice.'

'Do you know the names of the captains who hold the keys?' asked Reiner.

Hals, Pavel and Gert looked at each other, frowning.

'Wasn't one of them Lossberg or Lassenhoff or...?' asked Gert.

'Bromelhoff?' asked Hals. 'Bramenhalt?'

'It was Lundhauer,' said Pavel definitively. 'Or... Loefler? Lannenger?'

'So we don't know their names,' said Reiner, sighing. 'We'll have to speak to more guards.'

'Captain,' said Hals, looking queasy. 'Ye'd have to carry us back if we was to drink answers out of more guards tonight.'

'And I doubt we'd remember the names even if we got 'em,' mumbled Pavel.

'I'll go,' said Reiner. 'You lads haven't learned the gambler's trick of only *seeming* to drink.'

'Bad news,' said Dieter's voice behind them.

The Blackhearts jumped. The thief stood at the bottom of the stair. No one had heard him approach.

'How unexpected,' said Reiner dryly.

Dieter crossed to the fire and dipped a cup into the open cask of beer. He took a swallow, then sat. 'I looked in on Scharnholt like you asked,' he said. 'Found a place outside his library window where I could listen to his comings and goings without being seen.' He grinned, showing sharp teeth. 'Not a happy jagger, Scharnholt. Someone he called his "master" ain't very pleased with him. Had a few messengers come by to tell him that.'

'That's bad news?' asked Gert. 'Trouble for Scharnholt ain't bad news to us.'

'I ain't got to the bad news,' said Dieter, annoyed. 'The bad news is that Teclis is recovered, or so says Scharnholt. And he means to work his magic on the stone tomorrow. It's to be locked somewhere deep down in the earth with wards and curses and spells so thick no one'll ever find it, let alone steal it.'

'So,' said Reiner, his heart sinking. 'We have tonight.'

'Tonight?' said Hals, dismayed. 'Captain, is that possible?'

'There's worse yet,' said Dieter.

Everybody turned to look at him.

'If we try for the stone tonight,' he said, 'we'll have company. This "master" has ordered Scharnholt to get it. He's called a meeting an hour past sundown to make their plans.'

There were groans from the Blackhearts, but Reiner smiled. 'Ha!' he said. 'That's better news than we've had.'

'Eh?' said Pavel. 'Why so?'

'Another gambler's maxim,' said Reiner. 'Out of confusion comes opportunity.' He looked at Dieter. 'We must attend this meeting. Do you know where it is?'

Dieter shook his head. 'No, but it won't be any trouble following Scharnholt to it.'

'Even with me along?'

Dieter gave him a contemptuous once over. 'We'll manage.'

* * *

REINER HAD EXPECTED Scharnholt to sneak out of his house by the back way, cloaked and masked and furtive, and consequently, they watched the back gate and almost missed Scharnholt when he left openly, in his coach, and made his way through the Manor district by the main streets.

Dieter and Reiner followed him to an old stone building built at the edge of a large green park called the Darkrook Downs. There were many such buildings around the edge of the park that bordered the Manor district, all with a banner hanging above their door. These were the chapter halls of Talabheim's knightly orders. Some were local chapters of orders that had knights all over the Empire. Some were orders founded by noble Talabec families or by bands of knights who had come together here for some great purpose in times past.

Reiner and Dieter watched from the shadow of a high yew hedge as Scharnholt entered the hall of the Knights of the Willing Heart, whose device was a crowned heart held in two red hands. More coaches arrived, as well as men on horseback and some on foot.

'Can it be here?' asked Reiner. 'Perhaps he just stops here on his way.'

'This is the hour,' said Dieter.

'A corrupted order?' wondered Reiner aloud. 'Or do they not know what is done under their roof?'

Dieter shrugged. 'Better have a look.'

Reiner looked sceptically at the hall. It had the proportions of a townhouse, but was built like a castle, with a courtyard behind a fortified gate and little more than arrow slots for windows. 'Are you certain you can get us in?'

'Always a way in,' said Dieter as he started down the street, away from the chapter hall. 'Although sometimes it's murder.'

He led Reiner half a block before crossing the street and slipping between two tall houses. Like all the chapter halls, they had large stable yards behind them, the

gates of which opened onto the park. This was divided
into common-held riding rings, tilting yards, racing ovals
and archery lanes, all deserted at this hour. Reiner and
Dieter crept along hedges back to the Order of the Willing Heart.

'Hold here,' said Dieter. 'Might be a patrol.'

And there was. Moments later two guards in the
colours of the house rounded the right corner of the stable yard, then turned into the grassy alley between the
chapter and its left-hand neighbour. Jutting from the left
wall was a small chapel of Sigmar. There was a faint glow
behind its stained-glass windows.

'In there, maybe,' said Dieter.

'In a chapel of Sigmar?' said Reiner. 'There's cheek for
you.'

Dieter sized up the chapel. The stained glass windows
rose up two storeys with griffin-capped buttresses
between them. 'An easy climb,' he said. 'I'll go up and
lower the rope. Tie it to your belt when you climb up, so
it comes with you, aye? Don't want it dangling where
they can see it.'

'Aye,' said Reiner.

When the guards had turned down the green alley
again, Dieter set off low and silent, then spidered up one
of the buttresses with no apparent effort. At the top he
took a rope from his sack and tied it around a gargoyle.

Reiner was about to start forwards when Dieter held up
a hand. Reiner hid until the guards once again appeared
and disappeared, then Dieter dropped the rope and
beckoned him on. He hurried forward, trying to be as
noiseless as Dieter, but his shoes thumped on the grass
and his elbows scraped noisily through the bushes. He
felt as quiet as an orc warband on the march.

Reiner reached the buttress and tucked the rope into his
belt, then began pulling himself up. For all his recent running and fighting and climbing, this was not easy. His
arms shook before he was halfway up. His foot rasped
across the masonry as he braced himself, and he heard a

disgusted grunt from above. At last, Dieter hauled him onto the buttress by his belt and he lay over it like a sack of flour, wheezing.

'Ye'll never make a second storey man, jagger,' Dieter whispered.

'Never wanted to,' answered Reiner. 'It's Manfred puts me in these undignified positions.'

'Hush.' Dieter drew up the rest of the rope as Reiner held his breath. The guards appeared below them, muttering to each other, then passed on without looking up.

'Now,' said Dieter. 'Let's see what we can see.'

He took a tiny stoppered jar from his pouch and pulled out a ball of putty, which he pressed against a square of stained glass. Next he drew a glazier's tool around the putty in a rough circle, then, holding the putty with one hand, he tapped the glass very gently. There was a click, Reiner froze. Dieter wiggled the putty and a disk of glass came out with it.

'Try your eye, jagger,' he said, edging behind Reiner on the narrow buttress.

Reiner braced his shoulder against the chapel wall, and leaned in toward the hole. A low mutter of voices reached him, but at first he could see nothing but crossbeams and pews. However, with a little shifting he found the altar – and nearly fell off the buttress.

It might have once been a chapel of Sigmar, but it was no longer. The plain altar had been covered by rich velvet of the deepest blue, embroidered in gold with eldritch symbols that seemed to twist before Reiner's eyes. Three shallow gold bowls sat on the cloth, coals of incense glowing in them. The hammer of Sigmar that should have hung above the altar had been replaced by what appeared to be a child's skeleton, hung by one ankle, and covered entirely in gold leaf and swirling lapis traceries – and it was this that had made Reiner's heart jump, for there were eyes in the skull and they seemed to look directly at him.

When the thing didn't stretch out a skeletal arm and point at him, Reiner steadied his breathing and continued perusing the room. A cluster of silhouetted men sat in the pews near the altar, facing another man who stood. All were dressed in robes, most of blue and gold, but a few in purple and black. The man who stood wore the richest robe of all, more gold than blue, and wore a mask as well. Though his face and every inch of him was covered in heavy cloth, he had a presence about him that was tangible even from Reiner's perch.

Reiner put his ear to the hole and the muttered words became clearer. He held his breath and listened as hard as he could.

'Master,' came Scharnholt's voice, whining. 'Master, in all humility I object to this alliance with the followers of the purple one. Did they not, only a few days ago, lead the forces of the accursed Hammer God to our secret invocation chamber and disrupt the ritual of unmaking?'

'They did,' said the master in a whispery hiss. 'And that is precisely why we invite them to this colloquy. The goals of the Changer of Ways and the Lord of Pleasure do not always coincide, but here our paths run parallel. It is foolish to fight one another when the return of Talabheim to Chaos honours both our patrons.'

'These are pretty words,' said another man whose face Reiner couldn't make out. 'But how can we trust you? It is not for nothing that Tzeentch is known as the God of Many Faces. This one shows a smile, but what of the others?'

Reiner's jaw dropped. It was Danziger's voice. The tight-laced little bookkeeper was a follower of Slaanesh?

'Have we not trusted you with the location of our secret headquarters?' asked the master. 'Could you not betray us to the countess with a word? Surely that is proof enough of our intentions.'

Danziger was silent for a moment, then said, 'Very well. And have you a plan to take the stone?'

'We do not take the stone,' said the master.

The hooded men looked up, surprised.

'Why risk having it taken from us again when there is a better alternative?' he continued. 'Unfettered by the unseating of the waystone, the warpstone gives the spells of our sorcerers more potency than they have ever had. Where once it took a hundred initiates to call forth even the most minor inhabitant of the void, now ten may raise a daemon lord. And that is what we will do. Once we open the vault, we will summon an infernal one within the manor, and beg him to take the waystone into the void with him, removing it from Teclis's reach forever.'

'A brilliant plan, master,' said Scharnholt obsequiously.

'But the vault is heavily protected,' said Danziger. 'Could the lord not break it open and take the stone for us?'

The master sighed. 'That is the trouble with the followers of the Lord of Pleasure. They dislike work. Unfortunately, only in the deepest levels, far below the dungeon beneath the countess's manor, will the emanations of the warpstone be strong enough to allow our magi to call forth a great one of sufficient power. We must bring the stone there or fail. Fortunately,' he said, 'our patrons have blessed you both with position and power that allows you to walk your men though the gates of the Taalist bitch's castle without question. We must therefore only find a way to pass through the door to the dungeons and open the vault.'

'We will easily defeat the men who guard the dungeon gate,' said Scharnholt. 'And if my men then hold it and say that the guards were killed by cultists who we chased away, we will divert the attention of von Pfaltzen's fools.'

'One of the captains who hold the keys to the vault is ours,' said Danziger, 'and will surrender it for the cause.'

'Then there are only two to steal, and the men at the vault to defeat,' said the master.

'We will take Captain Lossenberg's key,' said Scharnholt.

'And we will take Captain Niedorf's,' said Danziger.

'And together you will defeat the men at the vault,' said the master. 'And then descend to the nether depths. Our goal will at last be attained. All glory to Tzeentch!'

'And Slaanesh,' said Danziger.

'Of course,' said the master.

Reiner pushed back from the hole, deep in thought, then turned to Dieter. 'We must find a place to watch them leave.'

'Lord Danziger!' Reiner called. 'A moment of your time!'

Reiner and Dieter had followed Danziger's coach, which, like Scharnholt's, had travelled openly to and from the Order of the Willing Heart, until its path had diverged from those of the other conspirators. Then Reiner had told Dieter to hang back out of sight, and ran after the lord, seemingly alone.

Danziger looked back, and his two guards, who sat with his coachman, stood with their hands on their hilts.

Danziger's eyes bulged when he saw who approached him. 'You!' he cried. 'You dare show your face, you dirty cultist? Horst! Orringer! Cut him down!'

Reiner stopped as the coach drew up and the swordsmen hopped from their perch. 'I am indeed a cultist, m'lord,' he said without raising his voice. 'Indeed, we attended a meeting of cultists just now, you and I.'

'What?' yelped Danziger. 'I a cultist? Preposterous!' The whites showed all around the lord's pupils. 'Kill him.'

'Kill me if you will, m'lord,' Reiner said, backing away from the guards. 'But you should know that Scharnholt means to betray you.'

'Eh? Betray...?' He waved his hand. 'Desist, Horst! Bring the villain to me. But take his sword and pin his arms.'

Reiner surrendered his sword belt and stepped into the coach. The two guards crushed him between them on the narrow bench opposite Danziger.

'Are you mad?' said the exchequer in a fierce whisper. 'Speaking such things in the street?'

'My apologies, m'lord,' said Reiner. 'But I was desperate to warn you of Scharnholt's treachery.'

Danziger looked Reiner up and down. 'Who are you, sir? It seems I have seen you on every side of this game. How do you know Scharnholt's business? The last I saw, you fought each other tooth and nail.'

Reiner inclined his head. 'M'lord, you are right to be cautious. And I admit that my actions may appear, from the outside, strange. Please, allow me to explain.'

'By all means,' said Danziger. 'And explain well, or you leave this coach with your throat cut.'

'Thank you, m'lord,' said Reiner, swallowing. 'Earlier this year, my master, the Changer of Ways, saw fit to allow me to place myself and my compatriots in the service of Count Valdenheim, one of the most influential men in the Empire. As his secretary, I was privy to the Emperor's most secret dealings, and I have used this knowledge to advance the glory of Tzeentch.'

'Go on,' said Danziger, sceptically.

'When the Reikland legation arrived in Talabheim, I intended to contact Lord Scharnholt and offer him what help I could, but before I was able, you approached Valdenheim, betraying your Tzeentchist rivals to him so that you might try for the stone for yourself.'

'It is only what he would have done to me,' huffed Danziger.

'Indeed, m'lord,' said Reiner. 'Unfortunately, this meant that I was forced, so as not to expose myself, to fight the very men I meant to help.' He sighed. 'Naturally, Lord Scharnholt, when we did at last meet, thought me a false Tzeentchist, saying that I should have turned on Manfred in the sewers and helped those who held the stone. I explained to him that this would have been suicide, which, because of my unique position, would be displeasing to Tzeentch. But he refused to see it,' Reiner sniffed. 'And would not include me in his plans for recovering the stone.'

'That does indeed sound like Scharnholt,' muttered Danziger. 'The pompous ass.'

'As you know, I then tricked von Pfaltzen and the others into the caves so that I might steal the stone while they were engaged with the ratmen, only to have Scharnholt attack me from behind and try to take it for himself. After that, I... well, I had had enough.'

Reiner sighed. 'Perhaps I am a poor student, but I had always thought the followers of the Great Betrayer were meant to betray unbelievers, not one another.' He looked sadly at Danziger. 'That is why I have come to you. I wish to learn more of Slaanesh, to whom treachery is not a sacrament, and to warn you that Scharnholt may once again endanger the cause of Chaos by trying to take all the glory for himself.'

The exchequer leaned forward. 'What does he intend?'

Reiner lowered his voice. 'He means, m'lord, to bring von Pfaltzen down upon you once the ceremony in the manor depths is done. He will help von Pfaltzen kill you, denouncing you as a cultist and making himself out a hero for discovering your plot.'

Danziger sneered. 'Always he has cared more for his worldly position than for the good of Chaos. He wants to both destroy the Empire and to rule it. But,' he bit his lip. 'But how will he do this?'

'You recall how he said that his men would guard the entrance to the lower levels?' asked Reiner. 'That is so they can let him out and trap you within, while he calls von Pfaltzen.'

Danziger paled. 'But... but how am I to keep this from occurring. We must destroy the stone, and yet–'

'It is simple,' said Reiner.

'Simple?' Danziger asked hopefully.

'Indeed.' Reiner spread his hands. 'Never let Scharnholt's men hold any position on their own. Say that you wish to share the honour of holding the stairs to the dungeon. If he says his men must go do such and such, you send your men too. Warn your men to be wary of a dagger in the back, and return any such attack tenfold, and swiftly, so no alarm is raised by your fighting.'

Danziger nodded. 'Yes. Yes, of course.'

'I will help you, if you wish,' said Reiner demurely. 'My men would welcome a chance to help Slaanesh, and get back a bit of our own.'

Danziger frowned. 'Surely Scharnholt will recognise you and know something is afoot?'

'He will not see our faces,' said Reiner. 'We have our own way into the manor, and will be masked when we meet you inside. You may tell Scharnholt that we are servants from the manor that dare not show our faces.'

Danziger nodded. 'Very well. Slaanesh is a welcoming god, and rewards loyalty and bravery. Help me bring down Talabheim and destroy Scharnholt, and you will find me generous. Betray me...' He looked into Reiner's eyes and Reiner flinched from his cold, lizard stare, 'and nothing you learned at the clawed feet of Tzeentch will prepare you for the exquisite agony a follower of Slaanesh can bestow with a single touch.' He sat back and waved a hand. 'Now go. We enter the manor at midnight.'

Reiner stood and bowed as the guards let go of his arms and returned his sword. 'Very good, m'lord.'

He nearly sank to his knees as he stepped down from the coach. His heart was pounding like an orc wardrum. He had done it. He had tricked Danziger into allowing him to ride his coat-tails through the dungeon gate, and hopefully into the vault as well. Now all he had to do was work out a way to sneak into the castle and back out again carrying a half-tonne rock. He laughed bitterly. Was that all?

SIXTEEN
I Will Not Betray My City

'Brothers!' cried Reiner, stepping out of an alley and falling in with seven priests of Morr who walked a plain casket through the rubble of the merchant district toward the Manor district gate. 'Do your labours take you to the Grand Manor this night?' He was dressed in black robes too, the Blackhearts having just relieved a Morrist corpse-burning detail of them not an hour ago.

'Aye, we do, brother,' said the lead priest. 'A sergeant of the guard has succumbed to the plague and his superiors wish him removed without anyone seeing his, er malformations.'

'Naturally,' said Reiner, his heart surging. At last! This was the fourth such procession he had asked this question, and the midnight hour was fast approaching. He signalled surreptitiously behind him.

'Why do you ask?' asked the priest.

'Er, we go the same way,' said Reiner. 'We thought we might travel together for safety.'

'We?' said the priest looking around. He shrieked as eight looming figures surged out of the alley and descended upon his fellows.

'ONE MOMENT, FATHER,' said a guard at the Hardtgelt gate. 'Where are you bound?'

'For the Grand Manor, my son,' Reiner said as the black-robed Blackhearts came to a halt, their stolen casket held between them. 'A sergeant of the guard awaits Morr's gate.'

'You have the order of removal?' asked the guard. He didn't seem eager to stand too close to the casket.

'One moment,' said Reiner. He withdrew a rolled parchment from his voluminous sleeve. He held it out, but the guard didn't take it.

'Open it, father. No offence meant,' he said.

'None taken,' said Reiner, and unrolled the scroll, pleased. The more disinclined the guards were to approach servants of Morr the better the Blackhearts' chances.

The guard gave the order a cursory glance. 'And the casket.'

'Certainly,' said Reiner. He lifted the lid so the guard could see in.

The guard stood on tip-toe so he didn't have to step nearer the casket, then waved them in. 'Carry on, father.'

'Bless you, my son,' said Reiner.

The Blackhearts started into the Manor district, Gert and Pavel and Hals moaning and weaving in the throes of savage hangovers. Behind them Reiner heard the guard mutter, 'They even stink of death.'

Reiner smiled, for there was a reason for the smell.

AS THEY APPROACHED the Grand Manor, Reiner saw Scharnholt and his men entering through the gate in. The gate guards saluted them. Reiner held back until they had entered, then approached. There was no sign of Danziger. Reiner hoped he was already within. It was almost midnight.

The scene at the Manor district gate was repeated with minor variations here, though the inspection was more thorough, and rather than passing them through, the chief guard assigned them an escort to take them where they were to go – a storeroom near a guardroom in the lower levels of the old barrel keep. Their escort was a sturdy young guard who seemed less than happy with his duty and hurried ahead of the Blackhearts as if he were trying to lose them.

Reiner did his best to memorise their route, and looked for stairs leading down. Their guide took them away from public areas of the manor, where the nobles might be offended by their presence, and into a maze of service corridors and back stairs.

After a while the hallways became tight passages of undressed stone, and Reiner knew they had entered the old keep. At the bottom of a twisting stair they passed a guardroom full of guards, talking and playing cards, then stopped just around a corner at a bolted wooden door with a sleepy guard before it.

'Jaffenberg,' said their guide. 'You're dismissed. They've come.'

'About time,' said the guard as he took a key from his pouch. 'Never done a duller watch.' He handed the key to the guide and saluted. 'See you at Elsa's later?'

'Aye, I suppose.'

Jaffenberg hurried off as their guide turned the key in the lock and pushed open the door, revealing a narrow storeroom filed with blankets and cakes of soap and jars of lamp oil. Lying on the floor was a dead guard with a second head, small as a baby's fist, peeking out of his collar next to the first.

The guide shivered at the sight. 'Poor beggar. Treat him well. He was a good man.'

'Better than we'll treat you,' said Reiner.

'Eh?' The boy turned and flinched as Reiner put his dagger against his jugular. 'What are you…?'

Gert covered the boy's mouth from behind with one big hand and pinned his sword arm with the other. He walked him backwards into the store room as Reiner kept the blade at his throat.

The others pushed in behind them. Ten people and a casket made it very crowded inside. Franka could barely close the door.

'Now, lad,' said Reiner, flashing the dagger in their guide's frightened eyes. 'Where are the stairs to the lower levels? And know that if you try to scream, you will die as you draw your breath.' He nodded to Gert. 'Let him speak.'

The boy took a breath. He was trembling. 'I... I won't tell you. I'd rather die.'

Reiner smiled kindly. 'Very brave, lad. But are you brave enough to not die?'

'To... to not die?' asked the boy, confused.

'Aye,' said Reiner. 'Dying is easy. It is over in a second. But Gert can break a man's neck so that he loses all movement in his limbs and yet doesn't die. Can you imagine it? Alive in the limp sack of your body, unable to move, or feed yourself, or wipe your own arse, or make love to your sweetheart, for the next fifty years? Are you brave enough to face that?'

'I will not betray the countess!' gabbled the boy. 'I will not betray my city–'

Gert twisted the boy's head, steadily increasing the pressure.

'Are you certain?' asked Reiner.

The boy's eyes were rimmed with white. His face was bright red. Gert twisted harder.

'To the right!' squeaked the boy. Gert relaxed the pressure. 'To the right until you pass the laundry, then left past the kitchens and down. It's below the store rooms, may Sigmar forgive me.'

'And may you forgive me,' said Reiner, and cracked the boy in the temple with the pommel of his dagger. He sagged in Gert's arms.

'Right,' Reiner said. 'Tie him up and give me his key. Then get out of these robes.'

Gert chuckled. 'Break his neck so he can't move? He bent to bind the boy's wrists. 'How do you invent these things, captain?'

Reiner shrugged. 'Desperation.'

'Bad business,' Augustus growled. 'Hurting an innocent boy.'

'He stood in our way,' said Reiner, coldly. 'We had no choice.'

'No choice but to die,' said Augustus.

'That isn't a choice.'

There followed a few moments of bumping elbows and muffled curses as the Blackhearts struggled out of their robes in the tight space.

'Put 'em in the casket,' said Reiner. 'The arm too. And leave the masks off for now. We'll look more suspicious with 'em on than off.'

Darius, looking queasy, took a long, lumpy, triple-wrapped parcel from a deep pocket in his robe, and dropped it with a thud into the casket.

'Good riddance,' he said.

When they were ready, Reiner squeezed to the door. A mask like a crow's beak hung from a ribbon around his belt. The others had similar masks. Reiner had bought them from a huckster who claimed they would protect them from the madness.

'Right,' he said, grinding out his torch. 'Dieter, on point. Jurgen, at the rear. To the right.' He opened the door a crack and looked out as Dieter joined him. A clatter of boots made him close it right back up. He waited until the sounds had faded away, then cracked the door again. Raised voices and reflected torchlight came from the guardroom around the left-hand corner, but the hall to the right was clear.

'Off we go.'

The Blackhearts followed Dieter into the unlit hall as quietly as they could. Reiner locked the door behind them and took up the rear. After a moment of feeling bindly along the stone walls, Dieter's silhouette became visible again and they heard women's voices and sloshing water ahead. On the left-hand wall an open door glowed with yellow light. There was a smell of steam and soap.

'He ain't my sweetheart,' said a shrill voice.

'Now don't lie, Gerdie,' cackled another. 'We saw ye makin' eyes at him. And he do look quite fetching in 'is uniform, don't he?'

Dieter edged forward until he could see into the door. He held up a palm. The others waited.

'So you fancy him, yerself, do ye?' said the first voice. 'Well, he don't like fat old… oh now look, this will never come out. That's blood, that is.'

Dieter beckoned Reiner across, and he tip-toed past the door, catching a glimpse of a handful of women stirring dirty clothes into boiling iron cauldrons with long wooden paddles. Another darned stockings in a corner.

Dieter pointed to the rest of the Blackhearts in turn, and they slipped across the opening one by one. The women never looked up from their gossiping.

Just beyond the laundry was the kitchen corridor. Dieter and Reiner looked down it. It was well lit, and voices came from it, rising over the clatter and hiss of a busy kitchen. As they watched, five footmen with large trays on their shoulders walked from a right-hand door and hurried toward a shadowy stair at the far end. A scullery maid crossed the hall, struggling with a huge skillet.

Dieter frowned, rubbing his chin. 'Bit more difficult, this. If we had one of them ratty smoke grenades…'

Reiner shook his head. 'I think this calls for brass, not stealth.'

'Brass?' asked Dieter.

'Aye.' Reiner turned to the others. 'Right lads, two abreast, weapons on shoulders. Dieter, Darius, er… do your best.'

The Blackhearts formed up, Hals and Pavel in front.

'Now,' said Reiner. 'Like you belong here. March.'

He plucked a torch from the wall and started forward with a brisk step. The Blackhearts tramped in unison behind him as if they were on an important duty.

Reiner waved back a footman carrying a platter. 'Stand clear, fellow.'

The man let them by with a look of surly patience, then followed after them. Cooks and kitchen assistants glanced up as they passed, but didn't give them a second look. When they reached the stairwell, Reiner led the Blackhearts down while the footman went up. Reiner breathed a sigh of relief. No one had sensed anything amiss.

As the noises of the kitchen faded behind them faint sounds came from below, growing louder with each step.

'That's a fight,' said Hals.

'Aye,' said Pavel. 'I hear it.'

'On your guard,' said Reiner, drawing his sword. 'But no need to hurry. Let Danziger and Scharnholt do the dirty work.'

They continued down the stairs, listening to the melee below as they descended past the storeroom level. Turning down the last flight, they saw shadows fighting in the light cast from a wide archway.

Reiner raised a hand, and the Blackhearts halted.

'Masks on,' he whispered.

The Blackhearts slipped their black crow-beaks on. Reiner hoped they wouldn't have to fight in them. He had no peripheral vision through the eyeholes.

As they started down again, a body flew backwards through the archway, spilling blood. A man in a black breastplate followed him in and stabbed him in the chest, finishing him off. The killer looked up, and jumped as he saw the men on the stairs. It was Danziger.

'Who?' he gasped, then relaxed. 'Ah, it's you. You're late. Come. We're in.'

They followed him into a low, square room with a stout, iron bound door in one wall. The place was crowded with Danziger's and Scharnholt's men, busy killing the twelve guards who manned the door. Scharnholt stood in the centre, directing with a casual hand

and mopping his round face with a white linen hand-kerchief. Reiner noticed that men in both Scharnholt's and Danziger's companies had short poles strapped to their backs for carrying the waystone.

'Pedermann, the door,' Scharnholt said. 'Dortig, cut every throat. These men know us. We can have no survivors.' He frowned as Danziger approached him with the Blackhearts. 'Who are these?'

'More of ours,' said Danziger. 'Servants who dare not show their faces.'

Reiner smiled to himself. Danziger was repeating his words to the letter.

'I see,' said Scharnholt, curling his lip. 'I hope they can fight as well as serve.'

'I assure you, m'lord,' said Danziger. 'They are most capable.'

'I will leave ten men here,' said Scharnholt as his men opened the door. 'With the story that they came upon some cultists slaughtering the guards and chased them off, then took it upon themselves to guard the door until more guards could be summoned.'

Danziger paused, shooting a knowing look at Reiner before smiling at Scharnholt. 'An admirable plan, brother. But let our men share this dangerous duty. I would feel remiss if you took the risk entirely upon yourself.'

Scharnholt raised an eyebrow. 'Do I sense mistrust, brother? Are we not united as one in this?'

'Indeed we are united,' said Danziger, indignant. 'It is why I offered to share the dangers with you. Perhaps it is you who are mistrustful. Or do you mistake concern for mistrust because you plan some treachery?'

'He speaks of treachery who betrayed my followers to Valdenheim and Teclis when we already had the stone?' asked Scharnholt, putting a hand on his hilt.

Danziger did the same.

Reiner stepped forward. 'M'lords,' he said, aping a slur-ring Talabheim accent to disguise his voice. 'Please. Remember our purpose here.' He wanted the two lords fighting, but not yet. Not before they opened the vault for him.

Scharnholt let go of his sword. 'Your man speaks wisdom. This is not the place to argue. Very well, we will share the duty.' He turned to the door. 'The dungeon is on the same level as the vault, and has its own guards. I will make it so that the noise of our battle does not carry, but you must not let the men we fight escape to warn the dungeon guards. Now let us go.'

SEVENTEEN
Kill Them

As THE COMPANIES lined up to enter the door, Reiner heard Augustus mutter 'Only doing their job,' under his breath as he looked around at the dead guards. His fists were balled at his sides, knuckles white.

Scharnholt and Danziger both left ten men behind to hold the door and led the rest down the steps. The Blackhearts marched in behind them, and started into the depths. The big door boomed closed above them. Reiner swallowed. No turning back now.

At the second landing, Scharnholt began muttering and waving his podgy fingers. The air around Reiner seemed to thicken and there was a pressure on his eardrums as if he had dived into deep water. The cultists and the Blackhearts were opening their mouths and wiggling their fingers in their ears, trying to clear the pressure, but it wouldn't go.

'What is it?' asked Franka, wincing.

Reiner could barely hear her. It sounded like she spoke from behind a thick pane of glass. All the noise around him was damped. The jingle and creak of the men around him was almost inaudible. The men followed. Their marching made as much noise as a cat walking through grass. It was as if the air had become a jelly and the sounds caught in it.

Three flights down, the stairs ended at a wide corridor that stretched away into darkness, other passages intersecting it at wide intervals. Were they still within the walls of the barrel keep, Reiner wondered? Surely the corridor carried on further than that. He shook his head. It was a wonder all of Talabheim didn't cave in, considering how much of it was riddled with tunnels.

Danziger pointed to a right-hand passage and the men filed in. It ended in an iron gate, through which they could see torchlight.

Scharnholt handed the key ring to Danziger without missing a beat in his mumbling. Danziger turned to the company and gave an order no one could hear. He rolled his eyes in annoyance and brandished his sword with an exaggerated motion.

The cultists and the Blackhearts drew their weapons as Danziger turned the key in the lock. It made no noise. Nor did the swinging of the gate. Danziger waved forward, and the men rushed into the room, as silent as a breeze.

Reiner took in the room as he ran. It was a vaulted rectangular chamber, longer than it was wide, with archways to the left and right, and ten guards standing in a line against a massive stone door at the far end, which was bound with iron bands.

The guards shouted in surprise as they saw the cultists. Their voices barely sounded in Scharnholt's bubble. They drew their weapons and met the charge valiantly, but they were too few. Danziger's and Scharnholt's men quickly chopped them to pieces in a horrible, silent bloodbath. Reiner and the Blackhearts hung back and took no part. Reiner felt ashamed nonetheless. Was standing aside to let good men be killed less villainous than swinging the sword oneself? Augustus was swearing out loud. Fortunately none could hear him.

'The keys!' said Danziger, shouting to be heard.

One of Danziger's men handed him two keys. One of Scharnholt's had another. But as he turned to the door, more than a score of guards poured out of the two archways, charging the cultists' rear.

'Kill them all!' cried Danziger, though it came out a whisper. 'Let none escape!'

Scharnholt stepped back to the door as the cultists turned to face their foes. He could give no orders, for he had to maintain his incantation. The two sides clashed together with almost no sound, mouths open like mummers miming shouts and screams.

Augustus glared at the backs of the cultists as they fought the guard, his hands gripping his spear as if he were about to attack. Reiner put a hand on his shoulder. The pikeman snarled and pulled away. The others looked nearly as mutinous. Reiner didn't blame them. But there was nothing for it. They had to get the waystone.

He stepped to Danziger and shouted almost inaudibly in his ear. 'M'lord. Give us the keys and defend us, and my men will open the vault so that we may be away all the quicker.'

'Aye,' said Danziger. 'Good. And make the stone ready to carry as well.'

'Of course, m'lord,' said Reiner. His heart leapt. The fool gave him more than he'd asked.

Reiner collected the keys and the poles from the men who carried them and motioned the Blackhearts to the door as Danziger's and Scharnholt's men formed a protective semi-circle around them, hacking and thrusting at the maddened guards. He gave keys to Franka, Darius and Dieter, then yelled to the others. 'Watch their backs,'

They nodded and faced out toward the melee, standing behind Danziger's men – all but Augustus, who only glared, spear at his side, at the carnage. Though they weren't invulnerable, as Scharnholt's men had been in the ratmen's caves, many of the cultists wore amulets written over with vile runes. Reiner saw a guardsman's sword veer away from a cultist's head as if pushed aside by an invisible hand.

The key plate was set into the floor before the vault door, an oblong steel plate decorated with geometric patterns. Franka, Darius and Dieter knelt over it. The designs that framed each keyhole were different, one was a square, one a circle, and one a diamond, which corresponded to the backs of the three keys.

Dieter shook his head as they inserted them into the locks. 'Dwarf work,' he shouted to Reiner. 'Glad y'haven't asked me to pick it.' He looked at the others. 'Now all together, or we'll have to go again.'

Franka, Darius and Dieter slowly turned their keys, and they hit home together. Reiner felt a heavy clunk under the floor.

Dieter smiled. 'Prettiest sound in the world.'

Reiner checked the battle. The guards were surrounded now, and falling fast. He slapped the backs of Hals, Pavel, Gert, Augustus and Jurgen. 'Here! Push!'

They turned and pushed on one of the massive stone doors. At first it didn't move and Reiner momentarily feared they hadn't unlocked it after all, then slowly it swung in.

When the gap widened enough to walk through, Reiner waved a halt. Pavel and Hals gathered up the poles and rope and the Blackhearts filed into the vault. The faint sounds of battle faded entirely beyond the door. They stopped and gaped in wonder. Augustus's torch glittered upon a thousand golden treasures. There were twenty gilded chairs and jewelled silver armour with a dragon helm. Swords with gold-chased scabbards and gemstone pommels sprouted like flowers from a Cathay vase. Beautiful paintings and statues and tapestries were piled everywhere. Caskets and chests lined each wall. The waystone stood among a grove of beautiful marble statues, looking out of place among them.

'Strewth,' said Pavel. But they were still within Scharnholt's circle of silence, so Reiner could barely hear him.

'Nice haul,' shouted Dieter. 'Like to have a peek in them chests.'

'We aren't here for that,' said Reiner. 'Unfortunately.' He pointed to the waystone. 'Get it ready. Once Scharnholt and Danziger defeat the guards, I will try to turn them against each other, and then we will kill the survivors.'

'Sigmar be praised,' said Hals.

'About damned time!' said Augustus.

The others nodded in agreement. They moved to the waystone and began to tip it down on the poles.

'Wait,' called Franka, suddenly. 'Wait! I have a better idea!'

'Eh?' said Augustus. 'There ain't a better idea than killing them cursed daemon-lovers.'

'It'll be better if we survive and escape, aye?' snapped Franka.

'What's the idea, lass?' bellowed Reiner.

Franka started to explain. Reiner couldn't hear her.

'What? You have to shout!'

Frustrated, Franka pointed to a statue of a buxom nymph next to the waystone, which was roughly the same height and circumference, then to a rolled rug.

Reiner laughed. It was a brilliant plan. They could get out without a fight. 'Yes! Good!' He waved to the others, shouting. 'Hide the stone and wrap that instead. Quickly. Jurgen, let no one in.'

Reiner helped Hals, Pavel, Augustus and Gert carry the waystone behind the stand of statues, as Franka and Darius unrolled a rug and draped it over the statue.

'Will it work?' shouted Gert as they lowered the wrapped statue onto the poles.

Reiner shrugged. 'If it doesn't, you'll get your fight.'

Gert grinned. They bound the statue to the poles, making sure that the ropes made it impossible to pull back the rug and see underneath.

'Good,' said Reiner when it was secured. 'Get it up. If all goes wrong, kill Scharnholt and Danziger first.'

He looked out as the others raised the wrapped statue. They were just in time. The cultists were killing the last of the guards and wiping their blades. Scharnholt ceased his incantation and turned toward the vault with Danziger. Reiner's ears popped and sound rushed into his head, battering his eardrums. Boot heels on flags, the laughter of the cultists, the moans of the dying, were suddenly unbearably loud.

Reiner beckoned the Blackhearts forward, then stepped out, waved at Danziger and Scharnholt. 'M'lords! We have it.'

The Blackhearts edged the covered statue through the partially open stone door. Reiner's palms were sweating. This was a dangerous moment. If the lords asked to see the stone they were in trouble. If they asked the Black-hearts to carry it, that was trouble as well.

'Lead on, m'lords,' he said with a wave of his hand. 'We will carry the stone.'

'Eh?' said Danziger, suddenly suspicious. '*You* will carry the stone?'

'What does he say?' said Scharnholt. 'Does your servant order us?'

'Your men have been fighting,' said Reiner. 'We are fresh and strong. Do not trouble yourselves. We have it well in hand.'

Danziger and Scharnholt exchanged a look, then turned back to Reiner.

'No, brother,' Danziger said. 'We will carry the stone. Since your fellows are fresh and unhurt, you will guard our backs in case we are followed.'

Reiner shrugged and bowed, hiding a smile. 'As your lordship wishes it.' He motioned for the Blackhearts to put down the stone.

After some argument, Scharnholt and Danziger agreed that their men would carry the stone together, and the party got underway, travelling without torches. As they neared the passage to the dungeons, Scharnholt resumed his muttering and silence again closed around them. Reiner looked down the corridor as they passed it. Not far down he saw the shadows of bars and of moving men in a square of light cast across the floor.

The main corridor dimmed into darkness beyond the dungeon passage. Scharnholt changed incantations and led the way with a faint blue light that flickered above his outstretched palm. The back of the column was in total darkness. Reiner motioned the Blackhearts to slow their steps, and by the time they reached the stairs to the bowels of the manor, they lagged twenty paces behind. They descended two flights in darkness, then Reiner stopped, listening. When no query came from below, he whispered, 'Back. To the stone. Quietly.'

The Blackhearts padded back up the steps, then along the corridor toward the torchlight. They slowed at the hall to the dungeons and crept past it. He waved them by. Augustus scraped his spear butt on the flagstones as he passed and it made a horrendous noise to their over-sensitive ears. Reiner wondered if he had done it on purpose.

When no reaction came from the dungeon corridor, they pressed on to the vault room. It was as they had left it, the vault door ajar, the bodies of the dead guards lying in spreading pools of blood. They hurried across the chamber, taking off their stifling beak masks and snatching up four spears with which to carry the stone.

They entered the vault, and Hals, Pavel, Gert and Jurgen covered the stone with another rug and lashed it to the spears while the others watched, nervous, and Dieter wandered the room, examining the treasures. But just as they lifted it, they heard movement from the guard chamber.

'Sigmar! What's this!' cried a voice. 'Captain! The Vault!'

'Blast it!' said Reiner, and rushed into the chamber, sword out.

But the guard was already in the hall, screaming at the top of his lungs. Reiner was about to race after him, when he stopped. He darted back into the vault and gestured at the Blackhearts. 'Set it down and stay hidden!'

He returned to the guard chamber. Voices and boot steps were approaching from the hall. He dropped and rolled in a puddle of blood, smearing it on his face, then flopped back as if dead just as a captain and ten dungeon guards ran in.

The captain stared. 'Sigmar! This… this is impossible! How did we not hear?'

'And the vault is open, captain,' said the first guard. 'Maybe they who did this are…'

Reiner spasmed up, groaning artistically. 'The thieves…' he said. 'They…' He looked around blindly for a moment as the guards turned to look at him, then flung out his hand. 'Captain! Cultists! They've stolen something! They took it to the basement and mean to do some strange magic with it! If you hurry, you might stop them!'

Reiner had hoped – prayed in fact, with fingers crossed to Ranald – that the captain would run off after the thieves in a screaming panic, but the cursed stoic barely raised an eyebrow.

'Yeager!' he said. 'Take two men into the cellar and see what's what! Krieghelm! Tell the boys up top the vault's been breached! Tell 'em von Pfaltzen's wanted. The rest stay with me. The vault cannot remain unguarded.'

The men raced off.

Reiner groaned. 'But, captain,' he said. 'There are more than thirty of 'em! Three men will not be enough!'

'Nor will fifteen, sir,' said the captain. 'Which is all I have.' He turned to the vault, motioning to his remaining men. 'Three of you with me.'

Reiner watched in horror as the captain and his three men started for the open vault. 'No! Beware!' he cried. 'They used some terrible magic to open the door. It is too dangerous!'

The captain ignored him and entered the vault, torch high. Reiner cursed, knowing what was coming. He got to his feet, still pretending to be hurt, and edged anxiously toward the door.

'Ho!' came the captain's voice. 'Stand forward, you!'

Something heavy smashed.

The guards in the chamber looked around, surprised. Reiner ran into the vault and came upon a frozen tableau. The captain and his three men were on guard, a toppled suit of armour at their feet, facing the Blackhearts who stood in a dark corner beyond the waystone, swords out.

'Captain, wait!' said Reiner, though what he meant to say after he had no idea.

'Guards! To me!' called the captain. 'The thieves are here!'

Reiner cursed. 'Kill them!' he said.

'Reiner, no!' cried Franka.

But when the captain lunged for Reiner, she came forwards with the rest. Only Augustus and Darius hung back, Darius hiding behind a stack of paintings, Augustus staring, mouth agape.

Reiner parried the captain's thrust and the man died with Jurgen's longsword in his back. His three men went down an instant later, impaled by Pavel and Hals's spears and butchered by the others' swords. But as they fell, nine more rushed into the vault. They cried out as they saw their captain dead and ran around the statues at the Blackhearts, who spread out to meet them.

'No!' cried Augustus. 'No, you damned traitor! I won't stand for it!' He lowered his spear and charged straight at Reiner.

EIGHTEEN
We Fight On The Wrong Side

REINER YELPED AND leapt aside, then fell sprawling across the waystone as Augustus's spear and the swords of two guardsmen passed above him. He rolled away, slashing about wildly. All around him the Blackhearts were crossing swords with the guards.

'Ye daft pike!' shouted Gert, and clubbed Augustus over the head with his heavy crossbow.

Augustus stumbled, grunting, and turned to stab Gert, but the crossbowman kicked him in the chest and he fell backward into a Cathay urn as big as a hogshead of ale. His arms and legs waved ridiculously as he struggled to get out.

Reiner staggered to his feet, parrying the guards' questing swords, and recovered himself. It was an awkward and horrible fight. The vault was so cluttered that there was hardly room to move and none to swing. Marble statues and suits of armour toppled and smashed, and priceless paintings were cut to ribbons.

The Blackhearts fought with a grim resignation Reiner had never seen in them before. They hated what they did.

Franka wept as she fought. Gert cursed Manfred with each swing. Pavel and Hals were tight-lipped with fury. Jurgen's face had even less expression than usual. Only Dieter seemed unaffected, stabbing men from behind with a superior smirk on his face.

Reiner backed into the thicket of statues to protect his flanks from his two opponents. Their swords skipped off marble shoulders and breasts. Reiner kicked a statue into one man and ran him through as he dodged. The other pressed forward, and he and Reiner fenced through the forest of frozen figures.

Jurgen fought like a machine, gutting one man with a down stoke, then backhanding another's head off before turning to face a third. None could touch him. Franka dumped a fortune in Reikmarks before her opponent and opened him up from knee to groin as he slipped on them. Gert had a jewel-encrusted ceremonial mace in one hand and his hatchet in the other. Both ran with blood, as did his chest.

Reiner ducked under a slash and cracked his head on the stone elbow of a former Elector Count of Talabecland. His eyes dimmed and he sat down suddenly. He threw his sword arm up, more to cover his head than to attack, and gutted his man by accident. He fell across him, vomiting blood. Reiner pushed him off, fearing another guard would take advantage, but none came. It appeared the battle was over. The Blackhearts stood panting over their kills. Franka's sobs were the only other sound.

Reiner looked at the guard he had killed. He was only a boy, his first beard just coming in, his dead eyes gazing sightlessly at the ceiling. Reiner stood, trying to clear the tightness in his throat. It wouldn't go.

'Are we all well?' He asked. He saw Jurgen kneeling in the middle of four bodies, his head down. 'Are you hurt, Rohmner?'

Jurgen looked up, and Reiner had never seen anything sadder than his scarred, solemn face. 'I am praying, captain.'

'Well?' growled Hals. 'We ain't well by a long stretch. This...' He spread his hands helplessly at the carnage.

Pavel shook so hard that he had to sit down. He glared at Reiner. 'Captain, we done some bad things before, but...' He made the sign of the hammer. 'Sigmar, forgive us.'

The others followed his example. Franka made Myrmidia's spear.

Reiner licked his lips. 'You heard me try,' he said. 'I tried to send them away. I didn't–' He choked and looked back at the boy he had killed, then away.

There was a smash and Augustus rose from the shards of the Cathay urn, shaking with rage. 'You'll die for this!' he said, his voice trembling. 'I'll bring the whole city down on you!' He started edging for the vault door.

'Don't be a fool, lad,' said Gert, as the others spread out. 'It's a bad thing we've done. But we had to do it. Manfred–'

'Damn Manfred! Damn the whole lot of you!' roared Augustus. 'We fight on the wrong side! He's made villains of us all!'

The others tried to calm him, but Reiner's heart was pounding. This was it! Or half of it at any rate. If Augustus ran, he could warn the authorities and they would come for Valaris. But no, Valaris would know the warning had been sent, and lower the boom. If only there were some way to make the dark elf think Augustus had been killed...

Reiner froze as inspiration suddenly flooded into him. By the gods! He had it! It was perfect, as long as the others played along.

'Do you think you can get by us?' Reiner shouted. 'Do you think we will just let you walk out and warn the countess of what we do and where we go?' Reiner laughed. 'You selfish little suicide! You may wish to sacrifice your life for the greater good, but as I told you before, we are blackhearts. We look out for our own skin. The rest of the world can go hang. Do you think I'll let some sentimental fool stop me when our salvation is at hand? We have the stone. All we must do is bring it to Valaris and we are free!'

'Then come ahead,' said Augustus, lowering his head like a bull. 'Least I'll die on the right side.'

He stooped to grab his spear, but Reiner was quicker. He snatched up a small bust of Magnus the Pious and leapt at the pikeman, bashing him in the head with it. Augustus fell back and Reiner kicked him in the groin. The pikeman moaned and squirmed like a beetle on its back, clutching himself.

The Blackhearts stared. Reiner laughed and tossed the bust aside, turning away nonchalantly. 'Kill him, Neff. Kill him as you killed that traitor Echert.'

'Eh?' said Dieter, and for a second Reiner thought he was going to give the game away. But then the thief smirked and drew his dagger. 'Oh aye. And my pleasure!' He motioned to Hals and Pavel. 'Hold him, lads. Let an artist work.'

The light slowly dawned in Hals's eyes. He grinned and nudged Pavel. 'Come on, lad. Just like Echert.'

'Oh,' said Pavel, getting it at last. 'Oh, right. Like Echert.'

They pinned August's arms as Dieter knelt on him and raised his knife.

'What are you doing?' screamed Franka, jumping in to grab his hand. 'Have you all gone mad? This isn't our way!'

Jurgen caught her and held her tight, clapping a hand over her mouth.

Reiner groaned. Franka had been serving Manfred dinner. She hadn't heard Dieter tell his story of faking the death of the merchant Echert. She didn't know it was a trick. She struggled in Jurgen's grip as Dieter's dagger rose and fell and rose above Augustus, blood spattering everywhere. Her eyes bored into Reiner's over Jurgen's thick fingers. Reiner's heart sunk to see the hate and despair there.

Reiner watched from a distance. He didn't want to be too close for fear of ruining the illusion. If they were smart, Hals and Pavel would be telling Augustus to play dead, and it was imperative that Reiner didn't hear their whispers or all was lost. It certainly looked savage enough from where he stood. In fact, it looked so real, Reiner had a sudden fear that Dieter had misread his command and was really killing the pikeman.

After a moment, Dieter stood, dagger and hands dripping blood. He grinned at Reiner. 'It's done, jagger.'

Reiner stepped forward, and still couldn't be sure Dieter hadn't killed Augustus. The Talabheimer lay motionless, his shirt shredded, and terrible, bloody gashes all over his breast. Reiner curled his lip and turned away quickly in case Augustus took a breath. 'And no more than he deserved, the swine,' he said. 'Come, let's finish this business.'

Franka stood slack in Jurgen's arms, staring at Augustus's body. There were tears in her eyes.

Reiner jabbed a finger at her. 'And not a word out of you, *boy*, or you'll be next! You understand me?' He took her from Jurgen, then motioned to the others. 'Pick it up.'

With Augustus 'dead', there were only six to carry the waystone, Pavel, Jurgen and Darius on one side; Hals, Gert and Dieter on the other. They grunted it up and walked it out of the vault. Franka stumbled along in a daze, Reiner guiding her with a hand on her shoulder.

Halfway across the guardroom they heard footsteps running in the hallway, and the guard the captain had sent upstairs burst in.

'Captain!' he said. 'Something's amiss. The men above wouldn't let me...' He froze as he saw the Blackhearts. He was another boy.

Jurgen let go of his spear-end and drew his sword. Reiner waved him back and faced the boy.

'Your captain is dying in the vault,' he said. 'Go to him.'

The boy hesitated. 'I don't…'

'Go to him, or die here!' shouted Reiner.

The boy flinched and ran for the vault, skirting wide around the Blackhearts.

Reiner took Dieter's place carrying the waystone. 'Lock him in.'

Dieter nodded, and when they had walked the stone through the guardroom gate, he knelt with his tools and locked it up.

They carried the waystone up the stairs to the last landing before the oaken door. It was already piled with the bodies of the guards Danziger's and Scharnholt's men had killed and replaced. Reiner motioned the Blackhearts to set it down.

'Here will be a fight more to our taste,' he whispered. 'Stay out of sight until I call.'

He slipped his beak mask on again and began crawling up the stairs as they drew their swords. When he reached the door he beat on it with his fist.

'Brothers!' he cried. 'Brothers! Open in the name of Lord Danziger! Open in the name of Slaanesh!'

There was a brief mumble of argument and then the key turned in the lock. Reiner hoped his dramatics here would be more successful than his last.

'Brothers!' he cried to Danziger's men as the door swung open. 'We are betrayed! Lord Scharnholt has slain Lord Danziger and stolen the stone! Kill the traitors!'

The Slaaneshi and the Tzeentchists looked at each other alarmed, hands on their hilts.

'Murderers!' cried one of Danziger's men.

'It is a lie.' shouted one of Scharnholt's men. 'A Slaaneshi lie. Show us the body!'

Reiner cursed. They were going to argue rather than fight! He surged up, charging the nearest Tzeentchist. 'I'll show you a body! To me, Slaaneshi!'

He hacked the man across the chest. The cultist was wearing a breastplate, so the strike did little damage, but it had the desired effect. The man slashed at Reiner, as did two of his comrades. Danziger's men bellowed, outraged, and leapt to Reiner's defence. The two sides came together, sword on sword, screaming curses and accusations.

Reiner parried his opponent's attack and fell back behind his Slaaneshi 'fellows.' No one paid him any attention. They were too intent on killing each other. He edged through the door, then hurried down to the Blackhearts, who looked up at him, concerned.

'Now we wait for a victor,' he said.

'And kill them,' said Gert.

'Aye.'

They listened as the sounds of battle rose and fell above them. Swords clashed. Men screeched. Bodies thudded to the ground. Then the sounds ceased.

'Lubeck, can you stand?' asked a voice. 'How many are we?'

'Is it true?' asked another. 'Did our lord mean to betray Danziger?'

'We must go below and see,' said the first.

'Now!' whispered Reiner.

The Blackhearts rushed up into the square room. Only Franka stayed behind, staring at nothing. The fight was over almost before it was begun. Only four of Scharnholt's men still stood, and not one of them was unwounded. Jurgen cut down two with one stroke, and Pavel and Hals ran the other two through with their spears. Dieter made sure they were dead.

'Now the most dangerous part of all,' said Reiner, as the others returned to the stone and he collected Franka. 'For if we are discovered before we reach the storeroom, no amount of murder will save us.'

They carried the waystone up the steps past the storeroom level to the kitchens. Reiner called a halt in the dark stairwell and looked down the long kitchen corridor, which had just as much traffic as before.

'We'll brass it out again,' said Reiner. 'Make out it's a dying man. Ready?'

But just then Danziger and Scharnholt's voices echoed up the stairs from below. Reiner could only hear snatches of words.

'...killed these too?' Scharnholt was shouting.

'...Hetsau must be...' Danziger was screaming.

'Curse it!' said Reiner. 'They've found our trick too soon. Hurry.'

They hurried down the kitchen passage, Reiner shouting, 'Make way! This man is dying! Stand aside!'

The cooks and serving maids scurried out of their way. Reiner thought he heard a rumble of running boots behind them, but it might have been his imagination. They turned right and passed the laundry, not bothering now to be silent, and Reiner saw the women look up disinterestedly. They had to tiptoe the last twenty yards to the store room, because the guardroom was just around the corner.

They were almost at the door when Reiner heard running boots again, and this time he was certain it wasn't his imagination. He let go of Franka and hurried ahead, fishing in his pouch for the storeroom key. He unlocked the door as quietly as he could and opened it.

'Did some men pass here?' came Scharnholt's voice. 'Carrying something?'

'Oh aye, m'lord,' a laundress replied. 'Just now.'

As the boot steps resumed, the Blackhearts angled around to walk the waystone through the door. They stopped short. The carrying spears were wider than the door.

Reiner cursed. 'Tip it!' he whispered. 'Pavel's side down! Hals's side up!'

Darius, Jurgen and Darius lowered their spear-ends almost to the floor, while Dieter, Gert and Hals struggled to raise theirs over their heads. Reiner helped Darius, who looked about to drop his end. In this awkward arrangement they walked forward again. Pavel's spear butt just caught the edge of the door.

'Left!' he hissed.

The party waddled a few inches left. Reiner thought his back would break. The boots were closing in. Reiner could see torchlight reflecting from the right.

'Now ahead.'

They started forward again, and this time just cleared the jam. The end of Reiner's spear juddered noisily along the ground and he strained to hold it up.

'On! On!' he breathed.

They continued forward, tripping over the casket. The bound guard gave a muffled cry as someone stepped on him. The Blackhearts set the stone down, grunting and hissing, and Reiner spun to close the door behind them. He fumbled his fingers under the door handle in the dark, but found no keyhole. It couldn't be locked from inside.

'Jurgen. Gert. Here!'

Reiner heard Jurgen and Gert feeling their way forward. The boots passed by outside. Reiner held his breath.

'You men,' came Scharnholt's voice. 'Have any men passed here, carrying a heavy burden?'

'No, m'lord,' said a voice from the guardroom.

Scharnholt cursed. 'Have we lost them? We must go back. Cultists have stolen a valuable relic from the vault!' he called to the guards. 'Let none pass unquestioned!'

'Aye, m'lord!'

Sounds of commotion came from the guardroom as the boots turned in the hall.

Reiner leaned in to Jurgen and Gert. 'Push on the door.'

Jurgen and Gert pressed their shoulders against the door with Reiner. Reiner felt pressure on the door as someone shook the handle.

'Locked,' said a voice, and the boots moved on.

Reiner waited until they had faded completely and the men in the guardroom had run off before he relaxed his pressure on the door.

'Right,' he said. 'Let's have a light.'

Hals lit Reiner's long-handled priest torch and they got to work – untying the covered waystone and putting it in the casket, then struggling once again into the black priest's robes while the gagged guard glared balefully at them from where he lay beside the dead, mutated sergeant.

'Where's the arm?' asked Reiner.

Darius held out the long, lumpy packet, wrinkling his nose. Reiner took it and stepped to the casket. He threaded a length of rope around the waystone at shoulder height then unrolled the packet, revealing a decaying, mutated arm with seven long sucker-tipped fingers. The stench of death rolled up from it in a solid wave, making them all gag. Reiner's eyes watered.

Wrapping his hands in a blanket from the storeroom shelves, he tied the arm to the waystone, so it looked like it had sprouted one greenish limb. The others draped more blankets over the carpet-wrapped waystone, making sure all of it was hidden, but leaving the arm exposed.

'There,' he said, standing. 'Now the final touch.'

He picked up the blanket with which he had handled the arm as Dieter continued fussing with the blankets. He stepped to Gert. The crossbowman shied away.

'What are you doing?' he cried.

'Shhh! You fool!' said Reiner. 'Hold still.'

As Gert cringed, Reiner wiped the blanket's slimy residue on his robe. He repeated the process with each of them and finished with himself. The reek was inescapable. 'Now we're ready. Lift it up.'

He listened at the door as Dieter closed the casket and the Blackhearts raised it. There were sounds of excitement and alarm coming from all over the manor, but none directly outside the door. He opened it and edged around the corner. The barracks room was deserted.

He hurried back and took up his torch. 'Right, ready.'

The Blackhearts walked out, the casket between them. Reiner locked the door behind them. 'Slow and dignified,' he said. 'The best way to be caught is to look like we're running.'

* * *

THEY WERE STOPPED as soon as they left the barrel keep and entered the modern part of the manor again. A sergeant of the guard with ten men at his back saw them coming out of a stairwell and raised his palm.

'Halt!' he said, striding forward, then stopped as if he had run into a wall. He backed off, covering his mouth and making the sign of the hammer. 'Death of Sigmar, what a reek!' he choked.

Reiner bowed. 'My apologies, sergeant. The corpse was in an advanced state of decay. It was being eaten by its own mutations.'

'Never mind that,' said the sergeant, as his men edged back unhappily. 'Where is your escort?'

'Er, he ran off, sir,' said Reiner. 'There was some uproar while we were fetching the body. He went to see what it was and never came back. Would you provide us with another? We seem to be lost.'

'Let me see your order of removal,' said the sergeant.

Reiner pulled it from his sleeve and stepped to the sergeant.

'Stay where you are!' The sergeant cried. He snatched the paper from Reiner's fingers and backed away to read it. He glanced unhappily at the casket. 'Er, I'll have to look inside. There's been a theft.'

'It's not a pretty sight sir,' said Reiner. 'He is much changed.'

'Open it, curse you.'

Reiner shrugged. 'Very well.'

He lifted the lid. The smell of death poured from it in a cloud. The sergeant retreated, gagging, then inched forward again. The suckered fingers of the rotting arm stuck up over the lip of the casket. They crawled with flies.

The sergeant retched. 'Sigmar preserve us!'

'Shall I pull back the blanket so you may see the face?' asked Reiner.

'Don't you dare!' The sergeant was furious. 'What is the matter with you, priest! Why did you wait so long to come! You endanger the whole manor! We might all catch the madness! Take it out! Hurry!'

'But sergeant,' whined Reiner. 'We have no escort. How are we to hurry when we will be stopped and asked to expose the body at every step?'

The sergeant's jaw clenched and unclenched. At last he growled. 'Right. Follow us. But stay far back, you hear me? Far back!'

'Of course, sergeant.'

The Blackhearts fell in behind the guards and followed them through the manor. Reiner crossed his fingers. With Ranald's luck, this was the last hurdle. The sergeant would walk them out and they would be free. But as they stepped out into the forecourt and approached the gate, Reiner saw von Pfaltzen and Danziger standing by it, talking with the chief gate guard.

'Heads down, lads,' Reiner whispered, and pulled his hood down over his eyes. The Blackhearts looked at their feet.

'No one is to leave the grounds,' von Pfaltzen was saying. 'No one, you understand. The thieves are still within. You will hold all visitors here until they are found.'

The chief gate guard saluted. 'Aye, sir.'

'I volunteer my men to help watch the gate,' said Danziger. 'The thieves may try to make a break.'

Reiner cursed. Five minutes earlier and they would have been through and gone.

The gate guard turned as the Blackhearts' escort approached the gate. 'Wait! No one is to go out, sergeant. The priests must bide.'

'But, captain, the corpse is diseased. It–'

'No exceptions, sergeant,' said the gate captain. 'Von Pfaltzen's ord–' He stopped as the Blackhearts' smell hit him. 'By Sigmar!'

'You see,' said the sergeant. 'It isn't safe.'

'Just a moment,' said von Pfaltzen, stepping forward with Danziger behind him. 'Open the casket.'

NINETEEN
There Is Blood To Be Spilled

THE SERGEANT SPREAD his hands. 'Sir, I have already seen in. I vouch for the contents. It would not be wise…'

'Open it.'

Reiner's hands shook as he lifted the lid. Flies buzzed up from within. Here was where he died. There was no escape. Curse Ranald. The old fraud had let him down again. Reiner held his torch high so the lid cast a shadow across the casket's interior and hung his head. Von Pfaltzen grimaced and covered his nose and mouth, but he kept coming, looking steadily into the casket. The torchlight glistened on the slimy arm.

'You see, captain,' said the sergeant.

Von Pfaltzen ignored him and reached his sword into the casket. Reiner groaned. It was all over. They were dead. They would be chopped to pieces. Von Pfaltzen prodded the blankets. Reiner expected a hard clink as his sword touched the stone, but the tip sunk in as if into a pillow. Reiner nearly yelped. He was glad for his cowl, for he was gaping like a peasant at a magic show. He heard Darius whimper with relief. Von Pfaltzen prodded again, then coughed and stepped back.

'Let them out,' he said, waving at the gate captain. 'They cannot stay.'

The gate captain nodded, relieved, and signalled his men to stand aside and let the Blackhearts out. Reiner led them forward in a daze. He was baffled. What had happened? Had Ranald sent a miracle after all? Had the stone softened? Had some hidden sorcerer caused von Pfaltzen to see what Reiner wanted him to see?

Reiner did not like the unexplained. And he was almost as frightened by their escape as he was thankful.

When they were out of earshot of the gate, everyone sighed and cursed.

'What was that?' said Hals. 'We should be dead.'

'It was a miracle,' said Pavel.

'Sorcery,' said Gert. 'Did ye cast a spell, witch?'

'I am not a witch,' said Darius.

'It was Sigmar's grace,' said Hals.

'Or Ranald's,' said Reiner.

'I only hope the filth didn't damage 'em,' muttered Dieter.

'Damage what?' asked Reiner.

Dieter said nothing. Reiner looked back, they were out of sight of the gate. There was a side street just ahead. 'Turn in there,' he said. 'And set it down.'

The Blackhearts angled into the side street and set the heavy casket down with groans of relief.

'Don't get any ideas I'll share,' said Dieter. 'I stole 'em fair and square.'

Reiner threw open the casket and flipped aside the blanket where von Pfaltzen had poked. Rolls of stiff canvas had been tucked down next to the stone. Reiner pulled them out.

'Easy, easy!' said Dieter, sharp.

Reiner uncurled the rolls and found that they were four paintings by famous masters, cut from their frames, which had been stacked with the others in the vault. There was a hole at the same spot on each painting.

'There!' said Dieter, disgusted. 'Cursed jagger ruined them with his poking. That was a fortune that was. Now they're worthless!'

'They saved our lives,' said Darius. 'I don't call that worthless.'

Dieter snorted.

Reiner re-rolled the paintings and stuffed them back under the blanket. 'Right,' he said. 'One more gate and we're free. Off we go.'

THE BLACKHEARTS PASSED through the Manor district gate with no difficulties, and made their way to the sewers and then the catacombs below them. It was a slow, silent trip. Slow because Reiner wanted to give Augustus as much time to get to the authorities as he could. It was quiet because, except for participating in the occasional argument about which was the right path, Reiner didn't care to speak for fear of saying something which might give away their ruse.

It seemed the others felt the same. Franka stumbled along like a sleepwalker, staring blankly ahead. It broke Reiner's heart to see her. He wanted more than anything to let her in on the trick, but he couldn't. His greatest fear was that she would run, but she seemed too stunned. His second greatest fear – after they had made several wrong turnings and had had to double back – was that Augustus would not remember the way either and lead their rescuers in circles in the catacombs while the dark elf destroyed the stone.

At last they came to the huge, glittering cave with the bridge over the chasm at one end, and the cyclopean arch at the other. The mutants came out of their hovels to surround them, even more deformed than before, and carried them, like a sea carries a bottle, into the chamber with the cages and the stone circle.

Valaris was waiting for them. In the days since they had left him he had built a home for himself. Beautiful if mismatched tables and chairs, vases and tapestries, all scavenged by his twisted slaves, were arranged against one wall. He had even managed to find a magnificent canopied bed in which to sleep.

To the right of this was a grand oak throne, and from this he rose to greet them, a wry smile on his cruel lips as they set down the casket.

'My friends,' he said. 'Your adventures have provided me with more amusement than a year's worth of blood sport. And had the success of your enterprise not meant so much to me, and the news that I had failed to kill Teclis not angered me, I would have laughed all the harder.'

He looked at Reiner with something akin to fondness. 'You in particular, captain, twisted more prettily than a snake pinned by a spear. So many times did I give up on you, so many times did I come within a hair's breadth of allowing your master to murder you before murdering him in turn, when suddenly you would pull an escape out of thin air and I would relent in order to see what fresh comedy was in store.' He chuckled. 'Never have I seen a man more torn between following his conscience or saving his own skin. For though you protest otherwise, I know you are not entirely the rogue you play, and your internal struggle was as entertaining as your fight with the Imperials. Thankfully your venality has won out at last, as I knew it would, and I was treated to the high drama and low farce that was the murder of your comrade. Beautiful. I almost wish...' He looked wistfully at them, then shrugged. 'But no, it is impossible. Khaine needs strong, pure blood in order to unmake the waystone.'

'Khaine needs... blood?' said Reiner, the brief flash of triumph in the knowledge that he had fooled the elf dying as he realised the elf had tricked him too. '*Our* blood?'

'Yes,' said Valaris. 'The mutants are too diseased. Their blood would be an insult.'

'But, Lord Valaris,' said Reiner, though he knew it was hopeless. 'You promised us our lives. You promised that we would go free with Count Manfred if we procured you the stone. It is the only reason we agreed to do it.'

'Naturally, I promised,' said Valaris, shrugging. 'Would you concern yourself with a promise made to a dog, no matter how clever its tricks?' He motioned to his slaves. 'Bring out the prisoner and tie them all to the stones. We will proceed at once.'

'Ye fish-belly cozener,' snarled Hals. 'Ye twist-tongued cheat!'

'Coward!' shouted Pavel. 'Tell yer dirty pets to stand off and face me sword to spear. I'll gut ye where ye stand.'

'But, lord,' said Reiner desperately. 'Our blood is tainted as well. Will Khaine accept poisoned blood?'

Valaris smiled. 'Khaine's sacrifices often die by poison.'

Manfred was led, blinking, out of one of the cages. He was gaunt and wild looking, his hair and beard matted and his clothes bedraggled and grimy.

His miserable expression changed to one of joy as he saw Reiner. 'By Sigmar,' he said, amazed. 'Have you done it? Have you freed me at last?'

Reiner laughed as the mutants dragged the Blackhearts to the tall basalt stones. 'No, m'lord. You have doomed us. The elf does not honour his bargain.' He wanted to add 'unless Augustus brings our rescue,' but even now he didn't dare speak, for fear of giving the dark elf warning.

'What!' cried Manfred, looking at Valaris. 'You devious deceiver! How dare you! I am a count of the Empire!'

Valaris was directing his slaves as they took the waystone from the casket and ignored Manfred.

'Come, m'lord,' said Reiner. 'You of all people should not be surprised by treachery.'

The mutants began to tie the Blackhearts tightly, if inexpertly, at chest and waist in coils of filthy rope, trapping their hands. Manfred was tied to the stone to Reiner's right. Franka was tied to his left.

'Franka,' Reiner whispered, but she only stared ahead.

When his slaves had raised the waystone on the central altar and withdrawn to the walls of the chamber, Valaris drew his dagger and approached Reiner. Reiner tensed, thinking this was the end, but instead of plunging the knife into his chest, instead Valaris gripped his wrist and cut out the sliver of crystal, flicking it carelessly to the ground. Instantly, the whispering warpstone buzz filled Reiner's mind again.

The dark elf moved around the circle, removing the crystals from each of them. When he had finished, he stripped to the waist, revealing a dead white, whipcord torso, and a blue crystal – mother to their slivers – on a chain around his neck. He began a chant, harsh and sibilant, while cutting himself at seven well-scarred points on his chest. He touched a finger to each of the wounds, then began to daub strange symbols across his chest and down his arms.

As he wrote the last symbol, Valaris's chant became a song, high and beautiful and terrifying. He moved around the waystone in a slow, sinuous dance, and with each move, it felt as if all Reiner's blood was being pulled to the front of his body. His pulse pounded behind his eyes and in his ears. His heart pounded as if he had run a ten mile race. His fingers and toes throbbed.

The song grew wilder, as did Valaris's movements, and the pressure increased inexorably. Dieter and Gert cried out. Darius vomited. Spatters of blood appeared on Valaris's chest and back, partially obscuring the symbols. Reiner thought at first that they came from the dark elf's seven wounds, but as he looked down at himself, he saw that the blood from his wounded wrist was dripping, not to the floor, but sideways toward Valaris. Drops flew at the elf from all the Blackhearts, as if he had become the centre of gravity.

That gravity was getting stronger. Reiner's whole body was being pulled forward. The ropes cut into his flesh cruelly. It felt as if his heart would burst from his chest, and it came to him with a nauseous shudder that this was exactly what was meant to happen – a tenfold coronary explosion that would bathe Valaris in heart-blood and give him the power to crack the waystone. Reiner suddenly knew he was going to die. Augustus would not arrive in time. This was the end.

He turned his head to Manfred. 'Valdenheim! For your pity, who was the spy?'

But Manfred had lost consciousness, his head bobbling at the end of his neck.

Reiner turned to Franka. 'Franka!'

She looked up. Her mouth drooled red and the whites of her eyes were flooded with blood.

'Franka!' he called. 'I beg you, beloved, before we die! Forgive me! Say you forgive me!

Franka's face twisted in disgust. 'Before we die?' she choked. 'I am already dead. You killed me when you killed Augustus.'

'No, listen!' He opened his mouth to tell her the truth, but with a jerk, the pressure increased violently. Blood streamed from his nose and mouth to splash on Valaris's torso. He couldn't breathe. Couldn't speak. The pain was incredible, but the agony of his mind was greater. He wanted to weep. It was so unfair. How could he die with Franka thinking him a cold-blooded murderer?

His head began to fill with screams and shrieks. At first he thought it was the others dying, or the mad whispers in his head calling to him, but then he heard the ring of steel above the shouting. Was Valaris striking the waystone with his knife?

He forced his eyes open. Valaris was looking over his shoulder. The pressure eased. The roaring in Reiner's brain faded.

As Valaris stopped altogether, Reiner and the others sagged in their ropes, sucking in great ragged breaths. Now Reiner could hear it – the clamour and clash of battle. The mutants were running into the huge cavern, waving their makeshift weapons.

Valaris stared after them, then turned burning eyes on Reiner, knife raised. 'You... you deceived me!' Reiner flinched and twisted in his ropes, but the dark elf paused as he drew back the knife, and raised his head like a wolf scenting blood on the wind. 'Teclis!' A leering smile spread across his face. 'You have brought me my prey, captain. For that, you shall die correctly.'

He crossed to his strange bedchamber and snatched up his sword and bow, then called to the few mutants that remained in the chamber. 'Come, slaves. There is blood to be spilled!' He strode into the big cavern at their head.

Hals laughed wearily. Blood ran in rivulets from his eyes, nose and mouth. 'So Augustus comes through at last.'

'And not before time,' said Pavel, spitting crimson.

'Au... Augustus?' said Franka, looking up, wide-eyed.

Reiner coughed blood. 'It was a trick. Dieter only pretended to kill him.' He swallowed. 'I couldn't tell you without telling Valaris. I'm sorry.'

Franka gaped at him, then looked away with a sob, trying to bury her face in her shoulder.

'You mean,' said Manfred groggily, 'you mean we are saved?'

'If Augustus brought enough troops,' said Reiner.

At that moment, Danziger came through the arch with his men. He smiled as he saw the Blackhearts' predicament. 'How convenient,' he said. 'We will be rid of your meddling once and for all.'

TWENTY
Spears To The Front

DANZIGER ENTERED AND motioned his men towards the waystone. 'Put it in the casket and hide it. We'll return for it when the others have gone.' He turned toward Reiner, grinning evilly. 'I reserve this pleasure for myself.'

'Lord Danziger,' said Manfred. 'What is the meaning of this?'

Danziger turned sharply, seeing Manfred for the first time. 'Count Manfred! We... we believed you dead.'

For a moment, Reiner thought Danziger would try to dissemble his earlier words, but then a cunning smile curled his lips and he looked back at the door.

'And why shouldn't you be?' He turned from Reiner to Danziger. 'What a coup this will be for Slaanesh! A count of the Empire.'

'You filthy cultist,' spat Manfred. 'You reveal yourself at last. You will burn for this.'

Danziger put his dagger to Manfred's chest and cut through the top button of his doublet as, behind him, his men waddled the waystone to the coffin. 'And who will know it was I? I will run out weeping that the elf has slain you, and–'

'Spears ready!' roared a voice from the door. 'Talabheimers, attack!'

Danziger and his men spun, groping for their swords. The waystone crashed down, smashing the coffin and crushing the legs of two of the men. Out of the shadows ran, not a company of spearmen, but a single man, his spear levelled. Augustus!

The pikeman ran past Danziger and the confused cultists, straight for Reiner. For a terrifying second, Reiner thought Augustus was coming to kill him, but then he saw the mad laughter in his eyes a realised he meant to cut him free.

'Not me, you fool!' Reiner shouted. 'Jurgen!'

Augustus veered right and chopped at Jurgen's ropes. The spear was an awkward tool for the job, but fortunately the ropes were rotten and Jurgen's strength immense. He heaved mightily at the partially cut cords and they popped and hung slack.

'Behind you!' shouted Reiner.

Augustus whirled about, swinging his spear like a sword and fanning back Danziger's men, who had run up behind him.

Jurgen drew his dagger and slashed at the ropes around his chest.

Augustus took a sword across the back of his breastplate and dodged behind Jurgen's stone. The cultists followed him.

'You imbeciles!' shrieked Danziger. 'Don't kill the free one! Kill the trapped ones before they're freed!'

And putting action to his words, he started toward Manfred again as his men tried to get around Augustus to the bound Blackhearts. Haggard as Manfred was, there was some fight in him. He kicked Danziger in the stomach.

Danziger cursed, and dodged aside to cut Manfred's throat from behind, but he was too late. Jurgen was free and leapt at him, sword drawn. Danziger shied away and Jurgen slashed through Manfred's bonds with a single stroke, then spun and did the same for Reiner before running to defend Pavel and Hals from three cultists. Augustus jumped before Dieter and Gert, fending off two others.

Reiner staggered forwards and fumbled out his sword, his arms numb and weak. His mouth and nose were still filled with blood and it was hard to breathe. On his right, Manfred wrestled Danziger for possession of a dagger. On his left, two cultists were approaching Franka's stone.

'No!' Reiner shouted. He lunged at them, but as they turned, he found he had little strength to fight them. Valaris's ceremony had left him trembling and sore. He managed to parry the left one's thrust, but the other nearly took his ear off.

Elsewhere, however, the tide was turning. Jurgen had freed Hals and felled another cultist, and Hals was freeing Pavel. Now in possession of Danziger's dagger, Manfred circled the cult leader, who jabbed at him with his sword.

Reiner wiped his nose and flicked the blood in the eyes of his left-hand opponent, then drove the one on the right back toward Franka. She raised both feet and kicked him in the spine. He stumbled forward, yelping, right into Reiner's out-thrust blade, and then Reiner faced only one.

As he saw Jurgen cut down another of his men, Danziger finally had enough. He sprang back from Manfred shouting, 'Fall back! This is foolishness. We will win another way!'

His men danced out of their engagements and raced with him for the door. Hals and Pavel gave chase.

'No! Regroup!' Reiner shouted over the battle beyond the door.

Pavel and Hals stopped and turned back, then helped Reiner and Augustus cut down Franka and the others as Dieter slit the throats of the men crushed by the way-stone.

'Thankee, lad,' said Reiner to Augustus. 'Wasn't sure you'd come back.'

Augustus's face darkened. 'I came for the stone.'

'Could ha' done that without cutting us down,' said Hals. 'We're obliged.'

Augustus snorted and glared at Reiner. 'Couldn't let the captain die. I owe 'im a kick in the eggs.'

'You have all done well,' said Manfred as they bound their wounds and gathered their weapons. 'If we survive this adventure, you shall all be richly rewarded.'

'Never mind that, jagger,' said Hals. 'Just free us like ye promised. That's all we ask.'

Manfred smiled. 'You need have no fear about that. Now, are we ready?'

Reiner frowned as the Blackhearts fell in behind Manfred. What had he meant, exactly? Gert also seemed to be wondering, for he was staring hard at Manfred's back.

Blinding flashes of blue and white light illuminated the door, and through it they could see the battle only in brief silhouetted flickers of seething bodies and glinting blades. The mutants surged around a square of men in a thick, undisciplined horde, more pouring into the cavern from the tunnels.

At the fore fought von Pfaltzen and the countess's guard, blood and black fluids staining their green and buff uniforms. On the far side of the battle Boellengen shouted orders at his handgunners as they emptied a volley into the churning mass. Scharnholt's men and Totkrieg's Hammers supported the handgunners, cutting down the mutants who survived their fusillades. A hundred Talabheimers under Hunter Lord Keinholtz defended the near side of the formation, spears in front, bowmen firing over their heads. Danziger, now returned to the main body of his men, encouraged them from the rear, shouting and waving his sword. Nearer the main entrance, Lord Schott's greatswords and Raichskell's Templars were doing butcher's work among the madmen. They were red to the elbows and mutants lay in waist high drifts around them.

But though the mutants died in droves, having only the crudest armour and weapons, they also fought with suicidal abandon, throwing themselves at the men without any regard for safety, and many a throat was torn out and gut ripped with their dying breath. They impaled themselves on swords and spears solely to drag them down so their brothers and sisters could rush over them and overwhelm their slayers.

In the centre of the conflict was the source of the blinding light. Like dark and light stars circling each other in a swirling celestial vortex, Teclis, in shining armour and Valaris, naked to the waist, attacked each other with spell and sword. Their blades glanced off each other's wards in showers of sparks, and their spells and counter spells met and burst against each other like colliding waves. Neither was making any headway against the other. It seemed the loser would be he who tired first, and Teclis, though no longer at death's door, looked feeble and exhausted.

Reiner was surprised to see Teclis without his guard, but then he saw them, lying at Valaris's feet, black bowshafts sprouting from their chests and throats.

'M'lord,' said Reiner to Manfred. 'The mutants only fight at the dark elf's bidding. Once he is killed, they will lose heart.'

Manfred nodded. 'Then you know your duty, captain. Kill him. I will join Boellengen and direct his men to cover your attack.'

'But... but m'lord,' said Reiner. 'He is warded by dark magics. We haven't a hope...'

'Then distract him and allow Teclis to prevail.'

Reiner saluted to keep himself from punching the count. 'Yes, m'lord. As you command, m'lord.' He turned to his companions. 'Blackhearts! Spears to the front! Forward!'

'Spiteful jagger,' grunted Hals. 'Wants to kill us before he has to let us go.'

Teclis and Valaris fought behind the mutants' line, the biggest, most monstrous mutants defending the dark elf from the spears of the Talabheim guard. Valaris's back was, however, entirely unprotected, and the Blackhearts charged for him across empty ground, Hals, Pavel and Augustus at the fore, Reiner, Dieter and Jurgen on the flanks with Franka and Gert at the back, nocking arrows. Darius stumbled along behind, whimpering as usual.

Jurgen, Reiner, Dieter and the spearmen stabbed and slashed at Valaris's naked back as one. Blinding sparks cracked, and their weapons bounced away as if they had swung them at granite. Reiner's hand stung like he had grabbed a thorn bush.

Valaris glanced back, and in that brief second Teclis pounced, battering him with a barrage of spells and sword strikes. The dark elf spun back, parrying and muttering madly to protect himself. At last he recovered and their stalemate resumed.

'Again!' called Reiner.

The Blackhearts struck another blow at Valaris, but this time his attention didn't leave Teclis. Instead, five of the massive mutants, each taller than Augustus and broader than Jurgen, turned like automatons from the battle line and attacked, swinging huge clubs and claws and rusty greatswords.

Pavel and Hals squared off against a towering thing with a horse-skull head and bones that grew through its skin in a lattice of armoured ridges, ducking its bony, hammer-like fists. Jurgen closed with a red, woolly-haired beast with four arms and four swords. Augustus plunged his spear into an obese doughy thing. It stuck like glue and the monster clawed the spearman as he tried to yank it out again. Dieter hacked at a walking flower. It had long legs and useless, shrivelled arms that flopped at its sides, but a head like a sea anemone with long ropy tentacles and a snapping beak at the centre. Gert and Franka stood back and peppered the things with bolts and arrows.

Reiner hacked at a broad, leather-skinned thing with a mouth that split its pumpkin head from ear to ear. It laughed at his attacks. One of Franka's arrows dangled harmlessly from its thick hide. Reiner cursed as he ducked the thing's claws. If the Blackhearts could reach Valaris again it might be enough. They had proved that a single distraction could be his undoing. But would they get a chance? Teclis was weaker than before. He had put too much into his last attack, hoping to end the fight, and was flagging. Valaris sensed this and pressed him hard, eyes shining. His crystal glowed like a star on his chest. Beyond the Talabheimers' line, Reiner saw Manfred directing Boellengen and Schott toward them. They would undoubtedly be too late.

Reiner blinked. The crystal. The crystal!

'Reiner! Look out!' screamed Franka.

Reiner flinched back and leather-skin's claws slashed his shoulder, knocking him to the ground. It raised its arms, roaring, then stumbled back, yelping, an arrow jutting from the roof of its mouth. Pavel and Hals gored it simultaneously, and it fell, spraying blood. Horse-head lay dead behind them, bloody spear wounds between its external ribs.

'Thankee, lads,' said Reiner as he picked himself up. His shoulder was shredded and bloody, but he couldn't take his eyes from Valaris. The crystal must help the dark elf absorb Teclis's magical attacks. If Reiner could take it… But that was impossible. A sword couldn't penetrate the assassin's defences, how could a hand?

Then he noticed something curious. As Jurgen pressed the four-armed thing, it stepped back into Valaris's sphere of protection and was not repulsed, though the wild swings of its four swords still bounced away.

Augustus, Hals and Dieter killed the sticky, blubbery thing. Hals and Augustus held it at arm's length with their spears and Dieter knifed it under the ear. They had to abandon their weapons though, for they could not withdraw them. They found shoddy replacements among the dead mutants and helped the others. Gert shot the flower thing through the heart and it died lashing its tentacles in violent spasms. Jurgen cut four-arms' legs out from under it, and pinned it to the ground as it fell on its face.

'All on Valaris!' said Reiner. 'And don't mind that you can't hit him.'

The Blackhearts attacked the dark elf's back and the flanks, though all their strikes rang on shimmering air long before they touched him.

'Back away!' called Teclis, angrily, before returning to his mumbling.

'No! Keep at it!' said Reiner, and stepped behind the dark elf, praying the others held his attention. He reached forward. It felt like he pushed his hand into a hot wind. The air glistened around his fingers. He moved slower and the wind lessened, but as he reached further, his hand began to prickle, and then to sizzle with pain. It felt as if he was reaching into boiling water. He expected to see his flesh blistering, but it looked no different.

The pain made him try to push harder, and he lost three inches as the barrier shoved his hand back. He forced himself to creep ahead, though he trembled with agony and sweat poured into his eyes. Another inch. He had to shift as Valaris and Teclis circled and the Blackhearts kept up their futile attacks. Another inch. He could almost touch the dark elf's shoulder. His arm was on fire to his shoulder. The pain made him dizzy. His knees shook. Another inch. His fingers rose toward the silver chain. Now his face was within the sphere. It felt as if the skin was peeling from his cheeks. His fingers closed on the silver chain. He shoved forward and was thrust back violently by the barrier. The chain snapped and came with him. He landed in a heap three yards away, spasming and dizzy.

'No!' screamed Valaris, spinning around. 'What have you…?'

Teclis's eyes flashed. He thrust his palms forward. The air around Valaris warped and his chest collapsed, his ribs snapping and jutting through his white skin. Air hissed from his slack mouth. He flopped to the ground, dead and staring, blood pooling around him.

Teclis fell to the ground too, utterly spent, and the Blackhearts made a protective ring around him. There was no need. With Valaris's death, the mutants' fury dissipated, and they fled from the assembled companies.

Teclis looked up at Reiner, breathing hoarsely. 'My thanks.' He took a vial from his pouch and drank it down. A shudder passed through him and he closed his eyes, then recovered somewhat. 'Now, where is the stone?'

Across the room, amid the weary soldiers, Manfred raised a bloody sword. 'Well done, men of Talabheim! Well done, Reiklanders!' he cried. 'But there is further work to be done.' He turned toward Danziger. 'We have traitors in our–'

'Followers of Tzeentch!' cried Scharnholt, interrupting. 'Kill the unbelievers! The stone will be ours!' He turned to von Pfaltzen, who stood beside him, and cut his throat from ear to ear.

TWENTY-ONE
The Gate Is Open

VON PFALTZEN TURNED uncomprehending eyes on Scharnholt, then crumpled, crimson jetting from his neck. At this signal, all of Scharnholt's followers, and some men of the other companies, turned on those next to them. Cries of shock and pain came from all over the chamber. Then, while the men of the companies tried desperately to defend themselves from those they had thought their fellows, Danziger, too, raised his voice.

'Followers of Slaanesh! Do thou likewise!' he cried. 'Take the stone and Talabheim falls! All glory to our delicious master!'

His men fell on those already fighting the Tzeentchists. As Reiner and the Blackhearts and Teclis watched, stunned, a quarter of the combined companies were murdered before they recovered enough to group together and defend themselves. Many cultists died as well, but as they fell, bloodthirsty cries echoed through the chamber and from the main tunnel burst a mob of masked figures waving swords and axes and spears. Half wore robes of blue and gold, while the others wore purple and red.

Teclis sighed as he stood. 'If it were not a matter of the stability of the world, I would let this city die.'

The companies fell back from the flood of cultists and clustered to the right of the main entrance. Scharnholt and Danziger and their men ran to join their masked comrades.

'Help me to Valdenheim,' said Teclis.

'Yes, lord.'

Reiner and the others carried him through the chaos to where Manfred stood with Boellengen, Schott, Raichskell and Hunter Lord Keinholtz, conferring with Magus Nichtladen. Father Totkrieg was dead. Their troops were close to panic. Their companions had turned on them. The battle they had thought won must now be fought all over again, against more dangerous enemies.

And it only got worse. As the cultists charged the companies, behind their lines, sorcerers commenced chanting. The air around them began to warp and shimmer.

'Magus!' called Manfred to Nichtladen. 'Protect us!'

The magus called orders to his few remaining initiates, and they began intoning warding spells. They appeared to be having difficulty. They stuttered their invocations. Their hands jerked and twitched. All at once one screamed. His eyes exploded, and he dropped, blood pouring from his mouth. Another began tearing the flesh from his face with his fingers. The air was tingling. Flames flickered around the feet of Boellengen's handgunners. They cried out in fear and fell back. The cultists advanced.

Teclis shook as he summoned his strength. 'The warpstone amplifies the cultists' powers,' he said, then spoke a single word and swept his hands apart.

At once the flames winked out around the handgunners' feet. The remaining magi recovered themselves.

Teclis was near to collapse. 'Your men and magi must slay the sorcerers,' he said wearily. 'I have only enough strength to keep them at bay.' He touched his chest where Valaris's arrow had pierced it. 'Naggaroth may have slain me after all.'

'Yes, Lord Teclis,' said Manfred. But even as he turned to order the men, columns of smoke began to rise with the circles of the Slaanesh and Tzeentch sorcerers.

'Quickly,' croaked Teclis. 'Attack them! Disrupt their ceremony!'

The troops pressed forward and the magi wove their spells, but they were too late. Things were moving within the columns of smoke, and the chamber filled with strange choking odours. From the Tzeentch side came a smell like sour milk, and from the Slaanesh side, an intoxicating perfume. Then things came out of the smoke. Reiner's eyes were repelled by the one and drawn by the other.

The Tzeentchists' conjuration literally hurt to look at. It was a shapeless, constantly changing pink mass. Horns and limbs and slavering mouths pushed out of its skin and sank away again like fish-heads bubbling to the top of a stew. It sweated pus, and moved by extruding a new leg before it and retracting an old one. Reiner wanted to run from it, to tear his eyes out.

The Slaaneshis' summoning, on the other hand, was so alluring Reiner found himself uncomfortably aroused – a lavender-skinned beauty with lush red lips and graceful horns. Her perfect, naked breasts swayed hypnotically with each sultry step and her almond eyes seemed to look at no one but Reiner. He took a step toward her, unlacing his doublet.

'He's beautiful,' said Franka. She too was stepping forward, her eyes glazed with lust.

'He?' said Reiner, dully. For the briefest second, Reiner saw something else where the purple wanton stood – still purple, but hard and chitinous. What he had thought were red lips was a mouth like a remora's. The almond eyes were black holes. Then the vision of beauty reasserted itself, but he could fight it now.

The companies were reacting as he had, backing away from the Tzeentch nightmare, and stepping toward the Slaaneshi temptress. The cultists cut down both the terrified and the mesmerised in droves.

Teclis groaned, then redoubled his chanting. The influence of the daemons lessened at once. Recovering, Manfred stepped forward, raising his sword.

'Hold fast, my Reiklanders! Hold fast, men of Talabheim!' he shouted. 'Steel your minds! Have we not faced these creatures before, and prevailed? Did we not push them and their filthy kind back to the Chaos Wastes? Fear not! The mighty Teclis will protect us! Kill the men and the horrors will fly! Now fight!'

The men fought.

On the left, Keinholtz and the Talabheimers charged into the Slaaneshi with renewed vigour, roaring, 'For von Pfaltzen and the countess!' While on the right Schott and Boellengen and Raichskell led their men against the Tzeentchists crying, 'Karl Franz! Karl Franz!' Even Reiner, who knew that Manfred had less honour than a common pimp, was stirred by his words. Whatever else he is, he thought, the old scoundrel is a leader.

But inspired as the men were, they were pitifully few, and they had just fought a pitched battle. The cultists were fresh. And the daemons, though their mental influence was diminished by Teclis's wards, slew all who stood before them with their claws and teeth and tentacles.

'I cannot protect them for long,' wheezed Teclis. 'If you cannot slay the sorcerers, we are finished.'

Manfred turned to Reiner. 'Hetsau! Add your men to the line. Cut through to the circles!'

'No, m'lord,' said Reiner. 'I've a better idea. This way, lads.'

As Manfred squawked, Reiner led the Blackhearts left to the cluster of shacks that ran around the chamber's wall. He gripped Darius's elbow.

'Listen, scholar,' he said as they ran. 'This is your moment. This is where you prove your worth.'

Darius gulped. 'What… what do you want me to do?'

The Blackhearts crept through the shacks, circling the Slaaneshi flank.

'Cast a spell at the fellows who called up the thing with the mouths,' said Reiner. 'It matters not what, so long as they know they are being attacked. Something with lots of flashes and smoke.'

'I am not a witch, curse you!' whined Darius. 'I've told you a thousand times.'

'And a thousand times I haven't believed you,' said Reiner.

They were behind both the Slaanesh and Tzeentch armies now, looking out from the hovels. The cultists had tightened their ring, and the companies' numbers were shrinking fast. The purple beauty raised a man on the tip of her sabre-like claw and flung him into Schott's greatswords. Two fell, and the cultists cut them to pieces before they could rise. The pink horror was gulping down three bodies with three different mouths.

'But it is true,' said Darius. 'I am a scholar. I know only theory. Not practice.'

Reiner shook him. 'Liar! Manfred chose you for a reason. He could have found a better surgeon anywhere. You're just too much a coward to do what he bade you. Is that it?'

'I… No, I cannot! I dare not!'

'So you do know something!' Reiner cried, triumphant. 'I knew it! Use it! Hurry!'

'No! I can't!'

'Damn you! Speak!' Reiner hissed. 'What is it? What can you do?'

'Nothing! It's useless. A way to make plants grow faster. I told him, but he wouldn't listen…'

'And you have plants in your pouch, I shouldn't wonder, though I told you to throw them away,' said Reiner. 'Make them grow.'

'I daren't!'

'Fool! Are you still afraid of our scorn? We need your skill!'

'It isn't that!' said Darius miserably. 'I am afraid of it!
I... I nearly lost myself the last time. That is how I was
caught. I was found by my landlady unconscious amongst
my circles and braziers, and–'

'So you are afraid of death?' asked Reiner.

Darius wailed. 'Of course I–'

'Good.' Reiner put dagger to his throat. 'For I will kill
you if you do not obey this order. And this is no game as
with Augustus. You can risk death and save a city, or you
can die now. Which will it be?'

Darius cringed from the blade. 'I– I will do it.' There
were tears in his eyes. 'I wish Manfred had never found
me.'

'Then you would have swung weeks ago,' said Hals. 'And
saved us all a lot of whining.'

'Hush, pikeman,' said Reiner. 'Now listen. This is what
we will do.'

MOMENTS LATER, REINER and Darius crept on their bellies
as close to the Slaaneshi rear as they dared. The
Tzeentchists were to their left. Reiner looked beyond them
and saw Franka and Gert getting into position in the shadows. Reiner prayed his gambit wasn't too late. It seemed
the Reikland and Talabheim lines must break any second.

'Ready?' he whispered.

Darius shrugged. His face was blank.

'Then go!'

Darius sat up and took a handful of plant cuttings from
his pouch. He muttered over them, moving his hands in
complicated patterns. At first nothing happened, but then
Reiner heard a tiny pop, and watched amazed as the cuttings began lengthening and sprouting tendrils. Darius's
words grew more guttural and the plants blackened and
twisted. He swayed as if dizzy. The words came hard and
harsh.

'Now?' asked Reiner.

Darius nodded and staggered up, hurling the rapidly
growing plants at the Tzeentchists with all his might.

'Come, plants!' cried Reiner at the top of his lungs. 'Do the bidding of thy master Slaanesh. Strike down these treacherous Tzeentchist heretics!'

Of course, thought Reiner, as he pulled Darius down and hid, the whole plan would collapse if the cuttings grew into daffodils and cabbages. He needn't have worried. The shoots had been cut from the mad plants of the Tallows, and under the influence of Darius's spell and the presence of so much warpstone, they exploded in rocketing spurts of mutated growth. Creepers undulated across the floor like serpents toward the Tzeentchists, sprouting questing tendrils and dagger thorns. Roots thrust into the hard ground and shot up like trees, branches bursting from their trunks and bearing unwholesome fruit in the wink of an eye.

Panting flowers drooled sap as they sniffed toward the cultists. Vines wrapped around ankles. Men were crushed in verdant embraces and impaled by foot-long thorns. Men who fell were instantly swarmed by the breathing flowers, which sucked at them like leeches.

The Tzeentchists chopped at the vines and looked for the culprits. Those who had heard Reiner's invocation pointed angry fingers at the Slaaneshi. Then an arrow shot from behind the Tzeentchists and buried itself in a Slaaneshi's neck.

'Slay the Slaaneshi scum!' bellowed a voice that sounded suspiciously like Gert's. 'See how they turn on us? Betrayers!'

Another Slaaneshi fell, clutching an arrow in his arm. His companions turned, looking toward the Tzeentchists, who were running toward them shaking their weapons. Cultists fell upon one another and the brawl began to spread. Reiner watched, gratified, as they turned from fighting the companies to fight their rivals. A Tzeentchist with an axe charged the circle of Slaaneshi sorcerers. He could not pierce their wards, but the sorcerers looked around at the confusion. The Tzeentchist sorcerers were turning as well, and the thing they had summoned began to pale. A rope of fire shot from the Slaaneshi to the Tzeentchists, burning all it touched. The Tzeentchists retaliated with a yellow cloud that caused men to choke and fall. The summoning circles broke in confusion, and with a thunderclap of displaced air, the pink horror and the purple beauty winked out of existence.

The Talabheimers and the Reiklanders cheered and renewed their attacks on the squabbling cultists.

'Well done, scholar!' cried Reiner. 'We've done it. Let's away.'

Darius lay whimpering on the ground, staring at his hands as if he'd never seen them before. Blood seeped from his nose and his tear ducts.

'Lad?'

Darius didn't respond. Reiner caught him under the arm. The scholar came up like a sleepwalker. Reiner led him back toward the shacks, joining Gert and Franka, who were creeping back as well.

'Good work!' he said.

'Hetsau!' cried a voice behind them. 'I might have known!'

Reiner turned. Danziger glared at him from behind a pile of rubbish where he and his men had taken refuge. He called toward the battle. 'Stop! Stop fighting! Manfred's dogs have duped us!'

No one heard. There was too much noise, and the cultists were fighting the plants and each other too fiercely.

Danziger cursed. 'Well, at least I shall have my revenge! At them!' He charged at Reiner, his men behind him.

Reiner turned to run with Franka and Gert, but Darius was on his knees, looking at his hands again.

'Damn you, lad! Up!' He grabbed the scholar's arm.

Darius shoved him, screeching.

Reiner fell, surprised, his sword skittering away. Danziger and his men were nearly on top of him.

'Reiner!' shouted Franka.

She turned back to cover him. Gert followed, cursing. Reiner scrabbled for his sword and grabbed the blade, cutting his palm. The rest of the Blackhearts were sprinting toward him from the shacks, but they were much too far away.

Franka lunged for Danziger, but one of his men swung at her head and she dived to the ground. Reiner fumbled for the right end of his sword. Danziger lunged at him. He couldn't twist away in time.

'Captain!' shouted Gert.

Gert jumped before Reiner, slashing at Danziger with his hatchet. The lord ducked and stabbed through Gert's groin. Another cultist gored him in the side. Gert collapsed against Reiner, clutching himself. Reiner thrust over the big man's shoulder and ran Danziger through the throat. The lord squealed and jerked his head, trying to escape the blade, and it tore out the side of his neck. He toppled, fountaining blood.

Gert fell as Franka sprang up, and she and Reiner stood over him, back to back in the centre of Danziger's six remaining men. Swords thrust at them from all directions. Reiner parried two and turned so another took him in his wounded shoulder instead of the heart. Franka dodged one blade, beat aside another, and raked a man's chest with a lunge, but took his riposte in the forearm.

But then the cultists were turning at the Blackhearts' thundering boot steps and they went down like straw before Jurgen's sword and the spears of Pavel, Hals and Augustus.

Reiner glanced to the battle to be sure no one else was coming for them, then squatted beside Gert. The crossbowman's breeks were crimson to his boots, and stuck wetly to his legs. 'All right, lad?' he asked, though he knew the answer.

'It's bad, I think,' said Gert. His face was paper-white. 'Captain, I–'

'Not here,' said Reiner. 'Too open. Jurgen. Augustus. Get him to the shacks.'

Augustus and Jurgen hauled Gert to his feet and put their shoulders under his arms. The big crossbowman looked like the stuffing had been pulled out of him. His face sagged. He moaned with each step.

Reiner touched Darius on the shoulder. He was still staring at his hands. 'Scholar.' Darius didn't look up, but allowed himself to be led away.

They had just reached the shacks when Scharnholt screamed behind them.

'Stop them!'

Reiner turned, cursing, but amazingly, Scharnholt wasn't pointing at them, but at a cluster of grey-robed figures who were creeping around the edge of the chamber toward the bridge that crossed the chasm. Two in front led the way. The others carried the waystone casket.

'Oh, now who are these?' Reiner groaned.

The thieves stepped onto the bridge. Franka fired an arrow after them. It hit the shorter of the two leaders in the upper arm. The figure stumbled and cried out in a voice Reiner thought he recognised. But the procession didn't slow.

Scharnholt's voice was rising, crying strange words. He thrust his hands forward and a column of fire shot from them and exploded on the bridge. The thieves were enveloped in a blossoming ball of fire.

As it dissipated Reiner and the others saw the casket bearers, mangled and on fire, tumbling into the chasm as their leaders ran into a dark tunnel on the far side, their cloaks smoking. The casket was aflame too, and teetered on the edge of the bridge.

The entire cavern gasped in horror. Tzeentchists, Slaaneshi and Empire men all rushed forward, but before any had taken five steps, the flaming casket tipped up like a sinking ship and slid off the bridge. There was utter silence among the combatants, as the object of the battle disappeared into the depths.

'Sigmar bugger a troll,' said Hals softly.

The tableau broke as a white light shot from the Empire ranks and Scharnholt screamed. He was held in a flickering penumbra of light, his back arched in agony. His skeleton glowed through his skin like phosphorus, brighter and brighter, and then with a blinding flash and thunderclap, he was gone. The Empire troops roared in triumph and fell upon the disheartened cultists.

Augustus and Jurgen laid Gert down among the shacks. He was barely conscious. His boots spilled blood. The others gathered around him.

'Scholar!' barked Reiner. 'Darius! Patch him up!'

'I know no spells,' Darius mumbled.

'I'm not asking for spells,' said Reiner. 'Doctor him, curse you!'

'I know no spells,' Darius repeated.

'Forget it, captain,' croaked Gert. 'Too late. Listen…'

'None of that,' said Reiner, kneeling and unbuckling his sword belt. 'We must tie off that leg. Help me.'

The others knelt as well, but Gert waved a feeble hand. 'No! Listen, damn you, Hetsau!' His eyes flashed. 'Let me speak!'

Reiner turned, surprised at the use of his proper name from a common soldier.

Gert glared up at him, grey and sweating. 'You were right. Manfred had a… spy.' He tapped his chest. 'He didn't trust you. 'Spected you would try some… trickery.'

Reiner's heart was pounding, shaken by a score of simultaneous emotions. The Blackhearts exchanged glances.

'Thought I was minding a villain.' Gert shook his head weakly. 'Yer less a villain than he, though we was comrades once.' He tapped his chest again. 'Captain Steingesser. Time was I would'a died for him, but he's changed. Now I…' He chuckled and looked up at Reiner. 'Well, seems I died for you, eh?'

Reiner's throat constricted. 'Gert, if you'd just shut up, you might not…'

'How did you kill Halsteig?' asked Hals, bluntly. 'Yer no sorcerer. You never said no spell.'

'Hush,' said Augustus. 'Let the man die in peace.'

'Ye weren't there,' said Pavel. 'Ye didn't see. We might have all died like that.'

Gert grimaced. His gums were white. 'Phylacteries,' he said. 'Made by Manfred's magus. Carry 'em in my pouch. Throw one in a fire and…' He made to snap his fingers but could barely raise his hand.

Reiner's blood chilled at the thought of the risks Gert had taken while wearing that pouch. But he said nothing, only clasped his hand. 'Thank you, captain. Sigmar welcome you. You've… eased our minds.'

When he let go, Gert's hand sank to his side. The crossbowman, or captain, or spy, or whatever he had been, was dead. Reiner wasn't sure when he had gone.

Hals and Pavel made the sign of the hammer. Augustus muttered a prayer to Taal. Franka made Myrmidia's spear. Reiner closed Gert's eyes and took his pouch. He opened it. At the bottom he found a rolled length of leather, sewn with nine little pockets. Inside each was a glass vial labelled in florid script. Reiner pulled out the one with his name as the others watched. Inside a lock of hair floated in a red liquid. Around the hair was a strip of parchment inscribed with arcane symbols. He shivered and slipped the vial back into its sheath, then put the roll in his pouch.

'Be careful with that, captain,' said Pavel.

'Indeed,' said Reiner. He looked beyond the shacks. The battle was over. The companies were chasing down the last cultists and cutting the throats of their wounded. 'Right, we'll take the old fellow back to Manfred. But we don't let on we know what's what, aye?'

The others nodded in agreement, but as Hals and Pavel began making a litter, Darius tugged on Reiner's sleeve.

'Captain,' he said. 'Captain.' He spoke with a feverish intensity.

'Have you returned to us, scholar?' asked Reiner.

'The gate lets in as well as out,' Darius said.

'Eh?'

'I cannot close it. I cannot close the gate. The wind.' His voice rose. 'It howls in me. It whispers through my skull. Whispers. Captain, the whispers. The whispers, captain.' There were tears in his staring eyes. The others watched him, uncomfortable.

'I'm here, lad.'

Darius crushed Reiner's wrist. 'Kill me, captain. I beg you. Kill me before I listen.'

'Come, lad,' said Reiner, his heart sinking. 'Is it that bad?' He didn't want to believe Darius had gone mad – didn't want to believe it was his fault.

'Captain, please,' said Darius. He held out his hands in supplication.

Reiner stepped back involuntarily. In the centre of each of Darius's palms was a mouth like a vertical slit, filled with sharp little fish teeth. It was 'that bad.' Reiner moaned and cursed himself for ever thinking he could be a leader of men. He'd forced the boy. Forced him.

'Please, captain,' said all three mouths. 'The gate is open. I cannot close it. I cannot.'

'Captain,' said Jurgen, drawing his long sword. 'Let me.'

Reiner shook his head, though he wanted more than anything to pass the responsibility. 'No. I caused this.' He drew his sword. 'Bow your head, scholar. I'll stop the wind.'

The mouths in Darius's hands were jabbering at him, telling him to run, to attack, to drink Reiner's blood, but with a great effort, Darius clenched his fists and lowered his head, exposing his neck.

Reiner raised his sword over his head with both hands, praying he would make a clean job of it. Franka turned her head. Reiner chopped down, felt the jar as his sword hit Darius's spine, and then he was through, and Darius's body fell forward onto his head.

'Well struck,' said Jurgen.

Reiner turned away, hiding his face. 'Right. Leave him. The priests won't bury him with those hands. Let's go.'

As Hals, Pavel, Jurgen and Augustus walked Gert's body back to the companies, Hals tried to catch Reiner's eye.

'Ye did what y'had to, captain.'

'Did I?' asked Reiner angrily. 'Was there a need for the spell? We might have accomplished the same thing with arrows and shouting.'

'And we might have not,' said Hals.

Reiner stepped ahead. He didn't want to speak of it.

There were less than fifty Talabheimers and Reiklanders left. In their centre Manfred, Boellengen, and Schott and Keinholtz stood around Teclis, who leaned against the cave wall as if he could not have stood without it. They were the only commanders left.

'We could lower men into the chasm,' Keinholtz was saying as the Blackhearts approached. 'Then fix ropes to the waystone and raise it.'

'If it isn't shattered,' said Boellengen.

Teclis raised his head. 'The waystone would not shatter.'

'But we know nothing of the chasm's depth, or what might be down there,' said Schott. 'It might be a river, or a lake of fire.'

'Then we will have to mount another expedition,' said Manfred with a weary sigh.

'We must return to the surface before any new venture,' said Teclis. 'I must restore myself.'

Manfred groaned. 'Days if not weeks.' He saw the Blackhearts setting Gert's body down and turned to them. 'Is… is he dead?'

'Aye,' said Reiner casually. 'As is your witch.' He smiled to himself as he saw Manfred looking for Gert's pouch.

'Did he have…' Manfred started, then thought better of it. 'Well, I'm sorry to hear it.'

'As am I,' said Reiner. 'He stopped a blade meant for me.'

'Did he?' Manfred looked uncomfortable. 'Well–'

'Quiet!' said Teclis. He looked around sharply. 'Listen.'

Manfred, Reiner and the others listened. At first Reiner heard nothing. Then came a vibration in the ground and a sound like far off rain. It grew steadily closer until Reiner recognised it as the rumble of an army on the march.

Manfred and Schott and Boellengen shouted to their troops to form up. The Blackhearts went on guard with the rest, looking from tunnel to tunnel, waiting to see from which this fresh menace would come.

It came from all of them – three endless columns of ratmen in green-grey jerkins armed with spears, swords, and long guns, spilling out in a silent flood that filled the enormous cavern from wall to wall. There were thousands of them. The fifty men huddled together, all facing out. The ratmen surrounded them entirely, staring at them with glossy black eyes.

TWENTY-TWO
The Hero Of The Hour

'WELL, LADS,' SAID Hals. 'Nice to know ye.'

'See ye in Sigmar's hall,' said Pavel.

'Lord Teclis?' said Manfred nervously.

'I am at the end of my strength, count,' said Teclis. 'I can kill many, but not all.'

Manfred firmed his jaw. 'Then we will sell our lives as dearly as we may.'

The other commanders nodded and their men dressed their lines, but still the ratmen stood motionless.

'Why don't they attack?' asked Franka.

A disturbance began at the rear of the vermin army, and out of the tunnel beyond the chasm came a cluster of ratmen. They crossed the bridge and pushed slowly toward the front. There were at least twenty of them, led by a tall, snow-white ratman who carried a long, verdigrised staff. The front line parted and the knot of ratmen stepped forward. The companies gasped. The vermin carried the waystone.

The white-furred ratman pointed imperiously at Teclis. 'You, sharp-ear,' he said with a voice like a knife on a plate. 'Fix elf-thing. Make good. Seer Hissith say!'

Manfred, Schott and Boellengen exchanged baffled glances.

Teclis frowned at the rat-mage. 'You wish me to reset the waystone?'

'I command!'

'Why?'

'No why!' spat Hissith. 'Do!'

'Why?' asked Teclis, calmly.

The rat-mage trembled with rage, and Reiner expected him to order his troops to attack, but at last he spoke. 'We Greenfang clan! Warpstone only for us! Then elf-thing break. Other clan smell warpstone. Come stealing. Crippletail Clan. Deadeater clan. We fight.' He pointed to Teclis. 'You fix elf-stone. They smell no more. Warpstone only for us again!'

Reiner exhaled, relieved and amazed. They weren't going to die. As insane as it sounded, the ratmen needed them.

'Lord Teclis,' said Schott, aghast. 'You cannot do this. The Empire does not treat with evil! We must fight them!' He looked to Manfred. 'Is it not what the Emperor would wish, count?'

'Er...' said Manfred. He looked like he wished to smash Schott in the face.

'Fortunately,' said Teclis. 'Your emperor does not rule me.' He nodded to the rat-mage. 'I will do this.'

'M'lord!' cried Schott, outraged.

'Silence, Schott!' hissed Manfred. 'Would you lose Talabheim and the stone for a point of honour?'

The rat-slaves set down the waystone and backed away as the rat-mage pointed at Teclis. 'You trick, you die! We come! Kill all! Hissith say it so!'

'He threatens us, lord count!' said Schott, eyes blazing.

'Let him,' said Manfred, and bowed, smiling, as the rat-mage returned to his troops.

Without a word, the horde of vermin withdrew into the tunnels again like an ebbing brown tide. The men looked around at each other as if they couldn't believe they were still alive.

'Don't stand there!' snapped Manfred at Reiner. 'Pick it up and let's be off before we lose it again!'

The Blackhearts picked up the waystone and, surrounded by the shattered remnants of the Talabheimers and Reiklanders, walked it wearily back to the surface.

FOUR DAYS LATER, deep under Talabheim, Teclis reset the waystone, binding it with powerful wards, then burying its crypt below thousands of tonnes of rock. He then cast a spell of forgetting upon all the labourers who had built the new vault so that they could tell none where it was, and a similar spell upon the vault itself, which would make any who came looking for it forget what they had come for.

Instantly upon the setting of the stone, the mad plants of the Tallows began to wilt, the clouds and strange aurora over the city dissipated, and the madness that had plagued Talabheim faded. There was still much to be put right – neighbourhoods to be rebuilt, mutants to be hunted down, cultists to be hung, but no new cases of mutation were reported and Taalagad was reopened to trade.

To celebrate, the countess threw a grand ball, to which Manfred and the Reikland legation were invited. Reiner did not expect to be invited. He thought Manfred would shove him into the shadows and take all the glory for himself, but to his surprise the count ordered him to attend, while Lord Schott was sent back to Altdorf early to inform the Emperor of their success.

'Damn stubborn bull wouldn't play the game,' Manfred said as they rode to the Grand Manor. 'In order to save the countess embarrassment and keep relations with Talabheim smooth, we must pretend that Scharnholt and Danziger died heroes' deaths fighting the mutants. There can be no suggestion that her court was plagued with cultists. Schott refused to cooperate in the deception, so I've sent him home.' Manfred glared at Reiner. 'Instead, you will be the hero of the hour – the noble secretary who led Scharnholt, Danziger, and von Pfaltzen to the lair of the evil elf. And if you don't play it just as I've said, and praise Scharnholt and Danziger to the heavens, I'll have your head, you understand?'

'Your lordship always makes himself perfectly clear,' said Reiner, bowing.

AFTER TELLING HIS story – or rather, Manfred's story – a dozen times, Reiner saw, across the countess's grand ballroom, Lord Rodick and Lady Magda, talking and laughing with the countess herself. Reiner broke off in the middle of a humourous anecdote. The cursed woman landed on her feet like a cat. How were the traitors back in the countess's good graces? Lack of evidence? Or did the countess not want one of her own family to be accused of treason?

Reiner had no such qualms. He excused himself from his audience and crossed to Manfred, who was talking to Talabheim's high priest of Taal.

'M'lord,' he whispered in his ear. 'If I might speak with you?'

Manfred finished his conversation then turned to Reiner. 'Yes? Why aren't you telling your tale?'

'M'lord, if you are still interested in destroying your brother's corrupter, I believe I have a way. Only invite me to tell our adventure before Magda, Rodick and the countess.'

Manfred nodded. 'Come.'

Magda and Rodick attempted to excuse themselves when Manfred approached the countess, but Manfred begged them to stay and hear the tale of his rescue and the waystone's retrieval. 'Reiner was the discoverer of the plot, and tells it so much better than I.'

And so they listened, fidgeting, while Reiner told how he had seen mutants dressed as priests of Morr sneaking from the Grand Manor and warned Danziger, Scharnholt and von Pfaltzen of the theft, then led them to the dark elf's lair. When he began to tell of the hooded thieves who had tried to steal the waystone in the middle of the battle he noticed that Magda's upper lip was sweating.

'My man Franz is a dead shot,' Reiner said. 'And when Scharnholt cried that thieves were taking the stone, he loosed an arrow after them. Unfortunately, the range was long and his shot only hit one of the leaders – a little fellow – in the arm, and he and the other escaped before the dark elf blasted the others off the bridge.' Reiner frowned, disappointed. 'I am mortally sorry those men got away. It would be a great service to Talabheim to learn what traitors had designs on that stone. Unfortunately, it is beyond practicality to ask every man in Talabheim if he had been shot in the arm just "here".'

As he said 'here,' he squeezed Magda's arm hard, just above the elbow. Magda shrieked. Her knees buckled.

Reiner gasped, as if shocked. 'Lady, I am terribly sorry! Are you wounded there? What an unfortunate coincidence!'

'Take your hands from her, you oaf!' cried Rodick angrily. 'You've crushed her arm.'

'M'lord, I swear I only touched her!' Reiner said. 'I meant no harm.'

'An unfortunate coincidence indeed,' said the countess, looking levelly at Magda. 'Come with me, lady. I will have my royal physician look at you.'

'There is no need,' said Magda, smiling though she was white as a sheet. 'He only surprised me. I am fine.'

'I insist,' said the countess, and there was no mistaking the threat in her voice. She turned and signalled her guards, who stood nearby. 'This way. Cousin Rodick, won't you join us?'

Magda shot a look of pure venom at Reiner as she was lead away.

Reiner bowed deeply. 'Goodbye, lady. The pleasure was all mine.'

AND SO, ON the morning that the Reikland legation left for Altdorf, Reiner and the other Blackhearts watched with satisfaction as Lady Magda Bandauer was hung from the gallows before the Grand Courthouse of Edicts. Lord Rodick, being cousin to the countess, had been allowed to take poison. Magda had then been charged with his murder – all neat and tidy with no awkward questions about waystones and statues of Shallya asked.

Magda carried herself with great poise on the gallows, and might have gone to her death with all dignity intact had she not, when the executioner offered her a chance to speak, begun to denounce the countess and the Talabheim parliament for covering up Scharnholt and Danziger's corruption and the threat of the ratmen who lived under the city.

Reiner chuckled as she was gagged and hooded and the noose snugged around her neck. Spiteful to the end, the bitch. He'd have done the same, of course.

'And that's for Captain Veirt,' said Pavel, as Magda dropped and jerked at the end of the rope.

'And poor Oskar,' said Franka.

'And Ulf,' said Reiner.

'Too bad she's that sack over her head,' said Hals. 'I want to see her face now she's tasted death herself.'

'And yet,' said Reiner. 'We have her to thank for our lives. Without her scheming we would have all been hung long ago in the Smallhof garrison.'

'This is a life?' asked Pavel.

The others, who hadn't known the men Magda had caused to die, watched silently as she twitched and fought under the gibbet.

Manfred seemed distracted throughout the proceedings. Reiner smiled, for he knew why. The night before,

after Reiner had helped pack Teclis's belongings – for
with his guard dead the elf had no servants – he had
done the same for Manfred. The count made Reiner go
through every case and box three times looking for a
small leather-bound journal. When it couldn't be found,
he had accused Reiner of stealing it, and searched his
belongings as thoroughly as he had searched his own,
but when he found nothing he had finally dismissed
Reiner, furious. Reiner had heard him rummaging all
night long.

TWENTY-THREE
Unfinished Business

THEY REACHED ALTDORF seven days later, and the Black-hearts were once again installed in Manfred's townhouse while the count closeted himself with the Emperor and his cabinet, explaining what had occurred in Talabheim.

The Blackhearts fidgeted and fumed, for nothing had been said of their release, and Manfred was never there to question. But at last, on the evening of the third day, Reiner was told the count would see him in the library.

Manfred sat in a high-backed chair by the fire when Reiner entered, flipping through official papers. Reiner stood at attention until, after a few moments, Manfred looked up, pretending he hadn't noticed him before.

'Ah, Hetsau,' he said. 'Sit. You wished to see me?'

Reiner cursed inwardly, for he knew then and there that Manfred did not intend to honour his promise. Still, he must ask. 'Yes, m'lord. Thank you.' He sat. 'I have come on behalf of the others, m'lord, about your promise. That if we freed you from the dark elf, you would free us.'

'Ah yes,' said Manfred. 'In the press of events I had nearly forgotten.'

'We have not, m'lord,' said Reiner.

Manfred paused for a long moment, then sighed. 'I'm afraid your success has defeated you, Hetsau.' He looked up at Reiner with a curious expression. 'What you did in Talabheim was impossible. The odds you overcame are not to be calculated. And because of this I… I find I cannot let you go. You are too valuable.'

Reiner nodded, resigned. 'I was afraid you would say that, m'lord. I have given up expecting honour from the nobility.'

Manfred stiffened. 'My position doesn't allow me honour, just as yours does not. If I am to keep the Emperor and the Empire safe, I must do what must be done.'

'And get a little of your own in as well, m'lord?' Reiner winked.

'Eh?' Manfred scowled. 'What's this impertinence?'

Reiner cleared his throat. '"It must be proved that Talabheim cannot rescue itself. And if 'evidence' could be found that the countess was behind the stone's disappearance, so much the better."'

'What did you say?' Manfred gripped the arms of his chair.

'"The Emperor wishes that Talabecland develop closer ties to the Reikland. How better than to have a Reiklander rule Talabheim? I have languished too long in the shadows. It is time to step into the sun."' Reiner shrugged. 'Forgive me, m'lord, if I have misquoted you, but I speak from memory.'

'So you *do* have the book,' said Manfred. 'Well, valuable as you are, you will die for its theft.'

'No m'lord, we will be released for its return.'

Manfred laughed. 'Blackmail? You are in no position. All your belongings are in my house. I will find the book and kill you all.'

'Fortunately,' said Reiner. 'I had the foresight to hide it outside the house before we returned here. It is in a place where your rivals will find it if we die.'

'And if I torture the location out of you?' asked Manfred.

Reiner shrugged. 'You may well, but looking for it where it is hidden may bring it unwanted scrutiny. You may lose it even as you retrieve it.'

'What have you done, you blackheart?'

'Merely taken precautions, m'lord, as one blackheart must when dealing with another.'

Manfred fumed silently. He looked like he wished to strangle Reiner where he sat.

'All you need do, m'lord,' said Reiner, 'is remove our poison and the book will be returned. I have no wish to destroy you, nor stand in the way of your ambitions. We only want you to honour your promise. We only want our freedom.'

Manfred glared at him, then chuckled. 'I think I am fortunate that you seem to have no ambitions of your own. Very well, Hetsau, the poison will be removed. I will speak to Magus Handfort in the morning. But know this,' he added. 'If you think to trick me on this. If you haven't the book, or you do not mean to return it, your freedom will be very short indeed.'

'Of course, m'lord.' Reiner stood and walked out.

MAGUS HANDFORT'S EXTRACTION of the poison was the most painful thing Reiner had ever endured, more excruciating even than reaching for Valaris's necklace. Indeed, at times Reiner wondered if Manfred had betrayed them after all, for it felt as if his blood were burning through his veins and his kidneys ached as if they had been battered with clubs. But at last it was over and the Blackhearts were returned, barely conscious, to Manfred's carriages.

'Now,' said the count, as he signalled his driver to return them to his townhouse. 'Where is the book?'

Reiner felt in no condition to carry on a conversation. He could barely open his eyes. 'Not yet, m'lord.'

'What! You promised me!' Manfred kicked Reiner in the leg. 'Wake up, curse you! I have done as you asked. Where is the book?'

Reiner flinched. His entire body felt as tender as a raw wound. 'I said I would give you the book when the poison was removed,' said Reiner. 'But is it? You may have tricked us.'

'Are you mad?' Manfred cried. 'Do you think I would go to such lengths to fool you?'

'I have read your journal, m'lord,' said Reiner. 'You have gone further to gain less. I want proof.'

'And what proof can I give you? Do you want me to swear by Sigmar? Do you want Magus Handfort to take an oath.'

'I want Lord Teclis to examine us,' said Reiner.

'Dog!' said Manfred. 'You cannot disturb so great a person for so paltry a reason. I refuse!'

Reiner shrugged. 'Then kill us and be prepared to hang when the book is found.'

Manfred glared at him, then with a vicious curse rapped on the ceiling of the coach. 'Kluger, turn about. Take us to Lord Teclis's residence.'

'AND HOW DID this poisoning occur?' asked Teclis. The high elf lay propped up in bed, in a white, sunlit room in the house Karl Franz had provided for him in Altdorf. He was still weak, but looked better than when Reiner had packed his trunks.

'It was the dark elf, m'lord,' said Reiner, smirking at Manfred. They sat at the mage's side while the Blackhearts stood uncomfortably at the door. 'He used it to force us to do his bidding.' Reiner pulled open his shirt, revealing Valaris's knife-work, still pink and raw. 'He said that with these he would know if we betrayed him, and would poison us from afar. He promised to provide an antidote when we brought him the stone, but he lied.'

'My magus, Handfort, attempted to remove the poison,' said Manfred. 'But such is my love for my men that I came to ask if you might confirm it.'

Teclis ignored him, looking at Reiner's scars. 'I am sorry I am too weak at the moment to remove those. Perhaps another day. Your arm.'

Reiner held out his arm. The elf took it and made a circular motion over it with his left hand. Reiner tensed, but there was no pain.

After a moment, Teclis looked up. 'There is no poison here. Bring the others.'

One by one the Blackhearts approached Teclis and offered their arms. At last he lay back, drained. 'They are free of poison.'

Manfred looked at Reiner. 'Are you satisfied?'

'Thank you, m'lord. I am.'

Manfred stood. 'Then take me to the book.'

'A moment, m'lord.' He turned to Teclis. 'Lord Teclis, your pardon.'

Manfred put a hand to his dagger, afraid of some treachery.

Teclis opened his eyes. 'I am tired, man. What is it?'

Reiner bowed. 'Forgive me, lord, but when I saw to your luggage in Talabheim, I inadvertently packed one of Lord Manfred's books among yours. May I retrieve it?'

'Of course,' said Teclis, closing his eyes. 'Then leave me, please.'

Reiner turned to Teclis's bookshelves. Two stacks of books, still tied with twine, sat before them. Reiner cut the twine from one and removed a slim, leather-bound volume.

'Here you are, m'lord.' He handed it to Manfred, who gaped like a fish.

'But... But, it might have been found. It...'

'It might have, m'lord. But it wasn't. Shall we go?'

WALKING OUT OF a door is an everyday act, but when he walked out of Manfred's front door with Franka, Pavel, Hals, Jurgen, Augustus and Dieter, it felt to Reiner a greater occasion than the coronation of a new emperor. He had been trying to walk out of that door for more than a year. His heart pounded like a drum. He wanted to leap for joy. He inhaled the smell of Altdorf, of cooking fires and piss, of rotting vegetation, cheap scent and sausages, and thought he had never smelled a more intoxicating perfume in all his life. He grinned from ear to ear. They had no minder. They had no mission. They had no leash. They were free. They could go where they pleased. And Reiner knew exactly where that was.

'To the Griffin, lads! And the drinks are on me!'

The others cheered. Even Jurgen smiled. They turned down the cobbled street, their packs over their shoulders and an unaccustomed swing in their step.

Half an hour later they were tucked into a corner table by the fireplace under the Griffin's smoke blackened beams. There were mugs of beer in their hands and a crispy brown goose lay on a platter before them.

Pavel raised his mug. 'A toast!' he said, but Reiner waved his hands.

'Wait!' he said. 'There is one last thing we must do.'

The others watched as he reached into his pouch and pulled out the rolled length of leather. He unrolled it and removed the phylactery with his name on it, then handed each of the others theirs. 'I am certain Teclis did not lie,' he said. 'All the same, I'd like to be sure.'

He turned to the fire, and though he knew there was no risk, it still took a fair amount of courage to throw the vial into the flames. There was a pop and a hiss, and then, nothing. Reiner let out a sigh. The others did too, then one by one, they solemnly threw their vials into the fire.

'Now the toast, pikeman!' said Reiner.

Pavel grinned and stood. 'There ain't no toast better than what our mumchance brother once gave,' he said, nodding to Jurgen. He raised his mug. 'To freedom!'

'To freedom!' The others cried as one, then downed their mugs in a single long draught.

'Barkeep!' roared Hals over their heads. 'Y'better bring the keg! We've been working up this thirst for a year!'

A FEW HOURS later, when Pavel and Hals and Augustus had reached the stage where they were singing marching songs and challenging everyone in the tavern to arm-wrestle,

Reiner whispered in Franka's ear. 'We have unfinished business. Will you join me upstairs?'

Franka gave him a shy look, then nodded.

They slipped away during the seventh chorus of 'The Pikeman's Shaft.'

'WELL,' SAID REINER as he closed the door of the small, plain room and faced Franka awkwardly. 'You asked me to ask you if you forgave me once we had returned to Altdorf and drank to Talabheim's memory. And, well, I'm certain we did that a few times just now, so…' He coughed. 'Do you forgive me for not trusting you?'

Franka looked at her boots. 'Do you forgive me for not trusting *you*?'

Reiner frowned. 'It added a nice bit of drama when you tried to stop Dieter killing Augustus, but it did hurt to think you didn't know me well enough to see it was a trick.'

'Well, good,' said Franka, sticking her chin out. 'Now you know how it felt.'

'Aye, aye, tit for tat,' he said. 'But did you truly believe I had turned murderer? Could you really think that of me?'

Franka looked at him, eyes glinting. 'In my heart I knew you were not, but…'

Reiner laughed. 'But only in your heart!' She had turned his own words against him. 'You, lass, are much too clever for your own good. It is one of the reasons that I…' He faltered as he realised what he was going to say. He had said the words many times when he didn't mean them, why were they so hard to say now? 'That I… I….'

Franka put a finger to his lips. 'Shhh. You don't have to say it.' She smirked up at him. 'I trust you.'

Reiner's throat closed up. His eyes glistened. 'Damn you, girl!'

He crushed her to him. They kissed. And this time there was no breaking away.

* * *

REINER AND FRANKA stumbled down to the Griffin's common room very late the next morning, for though they had awoken hungry, they had also been so delighted with their newfound freedom that they'd had to partake of it all over again. The others were already there, clutching their heads and trying to eat their eggs and trout as quietly as possible.

'Morning,' said Reiner cheerily.

Hals glared up at him. 'You two look very pleased with yerselves.'

'We're certainly very pleased with each other,' said Reiner.

Franka elbowed him in the ribs, blushing furiously, as the landlord brought more plates. They tucked in, and Reiner looked at Franka as if for the first time. He smiled. I will be having breakfast with this beauty for the rest of my life, he thought. But then he began to wonder what that life would be like. What would they do? How were they to support themselves? Reiner was a gambler by trade. Would Franka stand for that? For the late hours? The life of cheating rubes? He supposed he could take her back home to his father and become a gentleman farmer. But he had run from that life as fast as he could. Altdorf was his home. The question was, could he make it hers as well?

It seemed the others were having similar thoughts.

'Wonder if me dad's farm's still there.' Hals said. 'And Breka, who lived toward Ferlangen. Fine girl, Breka.'

'Weren't much there when we went through last year,' said Pavel glumly. 'Our people all dead most likely. Could go up and start again, I suppose.'

Hals frowned. 'Lot of work, that.'

'The Talabheim I knew is gone,' said Augustus. 'And they'd lock me up again if I went back to my company.'

'And ye, swordsman?' asked Hals looking up at Jurgen. 'Y'have a girl somewhere? A farm?'

Jurgen stared at his plate. 'I... cannot go home.'

There was an awkward silence, then Dieter stood.

'I can,' he said. 'And I will.' He wiped his mouth. 'My old digs ain't a stone's throw from here, and the watch thinks I'm dead. Time I pay them what sold me out a visit.' He picked up his pack and made a smirking bow. 'A pleasure making yer acquaintances, I'm sure, but I'm for home.' And with that he walked out.

The Blackhearts watched him go, then returned to their food.

'Wish I was certain as that fellow,' said Pavel.

'Aye,' said Augustus. 'Nice to know what ye want.'

Franka and Reiner looked at each other uneasily. Reiner could see that some of the things he had been worrying about where occurring to her too.

He grunted annoyed. 'There's a whole world out there,' he said. 'Surely we can all find something to do.'

But at the moment he couldn't think of anything, and apparently neither could the others, for they just carried on eating in silence.

At last Hals snorted. 'Maybe Manfred is hiring.'

The others laughed. Reiner nearly spat trout across the table. Then the laughter died away and they all fell silent again.

Nathan Long has worked as a screenwriter for fifteen years, during which time he has had three movies made and a handful of live-action and animated TV episodes produced. He has also written several award-winning short stories. When these lofty pursuits have failed to make him a living, he has also been a taxi driver, limo driver, graphic designer, dishwasher and lead singer for a rockabilly band. He lives in Hollywood.